THE
FOUNDING
FATHERS
RETURN

A Novel

BOOKS BY LAWRENCE ROWE

FICTION

The Tesla Paradox

NON-FICTION

Bubblenomics

Bubblenomics 2

SATIRE

Another Modest Proposal

VISIT LAWRENCE ONLINE

LawrenceRowe.com

THE
FOUNDING
FATHERS
RETURN

Part the Second

Lawrence Rowe

New York

ISBN-13: 978-0-9767668-4-1

The Founding Fathers Return: Part the Second may be purchased at special bulk quantity discounts for educational or promotional use. For information, e-mail: specialmarkets@mdrpress.com.

First paperback printing: July, 2021.

10 9 8 7 6 5 4 3 2 1

For My Uncle

PREFACE

It is a contentious time in America. Liberty is waning. Present leaders seem unequal to the challenges which America faces. At this precarious juncture in United States history, the wisdom of the Founding Fathers is more relevant than ever.

I have spent years studying America's Founding Fathers via primary sources and am awed by the prescience of their observations, many of which might have been uttered today rather than centuries ago. *The Founding Fathers Return* offers readers the singular opportunity to hang out with the Founders in the present day, to get to know them, and to solve America's problems with them.

America is great, but its problems run deep. True solutions are neither simple nor easy. This journey with the Founders in the present will be a long one spanning several volumes, but it will also be entertaining and enlightening. I hope you will enter the veil with America's Founding Fathers and embark upon their Odyssey with them.

LR
04Jul2021

ACKNOWLEDGEMENTS

America's Founding Fathers are among the greatest individuals to ever trod the Earth. Portraying them accurately is a responsibility I take extremely seriously, one which requires massive time and effort, as well as the help of others.

I prefer privy. The people who have helped me return the Founding Fathers know who they are, what they have done, and how thankful I am.

I am especially thankful to Karie Diethorn, Chief Curator of Independence National Historical Park, who provided information which was indispensable for writing the Constitutional Convention in immediate scene. I am also thankful to Bob Terrio for granting permission to use maps of colonial Philadelphia which he created for the 1976 Bicentennial at Independence Hall.

INTRODUCTION

Part the Second of *The Founding Fathers Return* contains the second portion of Chapter the Third. Chapter the Third may be the longest in the history of literature. If ever a scene warranted such length, it is the Fœderal Convention of 1787, the seminal event of the last several centuries. At present, every free government in the world utilizes some derivative of the Constitution of Government wrought at the Fœderal Convention. At present, America is in decline because it is forsaking said Constitution of Government.

Mainstream fiction usually resorts to short chapters. The problem I encountered in trying to write the Fœderal Convention in immediate scene is that any short treatment was so hopeless superficial as to be a waste of time. A historian friend who I explained my dilemma to encouraged me to simply write the Founders as I found them and not concern myself with length.

I did so.

This is the result.

No one has ever written the Constitutional Convention in immediate scene as novel chapters—until now. Understanding the Constitution and government that our Founders intended, and how and where it succeeded and failed, is essential to solving America's present problems.

America's Founding Fathers were not Gods, but rather imperfect mortals with foibles. I have written the Founders as I found them in primary sources, warts and all. This includes some curdling portrayals of their racism and chauvinism. My brutally realistic depiction of antiquated norms should not be construed as approval or advocation of them.

Spelling, punctuation, and grammar irregularities in *The Founding Fathers Return* are intentional. Though these irregularities may seem strange to the modern ear, and eye, they are authentic colonial usage.

I hope you enjoy this one-of-a-kind opportunity to hob and knob America's Founding Fathers and frame our Constitution of Government with them.

Your most humble and obedient servant,
Lawrence Rowe

THREE

Benjamin Franklin took measure of the Dissidents again. Of George Mason, who turned a moment, revealing a face that belonged at Versailles and the lips of an irritate wife. Of Edmund Randolph, face rectanglish, like a figurine chiseled out of a tree, the acreage dominated by a gargantuan nose and introspective yet indecisite eyes. Of the ghoulish, ever-squinting Elbridge Gerry, he of the endless forehead and indefatigate obstinancey.

No satisfaction on Dissident's faces, as with most Deputies.

All three men looked troubled.

Increasing troubled.

1

Franklin again felt gratitude for the absence of Luther Martin, Patrick Henry, Governour Clinton, Samuel Adams, and cetera. He was also pleased that Robert Yates and John Lansing of New York had absented Convention in disgust months ago. Yates, a Justice of the New York supreme Court, and Lansing, once Speaker of the New York Assembly and present Mayor of Albany, were among that cabal of Deputies who felt the Convention treasonous. State Legislatures that appointed Deputies gave instructions circumscribing their behaviour. Governour Clinton had ensured that the powers granted to the New York Deputation were minimal. Yates and Lansing had curtly informed the Convention that their instructions authorized only revision of the Articles of Confederacy, not the creation of an entire new Constitution, and had repaired to their country, to New York, to slander the Convention and Constitution.

In levying accusation of Treason, Yates and Lansing was hardly being preposterous. Congress and the States had authorized revision of the Articles of Confederacy, not the creation of a new government from scratch. Had every Deputation been as scrupulous in adhering to the instructions of their Assembly as Yates and Lansing, the Convention would have never attained to a Quorum.

Most Deputies did not feel bound to mere amend the Articles of Confederacy. The Articles were untenable, revising them futile. Deputies ought be free to Design a structure they felt most likely to secure Natural Rights. With the salvation of the Union and Revolution at stake, it would be treason to Deputies' trust not to propose what they found necessary.

Though an accusation of Treason was distant from ridiculous, 'twas also a far remove-ed from legitimate. With Washington and Franklin lending the Convention the gravity of their Reputation, no critick could make the Public believe it Ignoble. Especially not with its proceedings still Secret.

Before the Constitution became binding, Congress had to approve it, and transmit it to States which had to ratify it. All opponents would have their voice during these processes. The Convention was hardly some Conspiracy to implement Absolutism. Or even Republicanism.

Deputies who were state-sovereignty Zealots nonetheless seized upon the revision requisite to impugn the Convention. If the States and The People had been told that the creation of a new Constitution was the intent of the Convention, it never would have been allowed!

True.

But was Liberty to be extinguished for a whole nation, a whole world, a whole millennium or more, on such a particular?

Nay!

Yates and Lansing sat in Convention more than a month before absenting in early July. With Yates and Lansing riding over the Little Lion's votes on every occasion, he absented the Convention in frustration in late June, for nigh all of July and August, more than half the Convention, though had repaired, an act of courage as he was defying the wishes of New York, which ordered Deputies not to attend once Yates and Lansing reported back.

In exacting legal terms, the Little Lion acting as a representative of his state was Fugitive, and he was in attendance as a private Citizen only. In exacting legal terms, the same was true of nigh every Deputy and Deputation, once they had begun creating a new Constitution in violation of instructions of State Legislatures and Congress. Whatever the legal niceties, they were a trifle politically. So long as Washington throned the Convention and Franklin was in attendance, it was unimpugnable Legitimate.

In most cases, New York's nay votes were inconsequential, as that Majority of states needed to approve motions was still attained. Today, however, a Nay vote by any state might be fatal.

The way information was first presented to The People was crucial. Their initial impression of a measure was a lasting impression, difficult to alter. If the Convention presented a Constitution to The People which had not a façade of unanimous approval by Deputies, it might be Suspect with Permanency and might never attain sufficient support for Ratification.

Had Yates and Lansing been present, they would have certain voted nay. Their absence was fortuitous, and Franklin wondered what they might have done if they knew their votes might murder the Constitution. Might they have intended the Flying Machine and made the ninety-mile journey from New York to Philadelphia in but two days? Whatever they might have done, they hadn't.

No Nay from New York!

Yet a Nay there still might be, to the ruin of all.

Dissent had to be quelled, but gentle, in such a way that the quelled felt not bully'd or oppressed, causing them to entrench out of spite.

An exceeding delicate proposition. Not an investment to be made by a General. One best undertaken by a crafty old Sage.

"Article Seven," Jackson read. "The Ratification of the Conventions of nine States shall be sufficient for the Establishment of this Constitution between the States so ratifying the Same."

It would be a far from absurd to interpret the Constitution as an Amendment of the Articles of Confederacy and enforce the Articles' requisite of unanimous approval for ratification of Amendments. This would make ratification impossible and doom America to Anarchy. Thus this Clause. Deputies would argue that since a new Constitution proposed, ratification provisions of the Articles of Confederacy were inapplicable. The Fugitive act of drafting a new Constitution which many would object would be used as justification for ignoring the ratification rules of the Articles of Confederacy.

This provision was disingenuous at best, and perhaps outright dishonest, from a certain narrow purview. The Constitution would be put to The People and was thus not an attempt to circumvent their Will. Deputies were not inclined to fret the tactical niceties necessitate to stave off a general Anarchy.

A requisite of nine of twelve or thirteen states to ratify, depending upon whether one accounted the absented Rogue Island or not, was the three quarters Majority the Constitution required for Amendment. The chief objection to non-unanimous ratification, that it enforced obnoxious measures upon a dissenting Minority, was alleviate by having the Constitution bind only those States that ratified. This was a ruze, as ratification by three quarters of States including large States would render non-ratifying States effective outcasts and enforce their ratification. The publick would not be told this truth.

Overall, Article VII was blatant Fugitive and would rankle many, but Franklin was too exuberant to care, for these were the very last words of the Constitution!

Jackson's Adam's apple contracted into the flesh of his throat and then expanded, repeated, as he swallowed several times. It seemed damn nigh a Crime to not have a bumper for him to imbibe, and a high Crime at that. The absence of Luther Martin had its disadvantages. He always had spirits on his person and could have proffered a quencher.

Several Deputies exhaled. Some closed their eyes. Others rubbed their foreheads. Edmund Randolph squinted, leaned forward, and pinched the bridge of his nose. George Mason turned his head and peered out the window ponderous, eyes dilated, as if a horse were galloping straight at him.

A bead of sweat dangled off the tip of Jackson's nose, threatening to drop like a mortar ball and defile the ink on the Constitution. Jackson put the parchment down, wiped his face with a kerchief, and then dried his hands with it. He swallowed deep, repeated, cleared this throat several times. And then picked up the Constitution, turned describing a quarter circle with military precision, walked up the two steps of the dais, and handed the Charta to Washington.

"Your Excellency," Jackson said. "General, Sir."

Washington took the Constitution. His hands looked massive next to Jackson's, small once they held the vellum.

"A right admirable reading, Major," Washington said. "Right admirable."

Deputies tapped their canes on the floor repeated. Governeur Morris tapped his peg Leg. It had no joint, as of a kneepan, so could be worked up and down with ease. Deputies without walking sticks clapped the table with the flats of their palms, usually with one hand, some-times with two. Wooden rapping reverberated through out the chambre.

"Here, here," someone said.

Washington nodded at Jackson while bowing slight at the waist. Warmth flooded Washington's face, his eyes especially. Jackson's face lit up and he curtsyed in return, a much deeper curtsy than Washington's, with more nod of the head and a sharper bend at the waist. As the rapping subsided, Jackson returned to his table and Washington's face recovered from its thaw.

Silence descended.

Ponderous silence.

Precarious silence.

At last, at long bloody last, the moment was upon them. Deputies sat up straighter. Chairs were pulled closer to tables. All eyes fixated on Washington.

Who looked at Franklin.

Franklin stood. Without his cane, the Gout grated his knee. Agony blurred his vision, but he was careful not to show any pain, lest he appear weak at the most inopportune moment. Franklin placed his hands upon on the table just past its front left corner, as if it were a natural speaking gesture, even tho' he preferred to keep his body compact and still during Oratory.

Franklin glanced about the East Room and surveyed the Deputies. Many great Orators were present, and they had shown their parts repeated. Attempting flights of Oratory amongst such Pericleses was folly. Franklin had first gained pre-eminency with his Pen. He was no speaker and shone not in public Councils. His voice was soft regardless, and the Gout and Stone made standing for a long speech as impossible as defeating Britain had once seemed. Franklin had therefore written out speeches during the Convention and had fellow Pennsylvanian James de Caledonia read them. Caledonia was seated immediate right of Robert Morris, situate left a front the right Pennsylvania table.

"Mister President, Sir," Franklin said. "I have some remarks which I have reduced to writing for my own conveniency. With your blessing I shall again have Mister Wilson proffer them."

Washington nodded curt. "Mister Wilson has the floor."

James Wilson stood. James de Caledonia. Caledonia James. Caledonia to most Deputies. An unremarkable man physically, but one whose facial features screamed Scottish. Caledonia was calm, studious, with an air of hauteur about him. His dark, engaging eyes conveyed wisdom and severity, and his lips seemed perpetual skeptical and primed for a tantrum. Except that Caledonia was far too self Governed and methodical to ever allow one.

Caledonia nigh always wore steel spectacles, tho' his were a bit greater, which was to say larger, than those of most gentlemen, and he tended to wear them high on the nose and close to the eyes, which was considered peculiar. Most men hung their spectacles low on their nose and looked through them primary to read, but Caledonia looked through his continual.

Like all spectacles, Caledonia's had round lenses, and the temples extended outward from the lense frame before moving rearward. Even then, the temples did not extend straight back from the edge of the frame, but rather angled outward severe, and hooked into Caledonia's wig exterior rather than the ear which it concealed. The angle was less severe than on typical spectacles though.

Spectacles was general reckont unmanly, and vainer Gentlemen, which was most, scrupled to use them only in public when absolute necessary. Deputies' glances thus lingered on Caledonia's spectacles. And his shoulders, which sloped downward slight as they moved outward from the body rather than staying level as on a more athletic man.

Deputies none the less had respect in their eyes when they looked at Caledonia.

Immence respect.

Which is why Franklin had chose Caledonia to read his letters rather than other esteemed Pennsylvania Deputies such as Governeur Morris, Robert Morris, or Major General Mifflin.

Franklin glanced at Gouverneur Morris, who met his gaze, arched an appraising eyebrow, and pursed his libertine lips. During The War when the Continental Congress attempted to remove Washington as Commander of the Army, and the vote of yeas and nays had been equal divided, Governeur Morris had cast the vote that maintained Washington in Power. After observing the suffering of Washington's Army at Valley Forge, Morris became a Paladin of funding the Army in Congress, and as undersupplyed as the Army was, it was terrific to think how much worse its plight might have been without him constant beating the drum.

So many Patriots like Governeur Morris, who had made so many critical contributions not accounted for in the emerging

simplification, and ultimately distortion, of history that deified
Washington, Franklin, and but a few others.

Governeur Morris had spoke more than any Deputy at the
Convention, and nigh always said some Thing relevant. Calling
his oratory brilliant would be overstatement, but he was the sort
of mule the cause required, a man to make the large number of
obvious but necessary arguments with vigour and lucidity. This
freed up more eminent Intellects such as Caledonia to speak
less frequent, that their eruditions on the most critical or contentious points carry'd more weight.

Governeur Morris was no profund Phylosopher like Chancellor Wythe, Caledonia, Mason, or Jemmy, yet at times Franklin thought him the most intelligent Deputy to have seated at
Convention. Governeur was an acute calculator of the motives
of men. He understood human propensities and had proffered
practicable analysis of the effects of the Constitution that more
theoretical and scholastic Deputies had at times overlooked.
Morris was also adept at assessing the leanings and reactions
of Deputies in debate and adjusting his oratory extempore so
'twas more appealing.

In general, Morris was esteemed despite being one of the
most notorious Libertines in all of America, and he would have
been an excelent choice to read Franklin's letters.

But not the best choice.

Franklin glanced at the other Morris, Robert Morris, Finan-
cier of the Revolution, perhaps the wealthiest man in America,
on parchment, save only William Bingham. Robert Morris was
seated direct right of Governeur Morris. He had crafty eyes, a
cunning expression, and a blockish face whose lower portion

vanished in the pudding of his chins. The cleft of Morris' chin was the only line visible upon his lower face, and even it seemed indistinct and fleeting, as if chalked in light by some artist to give the illusion of dimensionality. Tho' Morris' hair seemed full from the front, hairs were drizzled over the rear scalp like plum sauce.

Franklin couldn't help smirking. Morris' bald rear pate was proof that wealth couldn't purchase every Thing.

If only respite from the Gout and Stone could be purchased. Franklin would become a pauper instantly for one hour without pain. Spend the rest of his days destitute to take one stroll unassisted absent agony. Languish in debtor's prison until his dying day if the Gout and Stone could be eradicate with finality. Thoughts of respite or cure were as foolish and frivolous as they were frustrating. Yet Franklin couldn't help but hope, even though there was none.

Baldness was considered exceeding unmanly, and most balding or bald men wore perukes. A wigless bald man was exceeding singular, especially at a formal event such as the Convention. Perpetual perukeless, Morris seemed to be saying that his wealth exempted him from vanity and decorum.

He perhaps had a point.

Wigs had gained prominence in the late 1500s when utilized to hide The Syphilis. The Syphilis plague at that time was the worst since The Black Death of the 1300s. The Syphilis could not be cured, and tens of Millions of its victims were ravaged by open sores, crusty rashes, blindness, insanity, and baldness. Rashes and sores on the neck and face made sexes fearfull of liaisons, as did hair loss, so the infinite multitudes of The Syphilis victims took to wearing long wigs. Festering sores and rabid rashes also tended to exude a foul odour, which led to the use of scented powders along with wigs. Powdered wigs endured long after The Syphilis plague passed, gradual shortening and becoming simpler over time, as they were needed only to hide baldness, not sores and rashes. And help keep the head free of lice.

Observing Morris' bald pate, Franklin could not help but think of The Syphilis. Morris had The Syphilis not, yet was so wealthy he probably could have flaunted it and still bedded many a beguiling Belle.

Morris' long, thin nose was flattish, seemed to plumb straight down the front of his face, and then ballooned sudden to accommodate large nostrils. His upper cheeks were corpulent to the point of seeming nigh swollen, causing the lines between the lower portion of the nose and the outside edge of the mouth to seem more distinct, as if the region between nose and mouth were a cavity.

Morris did much good living, excessive good, and it shewed.

Yet he had sacrificed much for the American cause. During some of the darkest moments of The War, Morris personal funded the Army, and it probably would have perished without his largesse. Morris gave Washington £10,000 to pay troops and keep the Army from disbanding just before the battle of Princeton. When the Congress emitted paper Continentals in such preposterous volumes they depreciated precipitous and were rejected as money, Morris had issued personal Bills of Credit to keep the Army afloat. These Morris Notes were the only American money in circulation at times during the Revolution.

Morris was brought to bed in Liverpool, England, emigrated to America at age 13, apprenticed to a prominent banking &

shipping firm, and was made a partner at age 24. He helped expand the firm aggressive, using its bank to purchase Land, and its shipping to traffick in Slaves, indentured Servants, sugar, spices, and any Thing else profitable.

Morris had voted against Independency in Congress, believing America could not best Britain and taking the pragmatic mercantile view that peace was better for trade and profit. Yet once the Congress voted for Independency, Morris signed the Declaration and supported the Cause. His basic view was to vote his Conscience but support the Majority whatever it decided.

Such pragmatism was typical of Morris—in the pursuit of profit especially.

Morris' firm had more than 250 ships during The War, making it one of the largest private Navys in the world. Morris used his Navy to smuggle supplies to America and engage in widespread espionage, providing Washington with critical Intelligence. Morris also profited handsome off Privateering, capturing British ships for America and keeping a per cent of the cargo obtained.

The Congress appointed Morris Superintendent of Finance as well as Agent of the Marine during the most critical years of The War. He was the Prime Minister and could obtain whatever he wanted for the public service with the scrip of a pen. Morris would accept the position only if granted massive powers, arguing that success would be impossible otherwise, but this led to fears he aspiret to Dictator.

Ridiculous.

Profiteer perhaps, Dictator never. Regardless, Morris was the second most powerful man in America after Washington.

For much of The War, Washington was Commander in Chief, Morris Administrator in Chief.

Morris brought business acumen to the inefficient Committees of Congress. He slashed the Civil List, forced Firms to bid for contracts, demanded exacting accounting, and hounded States for their promised contributions. Morris also created a National Bank that issued Bills of Credit which helped fund The War.

Since The War, Morris had proposed a radickal National Credit & Commerce System for America. Some such as Thomas derogated it. Others such as the Little Lion considered it indispensable to American survival.

Morris had been accused of Profiteering, of profiting wanton off war, treating it as a jobbing opportunity rather than a patriotic cause. There were few more damning slanders one could hurl at a gentleman than Profiteer. Morris had been investigated by Congress, and though acquitted of wrongdoing in a technical legal sense, the exorbitant profits he had accumulate during The War rankled many, eroding his esteem.

Morris had never asked for repayment of the exorbitant sums he gave Washington to fund his Army, nor for the ships he gave to the nation to help it amass a Navy, or his myriad other assistances. He had once been viewed as a nigh divine generous benefactor, but once his Profiteering upon The War was revealed, his gifts and character were viewed in a darker light. To many Americans, and many Deputies, Morris was and always would be a mere Profiteer.

Whatever one ultimate thought of Morris' Profiteering, he was a formidable man. A close friend of Washington, he had won the jockeying among the Philadelphia elite and had the supreme honor of hosting The General at his mansion during the Convention. Franklin was supposed to nominate Washington as Chair of the Convention, but when he missed the first quorumed day, Morris nominated Washington.

Washington was nigh certain to proffer Morris the senior Treasury, Finance, or Exchequer position in the new government. Whether Morris would accept it, condescend to have his every decision scrutinized and perhaps slandered for Profiteering or Interest, and perhaps have his future Profiteering and Speculation hampered, was uncertain, yet doubtful.

Franklin did not simplistic judge either Morris, not Governeur Morris for his Voluptuousness, nor Robert Morris for his Profiteering. Yet Franklin was not fully comfortable latching his Reputation to either by choosing them to read his speeches. Deputies hearing a speech reading by another Deputy coloured their perception based upon their sensibilities towards that Deputy. Neither Morris was an ideal selection, for both Morrises were resented by Factions of Deputies.

Franklin glanced at Thomas Mifflin, Major General Mifflin during The War. He was seated right next to Caledonia, a middle the right table of the Pennsylvania Deputation. Mifflin glanced at Washington with a sort of mild wonderment, and also a trifle of scarce-perceptible perturbation, as if he still couldn't believe Washington had attained Victory and was perplexed by the Fame heaped upon him.

When wearing a white wig, which Mifflin was, his face seemed like a softer-featured and more handsome version of Washington's. Though no one would ever mistake one for the

other—Washington's eye sockets, nose, and forehead were too
singular—the face of Mifflin at a distance seemed like a version
of Washington that a painter exceeding Sycophantic might draw.
Mifflin's nose was more balanced than Washington's, the eye
sockets less deep, and his lower face was not deformed by false
teeth. He also generally seemed less serious than Washington,
did not emanate aggression like Washington, and his eyes had
a compleat different character, conveying earnestness.

Mifflin was born in Philadelphia to a wealthy Quaker family,
educated at the College of Philadelphia, worked four years at a
counting House, spent two years in England, and then entered
his family's mercantile business. When The War for Independency began, Mifflin raised troops, causing him to be expeled
from the pacifistic Quaker church. He was commissioned a
Major in the Army, served on Washington's staff as an Aide-
de-Camp, and Washington appointed him the first Quartermaster General.

Quartermaster General. Responsible for provisioning the
Army. In an Army with few supplies and little money to obtain
them, a more thankless position was difficult to imagine. Yet
Mifflin exceled as much as was possible.

Most Americans were Yeomen or Aprons. There were few
truly brilliant American merchants, especially those with formal
education and training, and merchants from extreme large firms
analogous to a government or Army were exceeding scarce. Thus
Mifflin, with his work at a counting House balancing ledgers
and experience running a large mercantile firm, was invaluable
to Washington, whose plantation had never been a financial suc-

cess, and who had limited knowledge of the advanced workings of banks, bourses, and the commerce clockwork.

Like Morris to Congress, Mifflin brought business acumen to an Army that had been sore wanting for it. He organized, budgeted, negotiated lower Prices, improved delivery, and most of all parlayed his connections, cajoling merchants he knew, preying upon their Patriotism, inducing them to provide supplies on credit. They was much more trusting dealing with one of they own.

Like the Little Lion, Mifflin detested labouring as an aide, preferring to seek Glory in combat. Like the Little Lion, Mifflin had difficulty obtaining combat Commands because he was such a skilled administrator and so indispensable to Washington. Mifflin nonetheless had better luck than Hamilton escaping the camp of aides. Washington finally paroled him from Quartermaster General and the Staff, and Mifflin disappointed not, excelling in combat.

The problem with Mifflin was that he was one of the officers who attempted to have Washington removed as Commander of the Army, via the legal means of having Congress appoint a new Commander. Like many officers, Mifflin considered Washington a rank Amateur as a General, which he was. Washington's inexperience cost the Army dear many times, early in The War especially, and many officers scrupled not to express their contempt for his Incompetency. These officers truly believed that the Army could be better commanded by a more experienced, skilled, formal-schooled officer.

Washington kept his command. He detested Mifflin's machinations, though forgave him after The War. Mifflin felt he was doing his patriotic duty in trying to have Washington removed and never shied from association with the action.

Mifflin was later accused of mismanagement and peculation while Quartermaster General. Some felt this was political Retribution for opposing Washington, not ordered by Washington, yet undertaken by those loyal to him. Others felt the investigation was power Jobbing, an attempt to save face and place blame for the inadequate funding and supplying of the Army anywhere except Congress. The Forge and other sufferings seemed to grow more Infamous by the day, and obfuscating blame for them was a natural political act.

Within doors, Mifflin laughed at the ridiculous allegations. Peculate what? The Army was usual so insolvent, embezzling from it would be like trying to bleed a stone. And he had a secure fortune regardless.

Without doors in public, Mifflin welcomed the investigation, confident no wrongdoing would be found. And none was. Unlike Robert Morris, who had made galling profits during the Revolution, Mifflin was exonerate absolute.

Mifflin had enjoyed a successful career after opposing Washington and being prosecuted. He was elected President of the Congress, and Washington tendered his resignation as Commander in Chief to Mifflin in 1783, four years ago. One of the right frigid moments of the Revolution, to be sure. And one of its blistering ironies. Mifflin was elected Speaker of the Pennsylvania Assembly in 1785 and served for a year. He would probably succeed Franklin as President of the Supreme Executive Council of Pennsylvania when Franklin retired or died in office. Dying in office seemed more probable to Franklin on days like this when the Gout and Stone ravaged him furious. Also more desirable.

Mifflin would be appointed not to the fœderal Government by Washington, and might not be elected to the House or Senate of the new Government for fear of alienating Washington, but he was still belove-ed in Pennsylvania. Pennsylvanians revered Washington, yet also remembered the capture of Philadelphia and much of the Pennsylvania by the British, and in more candid moments, in whispers, some Pennsylvanians dared to think and utter the unthinkable: Mifflin and others had been right about Washington's incompetency to some degree, and victory might have been obtained more quick and with less bloodshed by a more competent Commander.

Franklin felt not the need to distance himself from Mifflin to appease Washington, as some Deputies, especially those not from Pennsylvania, did. Yet Franklin knew it would be impolitick to have a man who had tried to knock the American Zeus off of Olympus read his speech. More than half of Deputies had served under Washington in the Army, most all revered him, and many disliked or at least distrusted Mifflin for his machinations against Washington and would not be receptive to anything he read. 'Twas also preferable not to grate Washington with Mifflin unnecessarily when more palatable options were available.

Franklin glanced at the Morrises. Despite sharing the same name, they were not related by blood, as anyone seeing their disparate facial features side by side could deduce. Governeur Morris was Robert Morris' assistant during his tenure as Superintendent of Finance, and they became friends. Robert Morris had ensured that Governeur Morris was appointed to the

Pennsylvania Deputation. Hamilton fancy'd himself a protégé of Robert Morris. Caledonia, who was about to read Franklin's speech, was Robert Morris' attorney.

To an attorney, Morris was perhaps the most lucrative client imagineable. Morris could have any counsel he wanted and was exacting in his expectations, yet had chose Caledonia. This said much.

For all their vaunted Intellect and Reputation, few Deputies were Classics expert in the theory and history of government. Most Deputies had served in government, but this was a far less Taxing proposition than understanding the theory which underlay government and was necessary to design a government. Many Deputies had helped craft Constitutions for their state, but crafting a government for all states was a much more daunting task. Especially a government that could preserve liberty across a Continent over epochas.

Most Deputies were well read, but few were exhaustive read. Even fewer were obsessive Phylosophers who had devoted a massive portion of their waking life to reading, study, penetrating contemplation. Of the obsessive Scholars who sat in Convention, only a handful had studied governmental Phylosophy, spent years reading the Histories, and pondered the theory of government deep, to its roots. John Adams and Thomas would have been accounted among this select number had they been able to attend the Convention. Chancellor Wythe had been among this group while he had been at the Convention, but he had vacated to tend to his ailing Lady, Elizabeth, who had passed in middling August.

Franklin glanced about the chambre. 'Twas filled with politicians proficient at the Practice of government, but he saw few Phylosophers expert in the theory of government. Caledonia, Mason, and Jemmy were the only three Phylosophers which Franklin would group in that select scholarly Echelon with Adams, Thomas, Chancellor Wythe, and cetera, and Jemmy might be debateable.

What a petrifying Irony! At a Convention to design a government, there were less than a half dozen Deputies with an exhaustive knowledge of the Phylosophy of government. If the Constitution failed, historians of futurity might condemn this deficiency mercyless. Would the great Mistake that caused the Constitution to fail be ignoring the advice of Caledonia, Mason, Chancellor Wythe, and Jemmy? Would futurity malign the fact that the Convention had been too thick and arrogant to respect its wisest Deputies sufficient? Malign the States for not appointing more such Phylosophers, that they were a more dominant Faction?

Theory and History were not all that signified. Politicians with practicable experience in government had proffered many useful criticisms of, and Improvements to, the structure of government espoused by Phylosophers, and without these a viable Edifice would not have emerged. Scholars less exhaustive read had also drawn many useful conclusions from Theory and History. Yet 'twas nonetheless true that Caledonia, Mason, Chancellor Wythe, and Jemmy possessed the rarest Wisdom of any Deputies. They were esteemed for it, even by Deputies that disagreed with their conclusions and had discarded most of their Advice.

Franklin again surveyed the Deputies in Convention assembled. So many eminent Scholars!

Yet in a chambre overflowing with the Educate, Caledonia was perhaps the most learn-ed.

Government had been Caledonia's peculiar Study. All the political Institutions of the world he knew in detail. He could trace the causes and effects of every Revolution from the earliest stages of the Græcian Commonwealth down to the present time. Caledonia also seem'd to have the best sense of any Deputy of how to meld national and fœderative Principles into a workable government of dual Sovereignty, though he aggravated many Deputies with his relentless insistence that a truly national Government was preferable, and by advocating a direct electored Senate and President. Caledonia wanted to intrust The People with more Power than most Deputies were comfortable with, yet he tended not to naïveté like Thomas nor distrusted men pathologic like John Adams. Caledonia did not let Emotion cloud his Perceptions, never drew conclusions unwarranted by facts, yet saw a future nigh limitless for America.

Middlers were cavalier in their use of the term Genius, but true Genius was exceeding rare, and Caledonia possessed it in Abundance. His mind was a blaze of Light. Of all Deputies, he was one of the deepest Thinkers and most exact Reasoners. Most Deputies mere regurgitated the opinions of others, granted they were usually the opinions of æsteemed scholars or historians. Caledonia was truly liberate in this thinking, and truly drew his own Conclusions, a gift much, much rarer than suppose-ed, among the Learned especially. Through relentless application of Reason validate by historical precedent, Caledonia came to conclusions which tended to enrage those of lesser Intellect, even learned men who were usual cool. Caledonia never scrupled to bombard with Reason and expoze the folly in ridiculous proposals, often doing so with Hauteur. The Little Lion was an epitome of humility compared to Caledonia.

As the byname Caledonia suggested, James Wilson was Scottish born, to a humble Presbyterian farming family. He earned a scholarship to the University of St. Andrews, the third most antient University in the western world. Only the Universities at Oxford and Cambridge were elder.

Caledonia then matriculated to the intellectual Meccas of Edinburgh and Glasgow, which also had antient Universities. Here Caledonia was educated by modern Aristotles such as Francis Hutcheson, David Hume, and Adam Smith. American scholars were enamour'd of these Enlightened Phylosophers, which had provided the intellectual underpinnings of the Revolution and the Rebirth of Republicanism. Caledonia had hobbed and nobbed with many of these Legends!

Caledonia naturally emigrated to America, where the Liberty he heard espoused in theory was implementing in Practice. Carrying letters of introduction from the Legends, he secured a teaching position at The Academy and College of Philadelphia, and he was so learn-ed and wise he was awarded an honorary Master's. He read the Law under the esteemed John Dickinson, opened a Practice, and was so skilled he secured a Fortune from it in just a few years.

Caledonia penned influencial Treatises that legitimized the Revolution, and he signed the Declaration of Independency. At the Convention he had served on the critical Committee of Detail with Brearly, and much of the Perspicaciousness of the Clauses it crafted was credited to him by Brearly. If Washington did not appoint Caledonia to the supreme Court of the new nation, lawyers across the land would be scratching their heads with Perplexion.

Yet Caledonia's Achille's heel, a heel so vulnerable it should have made his foot seem clubb-ed, was an affliction for Speculation. The bloody Scotch. If they weren't mad for pulling the cork or War, they were mad for some Thing. Caledonia was already overextended in western land-company Shares and was continuing to extend with a reckless Abandon that was right curdling to behold.

'Twas easy to grab Land in the West. Most any gentleman could obtain Credit to do so, often by creating a company, selling Shares, and using proceeds from those Shares to buy Land upon Credit, far in excess of proceeds. The snare was that Land could be arduous to exploit, to develop into a Farm, Fishery, or other income-begetting entity, much more arduous than the naïve or optimistic realized. Even prudential Speculators often ended up oweing payments on Loans or Shares, being unable to make such payments, and calling upon by their Creditors and bankrupting despite being land rich.

There was nothing prudential about Caledonia's Speculations. Land Fever had ruined many an otherwise judicious man, and Caledonia was proof that even the mightiest Intellects could still succumb the basest Follys and Vices. It did not take an animate imagination to see Caledonia one day facing Ruin, a Fugitive from creditors, or perhaps even languishing in Debtor's Prison. Yet few Deputies knew how overextended Caledonia was.

Superficial, to those outside Pennsylvania especially, he seemed just another aggressive land Speculator, and his association with Robert Morris meant that no one scrupled his Solvency.

The longer Deputies' gazes lingered on Caledonia, the more they seemed to venerate him. Franklin looked Caledonia in the eyes and saw the same measured Brilliance he always did. Franklin also felt the Hauteur which Caledonia nigh always exuded. Caledonia wore a shirt with a cambric ruffled front sim'l'r to that of most Deputies, but his seemed neater than most.

Franklin handed Caledonia his speech with his left hand, careful to keep his right hand on the table for Support. The paper Caledonia held was puny compared to the Constitution. He smiled at Franklin, opened the paper, and waited for Franklin to sit.

Franklin wanted to simple drop into his Chair, but this would make him appear decrepit. And his Girth was such he might break his Chair. Even Philadelphia Windsors made of the stoutest hardwood had their limits. Franklin could not sit without grabbing some-thing, however, and with no cane he needed the Table. He pressed his teeth together tight before bending at the knees, but as it had so many times during the Revolution, Providence smiled. No agony from the Gout or Stone, mere the usual Throbbing. Franklin settled into his Seat. He peered intent at Caledonia, as if he were unaware what would be read and were curious.

Out his periphery, Franklin saw the small, thin, perpetual-offended Elbridge Gerry roll his eyes skyward. The oafish, busy-eyed Edmund Randolph seemed equal perturb-ed. Both men seemed to sense they were observing a Contrivance.

"Mister President," Caledonia read. "I confess that there are several parts of this Constitution which I approve not at present, but I am not sure I shall never approve them."

Caledonia had a pronounced Scottish burr. It had been weakened somewhat by his residency in America, so was less severe than that of his native countrymen, when reading rather than speaking phrases he had formulate especially, though 'twas still peculiar to the American ear. Caledonia pronounced many vowels different from the English. He also compleat omitted the English emphasis on certain vowels in the middle of words and de-emphasized or eliminated consonants at the end of words. There was thaur. This was thes. Or was ur. Shall was shaa. And cetera.

Deputies had long ago grown a customed to Caledonia's clipping of the king's Tongue and were no longer distracted by it. They were gandering Franklin. He had advocated Measures such as a single-chambred Legislature, elected officials that served without Pay, and an Executive Council rather than a President. The Convention wanted Franklin's figure heading it to impart stature, and flattered his Reputation, but ignored his every Recommendation. All Deputies knew it.

"For having lived long," Caledonia read, "I have experienced many instances of being obliged by better information or fuller Consideration to change Opinions even on important sub-jects which I once thought right, but found to be otherwise. It is therefore that the older I grow, the more apt I am to doubt my own Judgment and to pay more Respect to the judgment of Others."

Long was lang, right was reit, found was foond, and Franklin was turned of 81, by far the eldest Deputy. Roger Sherman, the next eldest Deputy, was turned of 66. 'Twas no accident that Sherman proposed the Compromise which saved the Convention. Other Deputies elder than 60, such as Chancellor Wythe and Colonel Mason, could be accounted on one hand. Most Deputies was turned of 30 or 40.

Franklin glanced at prominent Deputies. Jemmy was turned of 36, the Little Lion turned of 30, Governeur Morris turned of 35, Charles Pinckney turned of a mere 29, though people oft assumed him younger and he did little to dispell this Misconception. Ever vain, Pinckney doubtless fancied being thought the youngest Deputy, as this would make him seem the Prodigy. Franklin wanted to chuckle. No one had engaged in deceit to appear elder and try'd to rob him of the "distinction" of being the eldest Deputy.

Even Washington the Demigod was but turned of 55. The difference between Franklin and Washington's ages was longer than the span which more than a quarter of Americans lived!

Increasing numbers of Deputies peer'd at Franklin. He stared into the table, at the chandles, that they could inspect him without feeling rude. Franklin felt Deputies staring at his paunch. At his drape-like chins. At his swollen kneepans. Franklin knew he was a pityable sight, the very personification of Age, without any posturing or affectation.

Fixating upon a chandle, Franklin could not but help ponder his youth. When Franklin was turned of 10, the age when common men were expected to begin Work and find their lifelong Trade, Franklin's father had pressed him to follow his footsteps and become a tallow Chandler. A tallow Chandler crafted chandles from tallow, animal renderings, as opposed to a wax Chandler, who made chandles from the wax of the bee or myrtle. A tallow Chandler was the lowliest of Trades, only the tanner or shambler perhaps being equal deplore-ed, and Franklin had despiz'd the prospect of dispencing his life rendering vats of rancid animal fat. His father had been chagrined when Franklin chose to become a Printer instead, apprenticing to his brother when he was turned of 12, the usual age of Indenture. The decision to learn such Trade proved prudential, as Printing and Writing had been the principal mean of Franklin's advancement. How many men had extinguished their Dreams by forsaking their Ambitions? Franklin liked to think he would have excelled in any Profession, but who could say? Had he succumbed to his father's Wishes, might he this instant be toiling rendering stinking chandles and soap rather than scripting scenes for the Stage of the World?

Franklin looked up at Washington slow, giving Deputies time to look away. Washington's trim Physique remaint a stark contrast to Franklin's. Franklin envied it, yet he had only his own laziness to blame for his Corpulence and Decrepitude. How many times over the years had he admonished himself to break from chess, from reading, from correspondency, and take the Exercise, even if just a short Walk.

Glancing about, Franklin saw that his remarks seemed to have their intended Effect. Deputies seemed to envision themselves as antient as him and wonder how different their views of the world and Constitution might be at such time.

"Most men as well as most sects in Religion," Caledonia read, "think themselves in possession of all Truth, and that wherever others differ from them it is so far Error. Steele, a Protestant, in a Dedication tells the Pope that the only difference between our Churches in their opinions of the certainty of their doctrines is the Church of Rome is infallible and the Church of England is never in the wrong."

Error was errur, wrong was wrang, and Steele was Richard Steele, Raconteur of the first Order. He was founder and principal writer of the journals The Spectator and The Tatler. In his youth, Franklin had modeled his writing after Steele, especially Steele's practice of writing from the perspective of contrived Personæ.

"Many private persons think almost as highly of their own Infallibility as of that of their sect," Caledonia read, "though few express it so naturally as a certain French lady. In a Dispute with her sister, she said, 'I don't know how it happens, Sister, but I meet with no body but myself, that's always in the right'."

Franklin had written the sister's words in French, which Caledonia read in French. French pronounced with a thick Scottish Burr was an absolute Atrocity, and many Deputies chuckled a bit. Even Caledonia grinned appreciable after the last syllable of French.

But some Deputies seemed irritate, including the Irish-born but French-faced James McHenry of Maryland, whose conniving eyes always seemed to be shifted to one side, exposing whites. Curious that Roger Sherman's eyes never seemed conniving, no matter how much a-shifted, yet McHenry's always did, even when scarce shifted.

Franklin knew the criticisms levyed by Backbiters. That he was over concerned about preserving his Reputation, enlarging his Fame. That his sagacity was exaggerate, his wisdom worn, and he regurgitated the same old Platitudes.

"In these sentiments, Sir," Caledonia read, "I agree to this Constitution with all its faults, if they are such. Because I think a general Government necessary for us, and there is no form of Government but what may be a blessing to The People if well administered. I believe farther that this Government is likely to be well administered for a course of years, and can only end in Despotism, as other forms have done before it, when The People shall become so corrupted as to need despotic Government, being incapable of any other."

To Franklin's left, Governeur Morris smirked, as he had when reviewing this portion of the speech previous.

Other Deputies seemed less amuse-ed, especially the Yale educate Minister Abraham Baldwin of Georgia, who was seated at the table direct right of the rightmost Pennsylvania table, in the left seat. Abraham was the only Minister at the Convention, though Hugh Williamson, Jemmy, and Oliver Ellsworth studyed theology. Baldwin was long-faced, had wavy black hair that looked wind swept and somewhat gallant even on a calm day, and sourpuss lips. He was handsome in a way, though with a softness about him, save a measure of Brimstone in his eyes and chin.

Like Franklin, Baldwin had humble beginnings, having been born to a blacksmith. He served as a Chaplain in the Army during The War. Baldwin had declined a Divinity Professorship at Yale to read the Law, but believed in education, public education especially, and had been chosen by the Governour of Georgia to create an educational Plan for the state. Baldwin was labouring diligent to found America's first state-chartered University. Thomas strong approved of this University of Georgia and wanted to found one in his country of Virginia. Luminaries like Thomas and Baldwin envisioned an America filled with publick Schools that diffused Knowledge. Ignorance and Liberty were incompatible, after all. Unfortunately, idealism and naïveté were not. As a Minister and Educator devoted to trying to improve people, Baldwin seemed galled by Franklin's insinuation that people were fundamental incapable of maintaining to morality or perpetuating freedom. With each passing instant, Baldwin's expression grew more dour, with more Brimstone in the eyes and more Puss in the sour lips.

Few other Deputies seemed galled tho'.

The Little Lion, still direct a front of Franklin, turned and faced him. His blue eyes twinkled with Amusement. Conceit ouzed out of him with greater rapidity than usual, making him seem more Lion-like.

On the right side of Chambre, numerous Deputies shot musket balls into Hamilton's back with their eyes. One was that voracious land Speculator William Blount of North Carolina.

Up close and at a distance, Blount seem'd like two different men. Up close, Blount was a modest attractive man with balanced facial features, a flat nose, earnest eyebrows and eyes, and a solemn pursing of the lips. At distance, Blount seemed more powdered, more pork-ed, more the Dandy. The more distant the View, the more womanish Blount's eyes seemed, the more powdered his face, and the more the pursing of his lips seemed like the calculate Contrivance of a Shuckster.

As Blount was seated at the rightmost Chair in the right front row, he was neither close nor distant. Franklin thus alternated between the two Blounts by narrowing or widening his vantage. Yet gradual the true Blount emerged, the over-powdered Dandy ready to scalp anyone for a few Scraps of Land.

Blount was reputed to have acquired upwards of a million Acres of land in the West, most all on Credit, often by shaving savages, and tended to view all issues through the prism of western Expansion and land Acquisition. He had opposed the Treaty of Hopewell that Congress recent ratified against the objections of North Carolina. The Treaty ceded acres that Speculators had claimed, repairing them to Savages. To Blount, this encroachment upon state Prerogatives by the fœderal Government was an omen of Tyrannys to follow.

Would Blount sign?

Would this speech sway him?

Could any Thing?

Franklin was tempted to stand and proffer Blount a few thousand Acres to sign. He was a disquieting man. The sort of sordid Species that seemed to accumulate in governments over time. Franklin imagined a Congress in futurity brimming with Blounts.

Despotism, indeed.

Yet every Deputy could not be a Wilson, a Wythe, a Washington. Franklin didn't have to like Blount, or even respect him, mere induce him to sign the Constitution.

"I doubt too whether any other Convention we can obtain may be able to make a better Constitution," Caledonia read. "For when you assemble a Number of Men to have the advantage of their joint Wisdom, you inevitably assemble with those men all their prejudices, their passions, their errors of Opinion, their local Interests, and their selfish Views. From such an Assembly can a perfect production be expected?"

Many Deputies shook their heads.

"It therefore astonishes me, Sir," Caledonia read, "to find this system approaching so near to perfection as it does."

Perfection was a necessary Embellishment. Not a single Deputy felt the Constitution perfect, or even approaching to such. Yet a few Deputies none the less nodded.

"And I think 'twill astonish our Enemies," Caledonia read, "who are waiting with confidence to hear that our councils are Confounded like those of the Builders of Babel and that our States are on the point of Separation, only to meet hereafter for the purpose of cutting one another's throats."

Chairs creaked and groaned as Deputies shifted their weight. Caledonia was no metronome like Major Jackson. He paused for emphasis, for dramatic effect, did not hesitate to stop and clear his throat or take a breath, even mid-word or sentence. During such breaks in the reading, Jemmy's quill could be heard scraping on paper like a groping bird Claw. A faint sound, yet discernable. And even when the quill could not be heard, its shaft continued to dance like the baton of a Maestro. Yet a measure of Fatigue seemed to have had crept into Jemmy's Stroke. He seemed to write less as the months passed, and with diminished Flourish, his Notes perhaps becoming less detailed.

The Chambre remained bright. Bright and hot. The air was still utter lifeless. Even the baize on the tables of the deep-south States, those on the extremity of the rear right row, was now dotted with Sweat. And even the faces of the deep-south Gentlemen glistened with Sweat. Even their light Camblet coats could not save them from the Spittle.

The fœtid Odour of body, of stink from Sweat, was now more noticeable, more dominant than stain, than plaster, than paint, though still secondary to the smells of soot, Fire, extinguisht candle.

"Thus I consent, Sir, to this Constitution," Caledonia read, "because I expect no better, and because I am not sure that it is not the best. The opinions I have had of its errors, I sacrifice to the public Good. I have never whispered a Syllable of them abroad. Within these walls they were born, and here they shall die."

Franklin had reworked the speech numerate times and felt satisfaction at his wording. I am not sure I shall never approve it. I am not sure that it is not the best. Multiple negatives, to create a greater sense of Uncertainty, and thus Humility.

"If every one of us in returning to our Constituents were to report the Objections he has had to this Constitution," Caledonia read, "and endeavor to gain Partizans in support of them, we might prevent its being generally received. And thereby lose all the salutary Effects and great Advantages resulting naturally in our favour among foreign Nations as well as among ourselves, from our real or apparent Unanimity."

Many Deputies nodded, including Eminents such as the Morrises and Dictator John.

"Much of the Strength and Efficiency of any Government in procuring and securing Happiness to The People depends on opinion," Caledonia read, "on the general opinion of the goodness of the Government, as well as of the wisdom and integrity of its Governours."

The end of the speech was nigh. Franklin focused on Caledonia more intent, once again the very Portrait of the apt Listener curious to hear what was said sequel.

"I hope therefore," Caledonia read, "that for our own sakes as a part of The People, and for the sake of Posterity, we shall act heartily and unanimously in recommending this Constitution wherever our Influence may extend, and turn our future thoughts and endeavors to the means of having it well administered."

In Franklin's speech, he had written, "recommending this Constitution, if approved by Congress and confirmed by the Conventions," but Caledonia skipped the second portion of the Clause. A pleasing deletion, as the speech was more molass-ed without it, and all Deputies knew the daunting difficultys that Ratification presented.

"On the whole, Sir," Caledonia read, "I cannot help expressing a Wish that every Member of the Convention who may still have Objections to it, would with me, on this occasion doubt a little of his own infallibility, and to make manifest our Unanimity, put his Name to this Instrument."

By the time Caledonia had placed the paper containing the speech back onto the table, walking sticks were a tapping, palms were a clapping, and wooden rapping once again reverberated throughout the chambre. Morris pounded his peg Leg with admirable fury, like a hound wagging its tail.

Yet a few walking sticks and palms remained silent. McHenry was scowling so severe he might have been diagnosing a terminal Patient. Franklin could envision the scathing criticisms of the back biters, McHenry especially. Doctor Franklin had been perverted by residing in Europe so long and America ought be suspicious of his motives and Patriotism. The speech was plain, insinuating, designed to guard The Doctor's fame.

As the tapping began to subside, Franklin stood, again without his walking stick, and again with mighty great difficulty. He waited for absolute Silence, and let it settle in for a few moments. He knew his voice tended to be soft and difficult to hear, so spoke loudly. Louder anyway.

"Mister President, Sir," Franklin said, "I hereby move that this Constitution of the United States of Americay be approved and signed by all Deputies present."

A dramatic pause.

Governeur Morris handed Franklin a piece of paper, as arranged. He had a solemn expression appropriate for the moment, and looked roosterish rather than cherubic, especially because of his arched eyebrows.

Franklin opened the letter. His double Spectacles hung low on his nose, and he pressed them up slight. Lubricate by sweat, they immediately slid back down a bit. Franklin looked through the tiny circles of glass. He had invented double Spectacles three years ago, in 1784. They enabled his failing eyes to view distant Objects as well as near ones, making them as useful as ever. Franklin constructed his double Spectacles by taking two circular lenses with different foci, cutting them in half, and then adjoining a half-circle of each to make one circular lens. But the double Spectacles were a far from Perfect. The most glaring Flaw was the horizon at the union of the two half-circles, which was extremely intrusive and tended to impede vision.

Franklin wished there were a more precise way to measure the deficiency of the eye and use this measurement to construct a lens with the precise foci required. And a way to lessen the seam between the lenses. Ideally, the upper, less-concave lens which was used more frequent for viewing general surroundings could be made larger, and the lower, more-concave lens which was used less frequent for reading could be made smaller. Perhaps a crescent moon shape for the upper lens, with a smaller ellipsis shaped lens under the Crescent? Unfortunately, Optics was not advanced enough to allow such Marvels. Even Franklin's close friend David Rittenhouse, the world-renowned astronomer, inventor, and clockmaker, had been unable to construct superior double Spectacles.

Franklin looked through the lower lens with the greater foci. The words of the letter became immediate larger, but they were hazy, as if Franklin were standing too close. He slid the spectacles up slow, until Governeur Morris' calligraphic Scrawl became clear, and then press'd them onto his nose more firm, to minimize sliding.

"I further move that this Convention adopt the following as a convenient form." Franklin read Morris' calligraphic scrawl, "Done in Convention by the unanimous consent of The States present. In Witness whereof we have hereunto subscribed our names."

Reading Morris' stratagem gave it the weight of Franklin's Reputation, that it might have a better Chance of success. As unanimity of Deputies was impossible, unanimity of States would have to be settled for. If the motion passed, the signed Constitution would not pretend that it was approved unanimous by all Deputies, but merely all States. Deputies would not be individually committed to uphold the Constitution, meaning Dissidents might sign even if they approved not the Constitution.

"I second Doctor Franklin's motions," Jemmy said.

His quill kept scrawling as he spoke and he did not look up.

Franklin sat, again careful to do so slow, as a younger, more vital man would. Gerry, Randolph, and Mason were frowning. They seemed not just irritate, but downright warm. The Sophistrys of language had beguiled them not.

Silence.

Anyone could rise, address the President, and speak to the Motion.

Everyone a rising to speak had to address the President first because this was one of the Rules which Deputies had agreed upon when the Convention opened. Before creating a government for others, they had first governed themselves.

Anyone could a rise, but no one did.

All eyes were upon the Dissidents. Surely one of them would object the Motion.

Instead Nathaniel Gorham of Massachusetts stood. He had a face one could forget. Nary a distinguishing feature, save a small cleft in the lip just below the centre of the nose. Not a deformity, more of a Dimple. Another face longer than ideal, with a nose more dominant than ideal, and a wig with short grey hair that was several inches higher on top than on the sides, like the plume of a bird. A small Crease of chin Fat extended out from Gorham's tye, his cravat, but 'twas well behind the front line of the chin.

Gorham was extreme likely, but general absent Gravitas. His prime Virtue was that he was Complaisant and scarce offended anyone.

Likelyness and Complaisancy were not a trifling Virtues.

For a politician especially.

And Gorham attained to the feat without resorting to Corruption or Sycophancy.

Gorham had few enemies, for he scarce had any Thing incisive or inciting to say and was habitual in forsaking contentious Debates. Yet he was also genuine Benevolent, and men were fond of him.

Likelyness notwithstanding, Gorham was an indifferent Massachusetts merchant with mediocre education who served as President of Congress in the previous year, 1786. He was a direct descendant of one of the Pilgrims who had fled english Tyranny on the Mayflower, sailt to America, and founded Plymouth. Liberty was in Gorham's blood, and having served as President of Congress, he was cognizant of the deficiencys of it and the Articles of Confederacy. He was thus a strong supporter of a strengthened Government, tho' he seemed to have no keen sense of how to create one.

Like many a Deputy, Gorham had been seduced by land Speculation, and it troubled Franklin to think such a likely man might end up like most Speculators, destitute, a Fugitive from creditors, or rotting in Debtor's Prison. The temptation to attain to wealth without Work could seduce even the kindest and seeming moral men!

A Massachusetts man who was not so pompous nor grating you wanted to run him through was a rarity. Massachusetts was one of the three largest States, along with Pennsylvania and Virginia. The Convention President, Washington, hailed from Virginia, as did many of the Convention Eminents, including Chancellor Wythe, Mason, and Randolph. Pennsylvania was host to the Convention, and with Franklin at its head and many Eminents, it needed not its vanity stroked. But Massachusetts was like a handsome Belle, in need of constant Affectation, and appointing one of its Deputies to a position of import was advantageous.

Thus Gorham the Massachusetts Man had been made Chair of the Convention when it moved into Committee of the Whole. As debate was contentious, a likely Chair known to be objective and disinterested was critical, that the impartiality of his rulings could not be question'd and Compromise could be brokered.

The Convention had proceeded in four main Phases. It had been scheduled to convoke on May 14 but could not mount a quorum. The Pennsylvania and Virginia Deputations had conspired the Randolph Plan while a waiting a quorum, from May 16 to May 24. On May 25, the Convention convoked and determined administrative peculiars and rules, including Secrecy, a process which should have taken but a day or two but which languished until the eve of June, foreshadowing the Sluggardness to follow. Throught June and July, the Convention consulted and contended, and determined the key principles and provisions of the Constitution by calling hundreds of questions. From July 27 to August 5, the Convention recessed whilst the Committee of Detail prepared the first Draught of the Constitution, using the yea and nay votes on the questions called as Guide. From August 6 until the present moment, the Committee of Detail draught had been honed and finalyzed, including a revision by the Committee of Stile.

The Convention had spent the majority of its time, the bulk of June and July and much of August, meeting as Committee of the Whole. For most of the Convention, Gorham had occupied the Speaker's throne, not Washington. For most of the Convention, Washington had stepped down from the dais and sat silent with the Virginia Deputation, the proverbial Pachyderm in the room. It had been advantageous for Washington not to chair all Debate, squandering his Stature governing warm Deputies.

When Gorham stood, Deputies saw an esteemed Old Patriot they had chose as a de facto Speaker of the Convention, one who, like Washington, scarce involved himself in Debate. Most Deputies seemed to sense that Gorham a rising at the very last instant of the Convention was hardly happenstance, and that he must have been serving the Interest of The General in great measure. While Chairing the Convention, Washington could not make a Motion, as this violated parliamentary Procedure. Franklin had already made several motions. Gorham was next in the line of succession as it were, and though Deputies peering at him evidenced fondness more than deep respect, they were clear intrigued.

"Mister President, Sir," Gorham said. "If 'tis not too late I wish that the clause declaring the number of Representatives shall not exceed one for every forty Thousand be reconsidered."

Gorham was nought fashionable nor elegant. He had no gift for oratory, no weighty reputation, minimal physical stature.

Yet there was something unaffected and genuine in the way he spoke that was endearing.

"This Clause has produced much discussion," Gorham said. "For the purpose of lessening objections to the Constitution, I would strike out forty Thousand and insert thirty Thousand."

Gorham meant objections to the Constitution by little States. They still felt marginalized by large States. Deputies glanced at the Congregation of little States at the left of the chambre, pupils of a few dilating with understanding. This was yet another preemptory Concession to little States to ensure that they old Jealousies was not rekindled, causing them to unwind the Compromise and Constitution in the final instant.

The Grand Committee compriz'd of one Deputy from each state had chose the 40 Thousand ratio when it wrought the Compromise on Representation, but the number of Representatives per Quota had been an ongoing cause of warmth. With a Quota of Tax of 2,568 Thousand Americans, some 2.568 Million, having each Representative represent 10 Thousand Quotas more or less altered the distribution of power among little States and large States in the lower House.

Rogue Island and Providence Plantations had a Quota of Tax of some 58 Thousand persons at present, and would nigh certain have 60 Thousand by the time of Census the First. New Hampshire had a Quota of Tax of some 102 Thousand at present, and might very well have 120 Thousand by the time of Census the First. With one Representative per 40 Thousand, Rogue Island would have but one Representative and its addition'l 20 Thousand persons would be frittered in terms of Representation. Assuming she reclaimed her Senses eventual and partook of the

Union. With one Representative per 30 Thousand, Rogue Island would have two Representatives and a much smaller number of its residents would be frittered in terms of Representation. Similarly, New Hampshire would have three Representatives rather than two, had she not already been ceded an extra Representative by the large States when the initial quantum of Representatives negotiate by the Grand Committee. At one Representative per 30 Thousand, New Hampshire might even qualify for four Representatives by the time of Census the First.

A single additional Representative was much more significant to little States than large States, owing their smaller number of Representatives. If Rogue Island gained a Representative, its number of Representatives doubled, while if Virginia gained a Representative, it merely had eleven Representatives instead of ten. Thus, this last-moment Increase in the number of Representatives of little States addressed their fundamental Objection to the Constitution, the fact that large States would overwhelm them in the Congress. It minimized the Discrepancy that they found so objectionable and terrific.

"This would not establish an absolute rule," Gorham said, "but only give Congress a greater latitude which is not unreasonable."

Deputies nodded. The Constitution specified that, "The Number of Representatives shall not exceed one for every forty Thousand." Two Representatives for every 40 Thousand persons exceeded, was more than, one Representative for every 40 Thousand persons, and thus prevented by the Constitution. But two Representatives for every 40 Thousand persons was also one Representative for every 20 Thousand persons, or 20 Thousand persons per Representative, and 20 Thousand persons per

Representative was less than 40 Thousand per Representative. These computations were elementary to all Deputies, who easily grasped the crux: 40 Thousand persons per Representative was the minimum allowed by the Constitution. During districting, or when passing Apportionment Acts which set the number of Representatives for each State, Congress could chuse a higher number of persons per Representative, but not a lower number. It could create a District or Apportionment with 45 Thousand persons per Representative, but not 35 Thousand persons per Representative. Decreasing the number of persons per Representative from 40 Thousand to 30 Thousand thus gave Congress greater latitude in districting and apportionment.

Franklin again wish'd for some upper Limitation on the persons per Representative, a lessening of Latitude in diluting Representation, but knew this fancyful.

Rufus King of Massachusetts a rose and seconded Gorham's motion. He looked Roman and patrician and might have been the corpulent cousin of Julius Cæsar. Turned of but 32, King was a younger Deputy, and paunch-ed for his age, yet in the absence of John and Samuel Adams, one of the more esteemed Massachusetts Deputies. Harvard educate, he had interrupted his reading of the Law to fight in the Revolution, serving as a Major under General Sullivan. After The War, he finished reading the Law, passed the Bar, opened a successful Practice, and become political active, serving in both the Massachusetts Legislature and the Continental Congress. A few Deputies only, such as Governeur Morris or Jemmy, had spoke more than King during Debate. Like Governeur Morris, King had been one of the Mules that trudged arguments. He had proved an eloquent and persuasive Advocate of a strong fœderal Government, earning significant esteem from Deputies despite his youth. King was probably just seconding the Motion of a fellow Massachusetts man, but his second nonetheless added Gravity.

Daniel Carroll of Maryland stood. His face always reminded Franklin of the antagonist in Marlowe's Doctor Faustus. Pointy nose, mischievous eyebrows, a dev'lish smile. Yet there was also a piggish aspect to Carroll's face. The Devil if he'd eaten too much pudding and too many cakes and pastries. Carroll's chin dimple might have been attractive had he been thinner, but on his corpulent Face it made the chin seem snout-like. Mephistopheles cross-bred with a Swine. That was Daniel Carroll, who extoll'd the virtues of Gorham's Motion. As Carroll had spoke less than a few dozen times during the entire Convention, and had shown Wisdom when he did, Deputies listen'd respectful.

Carroll finished speaking and sat.

And then something signal happened.

George Washington stood.

Utter surprize on the faces of most Deputies. In the four months of the Convention, Washington had spoke frequent in his capacity as President, to supervise the proceedings. But he hadn't uttered a single syllable in Debate.

Until now.

"My situation," Washington said, "has hitherto restrained me from offering sentiments on questions depending in the House. And it perhaps ought to now impose Silence on me."

Washington's shoulders were thrown back, as lesser men when strutting. Except this was the way he stood natural. Like

Franklin, some Deputies couldn't help smiling, finding the person of Washington awe some.

"Yet I cannot forbear," Washington said, "expressing my Wish that the alteration proposed take place. 'Tis much desired that Objections to the Constitution recommended be made as few as possible."

Washington spoke halting, pausing in places to find words. Those he chose seemed imprecise to Franklin.

"The smallness of the proportion of Representatives," Washington said, "has been considered by many members of this Convention an insufficient security for the rights and interests of The People. It has always appeared to me among the exceptionable parts of the Plan."

Deputies nodded. When the Constitution was put to Ratification by the several States, enemies would pretend it diluted Representation so grievous that The People would have scant ability to instruct their Representatives. Deputies would be able to make honest Pretense that the Convention had consider'd this defect, and had concentrated Representation as much as feasible as their final alteration of the Charta, at the behest of no less than Washington himself. If Washington found the Concentration of Representation adequate, was that not insurance enough for America?

Washington was standing slight right of the centre of his throne, allowing Franklin to once again eye the gold Sun on the back of it. The Sol's glance seemed mocking. Was it a rising Sun or a setting Sun?

"Late as the present moment is for admitting Amendments," Washington said, "I think this of so much consequence that it would give much satisfaction to see it adopted."

The American Zeus sat and waited respectful, giving anyone who opposed the measure a chance to a rise and be heard.

The silence was nigh comickal. As if any Deputy had Brass enough to oppose Washington. Who could refuse him, both out of Love of the man and all he had done, and out of Fear that he might refuse to condescend the Executive. Or deny critics a Station in the new government.

Glances were inevitable heaved Franklin's way. Only he had sufficient Prestige to even contemplate opposing Washington. Doing so had never been necessary, and never would be.

As Deputies eyed him, Franklin couldn't help but admire Washington's shrewdness. Wise enough to use his Prestige judicious, once only, in the last and most critical instance, when of maximal value. His only Comment of the Convention address'd its core issue: the degree to which The People would represent themselves. Yet if Washington had stood and asked that the Chief Justice of the supreme Court be chose from the Felons in Walnut Gaol, that the President be given a Jester, or that the Vice President be a Billygoat, the silence probably would have been similar.

The very brevity of his remarks spoke to Washington's eminency. Deputies usual spoke for a quarter hour or more making their points, and some Times for hours.

Not Washington.

His presence was enough. His reputation enough. The Fear and Respect he commanded and most of all the Love he inspired were enough.

Yet the motion was easy to approve, for it was prudential, as most every Thing Washington advocated was. Washington would never expend his Stature for any ignoble, naïve, or imprudential undertaking. Which was why he had such Stature.

Power emanate from The People was the fundamental principle of Republicanism. With fewer persons per Representative, America would be more Republican. Washington had taken a measure which seem'd Partizan and placed it firm on Principle.

"Would any Gentlemen," Washington said, "like to be heard ere Mister Gorham's Motion is voted?"

Washington seemed conscious of the potential disaccord of Interest in the Chair speaking in Debate, and waited a considerable span, more than a full minute.

Governeur Morris a rose, planting his peg Leg with an audible thump. Washington recognized him.

"Mister President, Sir," Governeur said. "I have no objection to the Amendment and will certain positive it, but the Representatives for Congress the First were computed at the prior ratio. If the Amendment is to be positived, 'twould seem prudential to recompute Apportionment at the new ratio."

Dictator John placed his palm over his forehead and eyes, pressed upon his eyebrows, and frowned. Dawning realization creased the countenance of many a Deputy, rapid replaced by dazed Gazes or Frowns.

Franklin felt the same Chagrin nigh all Deputies did. The Quota of Contribution for all thirteen States, for all of America, was some 2,568 Thousand. At 40 Thousand per Representative, simple Ciphering, division of 2,568 into parts each of 40, gave some 64.2, which Deputies had rounded up to 65, not wanting to deny any State its just Representation by rounding down and discounting their persons. There would be 65 Representatives in Congress the First, if all thirteen States ratified, with the Apportionments for each State, its number of Representatives, having been enumerate in Article I Section 2.

The math was not so neat and simple as it might seem, however, for few States had Quotas of Tax which were round multiples of 40 Thousand. Dividing a State's Quota of Tax by 40 Thousand result'd in a decimal number, not a round number, and determining how to round decimal numbers of each State had been a political process negotiate in the Grand Committee. Large States had general agreed to round down, and in some instances even surrender Representatives, to appease the little States and allow them to round up. Massachusetts and Pennsylvania each had a Quota of Tax of some 360 Thousand, by way of example, which divided by 40 Thousand yielded 9. Massachusetts and Pennsylvania had been entitled to 9 Representatives, but had agreed to accept but 8. Virginia had a Quota of Tax of some 420 Thousand, which divided by 40 Thousand yielded a decimal of 10.5. Mathematics would general round 10.5 up to 11, and most States would want such apportion rounded up to 11, but Virginia had agreed to 10 Representatives rather than agitating for 11.

Georgia's decimal had been 2.25, and New Hampshire's decimal was 2.55, but both had 3 Representatives. Delaware's decimal was 0.92 or 0.93—Franklin could not recall certain—

and it had 1 Representative, the fewest the Constitution allowed. Maryland's decimal was 5.45 and it had 6 Representatives. New Jersey's decimal was 3.45 and it had 4 Representatives. South Carolina's decimal was 3.75 and it had 5 Representatives!

New York's decimal was 5.8—5.8—5.8 what? Franklin could not remember the second decimal, but New York had been given 6 Representatives. Connecticut's decimal was 5.05 and it had 5 Representatives, the only little State that had rounded down, save Rogue Island. Rogue Island's decimal was 1.45 but it had been given 1 Representative, it not being in Convention to agitate for itself and perhaps attain to 2.

If the ratio of Representatives was to be altered from one for every forty Thousand to one for every thirty Thousand, then it was indeed prudential to recompute the Apportionment, dividing each State's Quota of Tax by thirty Thousand instead of forty Thousand. The decimals would all be different, however, meaning Apportionment and the number of Representatives of each State would have to be renegotiate. The increased quantum of Representatives at the lower Ratio would also mandate such. At 30 Thousand per Representative, simple Ciphering, division of 2,568 into parts each of 30, gave some 85.6, which Deputies would round up to 86. This was a rough Hazard, using the population for the whole of America rather than those of each individual States. Even as a rough Hazard, 21 additional Representatives, a nigh one third Increase above the original quantum of 65, was no trifle. Such Apportionment was best negotiate by a Committee of Twelve comprised of one Deputy from each State rather than the Committee of the Whole or the Convention.

The prudential course would be to constitute such Committee of Twelve, or Committee of Eleven if Hamilton seated not for New York, to adjourn, and to reseat later in the day or the next day when the Committee had renegotiated Apportionment, which the Convention could then positive. Many Deputies doubtless evidenced distraught expressions because they contemplated such necessity, and the attendant delay of that Intention homeward of which all Deputies anxious.

Even if new Apportionment could be magickal and miraculous negotiate right rapid in just a few minutes, which was not unthinkable, Deputies being liable to dispence with their usual Blatherings and Agitations to expedite their escape from Philadelphia, the engross'd Constitution would have to be amended in some fourteen Places minimum. A few Amendations to the engross'd Charta could be countenanced, but it could not be transmitted to the Congress looking like some patchwork rough Draught, riddled with Erazures and Scribblework. This would beget a subtle yet pervasive tendency to view the Convention as fraught with uncertainty and Doubt, and the Constitution of Government as hurried, incompleat, a Charta to be scrutinized with Suspicion, and one probably in need of additional Amendment. Thus, if the number of Representatives apportion'd to each State be altered, the Constitution of Government would nigh certain need to be engrossed a fresh by the Scribe, Mr. Shallus. Even if Shallus had to fresh engross only a single parchment, page the first where Representatives apportion'd in Article I Section 2, this would take hours, and probably require adjournment until the morrow, delaying the Intention of Deputies homeward.

Several Deputies a rose to address and re-dress the issue, and made the points Franklin had contemplate. Deputies argued that the same essencial Proportions of Representation among the several States would be wrought by a new Apportionment, and it was thus unnecessary. Other Deputies retorted that the Spirit of the Amendment was that each Representative serve a small enough quantum of The People that they might instruct such Representative vigorous, and that this requisite had nothing to do with relative apportions of Representative allocate the several States. 'Twas rather a question of the quantum of persons per Representative. Deputies of several little States expressed pleasure with the present Apportionment and saw no need to effect alteration of it. Deputies questioned the Admission of new States to the Union at the thirty Thousand ratio, when existing Representation computed at the forty Thousand ratio, to which other Deputies replied that in the dernier Resort, new states could be apportion'd with additional Representatives at the forty Thousand ratio to ensure consistency. Other Deputies thought a violation of the Constitution a dangerous Precedent to inaguarate, even in such a seeming insignificant peculiar.

Some Deputies argued that as Congress the First would pass nigh all formative Laws, instigating fœderal Taxes, establishing Departments, constructing the Judiciary, and legislating upon Patents, crimes, census, naturalization, copyright, residency, Intercourse with Savages, and cetera, reapportionment was worth the time. 'Twas crucial that The People have the Power to instruct their Representatives on such plenitude of foundational Decisions, even if Intention homeward delayed a day. At mention of delaying Intention, Deputies affixed other Deputies proffering such sentiments with murd'rous Glares and seemed to want to run them through.

Whilst Deputies debated as hens a-clucking, Franklin pondered the provisions of the Constitution pursuant to Apportionment. Months prior, little States had pressed for a minimum of 2 Representatives for each State in the lower House, a mode which was thankful rejected, else Apportionment would have been a bloody cock Pit fight. The absence of a Clause specifying rounding for Apportionment struck Franklin as curious though, even making allowance for the fact that Constitutions was not Principia Mathematicas. Such Clause would have allowed a simple recomputation of Apportionment, in a mode strict mathematic, without any political Barter, and attendant Corruption, requisite.

Alas, Politicians in Convention assembled had evidenced a grievous Antipathy to a mode which favoured the mathematic to compleat exclusion of the political. Little States had object'd to a Clause requiring all decimal divisions to be rounded down, which would diminish their Representatives. Some pondering Principle rather than sole Interest also questioned the Justice of such mode, arguing that exclusion of all remainders of division served to dilute—and in some measure negative—the Representation of significant quantums of persons. A Clause enforcing a rounding up of decimal divisions in all instancys seemed to answer the Need, but might enforce Districts which violated the one Representative per forty Thousand—or thirty Thousand—rule, with too few persons per District. In point of fact, rounding up must produce such Violation in every instance, even the rounding up of the total quantum of Representatives of the several States, the 64.2 rounded up to 65 or the 85.6 rounded up to 86. This before the Imprecision of the three fifths Clause accounted, which made a Mockery of the entire proposition. The three fifths Atrocity notwithstanding, once the mode of rounding down forsaken, Apportionment could not be ciphered exact as if a Newtonian Force, if it were to be consonant with the ratio Clause.

Nor, by the reckon of most Deputies, ought Apportionment be ciphered so. The chief objection to such mode had been the Determination to enumerate essential principles only, and confine to general propositions. Most Deputies seemed to reckon that the Quota of Tax of the several States, or of each individual State, ought be divided by 40 Thousand—or 30 Thousand—and that the Latitude to round up or down from decimal results ought devolve to the Congress. Whatever ought be, this is what was, yet the Imprecision still irked the natural Phylosopher in Franklin.

Listening to the Debate made Franklin exceeding conscious of the delicacy intrinsic to the Amendation of a Constitution. The seeming simplest Clauses, or Amendations, were scarce such, for each Clause was part of an interlocking Clockwork. All Deputies within chambre agreed that a quantum in excess of 30,000 persons could not be adequate represented by one Person, and that the apportionment Ratio ought be lowered to this quantum, but the implementation of such principle, the addition of a gear to the extant Clockwork, or even the alteration of the gear's size within Clockwork, was not so simple as it seemed.

Franklin refocused upon the debate. Deputies argued that a Census would nigh certain be ordered by Congress the First, with its Enumeration reported to Congress the Second, which would then pass an Apportionment Act that would reapportion Congress the Third. Congress the First and Congress the Second could be apportioned at the 40 Thousand ratio, and Congress the Third at the 30 Thousand ratio using an accurate Enumeration rather than the hazards the Convention had been enforced to resort to. While a reapportionment at the present instance, and Perfection in every partickular, would have certain been preferential, they were not requisites, and nigh impossible. The 40 Thousand ratio would be adequate for a Congress or two. 'Twas not as if Tyranny need be feared immediate, as nigh half the Senate and perhaps a tenth the House was seated in Convention at present, and would check any attempts at Abuse in Congress the First or Second. As Mr. Gorham rightful observe-ed, the 30 Thousand ratio was not an absolute Rule but only a Latitude granted to Congress. Let Congress make utility of it, once constitute, if they of such a mind, but there was no need to alter the quantum of Representatives apportion'd in the present Charta.

Politicians being politicians, other Deputies felt the need to show their Parts, and regurgitated what others had spoke for some half Hour, at the least. It seemed as Hours. The more Deputies a rose to speak, the more other Deputies saw their Intention homeward in the morrow slipping away.

Franklin could not help but ponder the size of Congress the Third at the 30 Thousand ratio, after Census the First accounted a mighty enlarged Population. House the Third would exceed 100 Representatives, nigh certain. A House so large early in the life of the Republic, before it had attained to even a fraction of its eventual size. Were Montesquieu present, he would probably be grievous vex'd, and might foredain a dilution of Representation fatal to the American Republic. What would be Census the Last of the American Republic? Census the Tenth? Census the Twentieth? Census the Fiftieth? Census the Hundredth? Would America morph into Empire, as Rome had, and continue its Census long after Liberty expired? When would be Census the Last of America, whatsoever its form?

Deputies continued showing their Parts, and a consensus on the 30 Thousand ratio eventual emerged. No opposition was made to the Amendment of Washington, but no attempt to alter other Clauses of the Constitution to make them consonant with said Amendment would be undertaken.

Bloody Assemblys.

Even defaulting to no action took a veritable Æternity.

Silence at last.

Washington stood.

"I put it again to the good Gentlemen," he said. "Would any Deputy like to be heard ere Mister Gorham's motion is voted?"

Silence.

Washington waited more than a full minute.

Silence still.

Washington ordered a Vote, which Major Jackon called. Mr. Gorham's motion—Washington's motion—passed unanimous. The support of little States, if any were wavering, was secured with finality, and the republican Character of the general Government was purified, though Franklin still feared that Representation a far too Dilute.

"Your Excellency," Jackson said. "Might I amend the engrossment?"

"You have leave," Washington said.

Jackson laid parchment the first down careful. His table was too small for such a task, and he looked left and right for a Place to lay the other three parchments. Washington condescended from the dais and held the engrossments for Jackson.

Jackson effected an Erazure as best he could, using a small piece of softish gum Elastic as a rubber. 'Twas irregular shaped yet vague spherickal, like a sponge or piece of coral. Jackson held the parchment taut with two fingers of one hand and rubbered gentle with the other hand. For the first time, Deputies seemed patient. Most all Deputies had torn paper or parchment by erazing careless, and no Deputy would want the Infamy of tearing the engrossment. Jackson proceeded slow and fastidious to avoid such erratum.

Jackson seemed dissatisfied with his Erazure, so resorted to a small pumice Stone, which he used exceeding gentle. Still dissatisfied, he unsheathed a small scraper which seemed a Cross between a chirurgeon's knife and a letter opener. It had a blade that resembled the spade or heart on a playing card. Jackson scraped the blade across the dried animal Hide, again careful to be exceeding gentle, and did so twice and then thrice. He blew on the parchment like a lover's ear and ink and parchment particles disperst. Jackson resorted the gum elastic once more, rubbered the parchment, presst his face within inches of the Erazure, examined it, and then pulled away and sat straight. He resheathed the scraper.

Jackson placed his inkstand immediate left of the parchment, atop a large piece of scrap paper which covered part of the engrossment. If the ink spilt or dript, it would not defile the engrossment. Jackson dipt his quill once, wiped it gentle on

the inkstand edge repeated, and drew on the paper. He dipt his
quill again, wiped it gentle on the inkstand edge repeated, and
then drew on the engrossment. He drew for but a few seconds,
his Amendation being brief. He replaced the quill in the inkstand. Washington peer'd down at the Amendation and nodded once curt.

Jackson waited several minutes to be certain the ink dry. The
Convention sat in absolute silence.

When the ink dry, Washington handed the three parchments
back to Jackson, ascended the dais, stood, and made the full
measure of his Stature evident. He peered down at the Deputies.
The raw Aggression usual emanate by Washington was much
more intense. This change seem'd not affected nor purposeful,
but rather involuntary.

"Would any Gentleman," Washington said, "like to be heard
on Doctor Franklin's first Motion to agree to the Constitution
enrolled that it may be signed? I would remind the Gentlemen
that this first Motion is distinct from Doctor Franklin's second
Motion on the mode of signing."

Franklin felt Fear and saw that other Deputies did. 'Twas not
as if Washington would leap from the dais, draw his sword, and
run dissenters through. Nor was he attempting to wanton intimidate Deputies and bully them into signing. Yet Washington
had that rare Fierceness usual found only in Savages, and when
it surfaced it affrightened non-warriors. And many Warriors.

Franklin glanced from Deputy to Deputy, one by one. Could
any kill Washington in melee combat? Many harden'd Veterans
of the Revolution was present, including Few, Butler, Pinckney, Gilman, Dayton, Mifflin. And Major Jackson. Mifflin had

shown prowess in Battle. Pierce Butler was a former Lobster, a former Redcoat, and a cunning commander. Colonel Charles Cotesworth Pinckney had served with distinction leading Grenadiers, among the strongest, largest, and most physical powerful soldiers. And the fiercest. Pinckney was perhaps the only soldier present with raw physical strength that might be a match for Washington's.

Yet in truth no Deputy present was as physical imposing as Washington. Many of the soldiers present were decades younger than Washington, yet 'twas difficult to envision any besting him one on one, even though he was now arthritick. If forced to match a Deputy against Washington, like Cocks in the Pit, Franklin would have chose the Little Lion. Though lithe and a mere 5'7" high, nigh 9" shorter than Washington, the Little Lion was exceeding fit and possessed of a lightning Quickness that might allow him to play David to the Washingtonian Goliath. Or perhaps Franklin's view was colour'd by the fact that the Little Lion seemed one of few men in the room both physically and morally capable of killing Washington.

Washington's aggressive Bearing made it clear that the time for niceties had passed. Not that there had been many at the Convention. As eventual happened in all Assemblies, when taking critical Votes especially, the time for the exercise of raw Power was at hand.

Away from the Convention and its Chair, Washington had made his support for the imperfect Constitution known. So had Franklin. Any Deputy opposing the Constitution was defying the two Demigods of the Revolution, and would have to stand against their combined Reputations, possibly incurring their permanent disfavour.

No trifle a consideration.

Especially in the case of Washington. Woe to the man that impugned Washington's precious Reputation, direct or indirect. Washington never forgave even miniscule Slights in this regard. Washington had risked his sacred Honor in backing the Convention and lending it the weight of his Prestige, and he was not to be rogered and scapegoated. 'Twas The General's view that anyone opposing the Constitution at this late date was trying to play him the Fool and trample his Reputation. All Deputies knew it. And felt it when they looked into Washington's cold, pitiless, prædatory Eyes.

Thus the brooding expressions of Deputies as they once again performed the mental Fluxions. Future career aspirations in the fœderal Government had to be weighed against prospects back home and the desire of Constituents. Every State had powerful anti-Fœderal Factions. Who the bloody hell wanted to surrender Sovereignty and pay more Taxes? There was no guarantee that the Constitution would be well received by The People. A Deputy standing for it might be slicing his political Throat and barring all prospect of local office permanent. If backlash were severe enough, lawyers or merchants that supported the Constitution might be boycotted, harming them financial, perhaps ruining them. Complicating these petty personal Calculations was the moral Imperative to secure Liberty for humanity, which ought trump all other concerns, yet might not. Men could be fickle in moments of import.

Deputies began to glance at the known Opponents of the Constitution. At Blount, at Gerry, at Randolph, at Mason. Would these Dissidents prostrate themselves to the wishes of The General and The Sage? If nay, they would have to speak soon. The Signing was nigh!

Washington waited more than a minute.

Tension built.

But no one a rose to speak.

"Ere I call for a Vote for Affirmation of the Constitution of Government of the United States of Americay," Washington said, "does any other Gentleman not wish to be heard?"

Washington waited almost another full minute.

The tension became bloody unbearable.

"Major Jackson," Washington said. "Call the Vote for Affirmation of the Constitution of Government of the United States of Americay."

Washington peered at the wary-eyed John Langdon, senior Deputy from New Hampshire, who sat in the left seat at the leftmost table in the front left row.

"New Hampshire," Jackson said. "How vote ye?"

Langdon's voice rang out like a cannon Clap.

"Yea," he said.

Washington peered at Nathaniel Gorham.

"Massachusetts Bay?" Jackson said.

"Yea," Gorham said.

Jackson called each State in turn, moving north to south geographic, and proceeding slow enough that Washington could peer at each senior Deputy before they were called.

As each additional state voted Yea, a palpable Exuberance built.

Finally, the last State, Georgia.

Washington peered at William Few, senior Deputy from Georgia.

"Georgiay?" Jackson said.

"Yea," Few said.

The bodies of many Deputies seemed to sigh sudden. Several lean'd back in their Windsors, and some allowed their heads to rock backwards. Others exhalt deep.

They had done it!

The vote was unanimous!

Yet also ambiguous. Without Convention, Deputations had voted to determine the ballot a State would cast, with the Majority prevalent. Deputations having determined their Vote in privy, Deputies who might have voted Nay were not known a certain.

Washington spoke immediate after Georgia voted, ere walking sticks could be tapped or Deputies could otherwise celebrate, probably to maintain the momentum which the Vote had built. Celebratory would have been a Violation of Procedure regardless, something Washington would not countenance, and which no Deputy would attempt. Certain not after twelve successions of The General's fearsome glances.

"Would any Gentleman," Washington said, "like to be heard on Doctor Franklin's second motion on the mode of signing?"

Tension returned. Gazes were fixed firm upon the most eminent and vocal Opponents of the Constitution. Blount. Gerry. Mason. And Randolph.

Randolph had helped Jemmy draft the Virginia Plan that the Convention used as a point of embarkment for its deliberations. Randolph had presented the Virginia Plan to the Convention, which is why some Deputies called it the Randolph Plan. Though many significant Changes had been made as the Convention proceeded, much of the Constitution just approved was in fact the Randolph Plan.

And now Randolph might oppose it!

The Fodder this would give enemies of the Constitution was horrific to contemplate. Franklin envisioned agitators like Samuel Adams and Patrick Henry a rousing The People with the most incendiary interpretation imaginable. Randolph, Governour of the largest state Virginia, a co-architect of the Virginia Plan, and one of the most eminent and able lawyers in America, couldn't even be made to sign the Constitution, despite inordinate Intimidation by The General and The Doctor. If Randolph scrupled to support the Constitution, why should anyone support it?

Like most Deputies, Randolph was scarce absent political Ambition, and like most Deputies, political Ambition coloured his View of the Constitution. He might have to face Patrick Henry in a future election, and Henry would harangue him merciless if he supported the Constitution. Few men could weather verbal Ambuscades from Henry and emerge with their reputations intact.

Yet Randolph had more to luse by opposing the Constitution than nigh any other Deputy. He had served as an Aide-de-Camp to Washington during the Revolution, earning the General's Trust, a difficult feat. The two were cordial acquaintances. As

Randolph was prodigious Eminent and trusted by Washington, 'twas not absurd to think he might attain one of the most senior Posts in the new government. Attorney General or even Secretary of Foreign Affairs, 'twas whisper'd. Franklin tended to think Attorney General more probable. Yet if Randolph stood and spoke now, all such prospects might be scuttled irreparable. And he wouldn't be able to slink away to some distant State, but would rather have to repair to Virginia, where Washington lived, and face the brunt of the General's Wrath square.

Randolph was born into a story'd family, had wealth, health, Station, a belle of a wife, and had cultivated a manly Character despite persistent Indecisiveness. He was an easy man to envy, but in this moment not a Deputy præsent would have wanted to be him.

Randolph's figurine of a Face was etched with anguish. His mild underbite jutted more than usual, changing the character of his countenance, making him seem the despondent Brooder. Randolph rose slow. Wearily. The language of his body reminded Franklin of a labourer trudging a Burden.

"The vast Majority and venerable Names have given sanction to the wisdom and worth of this Constitution," Randolph said. "But I cannot sign it. For this, I apologize."

Randolph's voice was riddled with emotion and certain syllables seemed right nasal. He might have been telling Deputies their families had been bombarded to death by the British.

"I mean not by this refusal," Randolph said, "to decide I shall oppose the Constitution without doors. I only mean to keep myself free to be governed by my Duty as prescribed by my future judgment."

Randolph peered at Washington for a long moment, and then glanced around at the Deputies, locking eyes with several in succession.

"I refuse to sign," Randolph said, "because I think the Object of the Convention will be frustrated by the alternative which it presents to The People. Nine States will fail to ratify the plan and Confusion must ensue."

Nine of thirteen states had to ratify the Constitution for it to be establish'd in those ratifying states. This was the final Clause of the Constitution.

"With such a view of the subject," Randolph said, "I ought not, I cannot, pledge myself to support the Plan. If I do, I restrain myself from taking steps that may appear to me most consistent with the publick Good."

Randolph peered into Washington's eyes one last time, and then sat.

Franklin saw Irritation on the faces of Hamilton, Jemmy, and other Deputies. One didn't need a soothsayer to deduce their thoughts. Fear of failure was not a Justification for opposition. With such thinking, Patriots would have presumed that Britain could not be best'd, and there would have been no Revolution. The Brass of Randolph! What a wanton, sexist View of the matter!

Attention turned to Franklin. Surely he would explode Randolph's cowardly Obfuscations. Expressions of Deputies were expectant, hopeful.

Franklin knew he had spoke enough for one day. The more one spoke, the less men listened.

Governeur Morris stood. There was an audible Thump as he planted his peg Leg on the floor. Morris was perhaps the tallest Deputy—save Washington. Yet his peg Leg made him appear taller for some illusory Reason. Tall Boy indeed.

The two belts used to strap the peg Leg to the stump of Morris' thigh were at Franklin's eye level. The stump was inserted in a cylindrical peg enclosement affix'd to the wooden leg. The enclosement was cut away in two sections opposite each other, which made it resemble a short cloathespin with a gaping central cavity and prongs prodigious thin. The belts were affixed to and encircled the prongs, and this allowed them to be tightend so as to shrink the diameter of the enclosement, clamping it secure to the Stump. The leather on the belts was worn.

Governeur faced Washington and nodded respectful.

"Mister President, Sir," he said.

Governeur opened his body to the Deputies and looked at Randolph.

"I too have Objections," Governeur said, "but I consider the present Plan as the best that is to be attained and take it with all its faults. The majority has determined in its favour and by that determination I shall abide."

Governeur had superb Balance, yet nonetheless oscillated fractional as he stood, like a Sail blowing ever so gentle by a slight breeze. His stump muscle flexed as it laboured to maintain balance.

"The moment this Plan goes forth," Governeur said, "all other considerations will be laid aside and one great question will be asked. Shall there be a national Government or not?"

Governeur let the weight of the question hang in the air. His face was aggressive and roosterish, not cherubic.

"There must be a national Government," Governeur said, "or a general Anarchy will be the alternative."

Deputies tapped walking sticks or clapped tables with hands, but brief only, that Governeur could continue speaking.

"The signing in the form proposed," Governeur said, "relates only to the fact that the States present were unanimous."

Governeur sat.

Randolph scowled. So did Mason. And Gerry. But not Blount!

Hugh Williamson of North Carolina stood. He sat in the left seat a front the rightmost table in the front row. Williamson was an elder Deputy at 52, and a hard man to look at. In a Convention with more than its just Share of unattractive Gentlemen, he stood out as the most absolute hideous.

Williamson's prodigious nose was sharp angled at the top and crooked into a less offensive angle about a quarter way down, giving it the profile of one side of a barn roof. Yet it also had a conspicuous flat ridge, and the pointy Tip was lower than the nostrils, as if it were a Beak.

Williamson's beak absolute consumed his Face, destroying any Hope of handsomeness, and the heightened forehead and thinning white hair combed sideways across the scalp did little to aide. The rear Portion of his cheeks behind the bones was sunk, as if he had Consumption, which he did not, and this made the frontal, non-sunken Portion of the face seem like a mask that could be removed.

Williamson had been plagued by ill Health his entire life, and looked it, with a ghoulish Cast to his complexion, like Washington, though with a-shriveled skin which Washington lacked. Williamson conveyed a singular Sense of fragility absent even in more diminutive men such as Jemmy or Paterson, and there was sympathetick softness in the eyes of many Deputies as they glanced at him.

Williamson was versatile. He was the only natural Phylosopher at the Convention besides Franklin, and one of only three Physicians, the other two being James McClurg and James McHenry. Brought to bed on the frontier to a cloathier who wanted him to become a Minister, Williamson entered the inaugural class of the College of Philadelphia and took his degree in 1757. His father never lived to see him become a Preacher, nor abandon the Calling before ordaining.

Williamson was too much of a natural Phylosopher to believe the prepost'rous and fantastical Claims of religions, and like Franklin viewed religions as pragmatic tools for instilling Virtue in weak-willed men. Williamson became a Professor of Mathematic at the College of Philadelphia. This soon bored him, so he travel'd abroad and studied Physick, a discipline that perhaps intrigued him because of his perpetual ill Health.

Williamson took his degree, returned to Pennsylvania, and plied himself as a Physician, but found it troubling, believing that many treatments did nothing to cure Disease and oft did Harm. He shared some of Franklin's unconventional Views about natural Phylosophy, especially about health, and had tried to make the Army adopt measures based on these principles so as to prevent Disease. Williamson became determined to start an

Academy that would study Physick and other disciplines from a natural Phylosophic perspective, emphasizing logic, Experiment, and Evidence, and discarding the Dogma and Superstition that prevail'd.

Whilst a waiting in Boston to sail for London to solicit Subscriptions for this Academy, Williamson saw Americans disguiz'd as Savages host The Tea Party, dumping 46 tons of East India Company tea in Boston Harbour, most of it choice Bohea. This infuriated Britain and made it vow to prosecute the American Rebellion no matter what the dispence.

How frenetic the Fish must have been from the Tonnage of tea. If only the ocean were a-sugared instead of a-salted. Then the sea denizens could have enjoyed tea in the true english Fashion. Would the Fish thus caught be sugar Fish rather than salt Fish? Have a sweet Taste rather than more tart, as if smoked and cured with molasses? Too bad a few frigates brimming with sugar hadn't been near those with tea. Though The Tea Party had been in defiance of the recent passed Tea Act. With the earlyer Sugar Act a decade distant, would "Savages" have jettisoned sugar?

Franklin was glib with his Lampoons, as was his nature, but in truth The Tea Party had been no jesting matter. It had agitated the entire british Nation into an irreconcilable anti-American Frenzy.

Samuel Adams and the Sons of Liberty, a Junto committed to inflicting Terrour upon the British, had perpetrated The Tea Party on December 16, 1773. Travel across the Atlantic was slow in winter, but word of such a notorious Crime nonetheless traversed it with extreme rapidity, and the crown learned of it 34 days later on January 19, 1774. Nigh a week later, on

29 January, Franklin was crucified in the Cockpit, which, some encounters with low Women notwithstanding, was the single most humiliating event of his life.

As America's de facto Minister to Britain, Franklin met with members of the House of Lords and House of Commons regular, and also corresponded with prominent Americans across the ocean, counseling Temper to both sides that a Breach might be avoided. It had always been an arduous Sell on both sides, but Franklin had been making modest inroads and was cautious optimistic that Insurrection could be averted—until word of The Tea Party arrived.

It felt curious to revisit the perspective Franklin held then, that of a British citizen. Benjamin Franklin the Loyal Subject seem'd like a different person, someone Benjamin Franklin the American might meet on travels abroad. At the time, the thought of America declaring Independency horrifyed Franklin. He had toiled mighty to prevent a Breach, and he wept when he finally accepted that Revolution was inevitable because the crown and Parliament would never respect the Natural Rights of Americans.

The turbulent years immediate before Independency was declared. So long ago. Lifetimes ago, seeming. Britain spent exorbitant sums to eject her enemy France from America and protect her Possessions there. She then made the reasonable request that Americans share in the dispence of this Defence by paying Taxes a trifle higher, and still prodigious less great than citizens in Britain paid to support the American defence. Britain was dumb-founded by the American refusal to submit to such Taxes, which precipitated the Revolution.

No matter how many times it was explained, Lords could not comprehend—or perhaps would not comprehend—the American view of the matter. Franklin would never forget the long hours spent in Haunts such as the Smyrna Coffee House, never forget stunned or perplex-ed expressions on the faces of prime Ministers, Lords, and Members of Parliament such as Messieurs North, Hillsborough, Grenville, Townshend, Granby, Dorchester, Cobham, and cetera, as he tried to expound the American perspective. These British political elite gaped at Franklin as if he were Ripe for Bedlam. How in the bloody Hell could Americans consider it tyrannical to pay such trifling Sums when they were but a fraction of the crown's total defence expenditures for America? Would the Colonists have rather been subjugate by France? What did the bloody American Brats expect, to hoard the bounty of their Continent and pay nothing for an exorbitant Defence which the crown funded entire?

Franklin felt his chest tighten a bit as he relived the Warmth of hundreds of such futile intercourses. Yet they was cool compared to the Intolerance unleashed by The Tea Party. Reliving that week was enough to make one expire.

Bloody Samuel Adams! A bankrupt brewer and Embezzler. A mere Agitator, one of the Violent Men. Nought more. Thank Providence yet again the bloody Bugger wasn't at the Convention, where he would certain have plied his one and only talent: a rousing men to Malcontentment.

To Franklin, one of the most curious aspects of the Revolution was the dismaying severity with which Parliament miscalculated America's responses to its policies. Most Lords and Members simply could not be made to believe that America would Revolt over trifling Taxes so just and reasonable. America would puff her chest, rattle the saber of Revolution, yet in the end come to her Senses and submit.

This was the prevailent british Delusion—until The Tea Party.

After the Tea Party, Britain at last understood that America was not mere posturing and would revolt rather than submit to Taxation without Representation in Parliament. At this juncture, Britain finally accepted what America truly wanted, but was unwilling to grant it. And in many ways unable to grant it, if the exploitation of Colonys which produced British prosperity was to be perpetuate.

To Americans, The Tea Party was an admirable act of Resistance against Tyranny, but to Franklin it would always be an abject act of Terrour. Upon learning of The Tea Party, Franklin immediately wrote a letter to Samuel Adams, John Hancock, and other prominent Rousers, reprimanding them and advising that they make immediate Reparations to the crown.

The bloody Vandals refused.

The East India Company reported losses of £9,659, a horrific Sum which was just the value of tea, irrespective of the reshipping dispence. Franklin proffered to make Reparations personal, or raise them in Boston if the crown preferred, and proffered an immediate payment of £4,000 out of his private Funds.

The crown refused curt.

A group of American Merchants including the prominent Robert Murray of New York proffered to make immediate Reparations to the crown equal to Double the loss.

This proffer was also refused curt.

After the crown learned of The Tea Party, Franklin was summon'd before the Privy Council, a body of advisors to the king
which was comprised of the most senior and eminent politicians
and nobles. The Privy Council met in the octagon-shaped Cockpit of Whitehall Palace, so named because 'twas surrounded by
vaulted balconies packed with observers, making it resemble a
Pit where Cocks were made to fight to the Death for sport. The
chambre had actual been used for cockfights centuries early'r
during the reign of king Henry VII.

The sobriquet Cockpit also had a darker connotation. For
political onlookers, Sport was to be found, Fights to the political Death. Many a fortune, career, and reputation and had been
murder'd in the Cockpit.

The British wanted Blood after The Tea Party, and as there
was only one famed American in England, he would be made
the example, to send a message to Americans. Franklin had to
stand before the Privy Council in his Manchester velvet suit, and
suffer Inquisition and Slander at the hands of Solicitor General Alexander Wedderburn for an unremittent hour. Whatever else might be said of Lord Wedderburn, he wanted not for
eloquencey, and he denigrated Franklin relentless with a nigh
poetic turn of Phrase. The upper rafters had been packed full
in a preconcerted manner, and Spectators howled, leered, and
laughed at Franklin. He was wise enough to realize that Rebuttal
would play into the crown's hand, so stood silent and suffered
the molestation of his Honor.

Franklin glanced around the East Room at Deputies. Like
most Americans, they had their moment, the exact instant they
knew they were no longer British. For more cautious Americans

such as Washington, always a difficult man to gauge, it seemed
to be just before the first outbreak of violence at Lexington
& Concord, when Lord Dunmore, His Majesty's Governour
of Virginia, upheld the voidation of Surveys intended to provide Land promised to veterans of the French & Indian War,
thereby denying Washington compensation for his military List-
ment. Thomas seemed to have made the transition earlyer than
Washington, after the Intolerable Acts passed, when he wrote
his renowned Summary View of the Rights of British America. Firebrands like John Adams had probably determined that
America must separate from Britain in the womb prior to birth.
For Franklin, the Cockpit was his demarkation. He entered
the Cockpit a British citizen and exited an American. The next
morning the crown terminated him as Postmaster General of
the American Colonys, cementing the Alienation.

Hugh Williamson arrived in Britain during this auspicious
time, and he and Franklin became friends. Franklin had been
anxious to hear an accounting of The Tea Party from an American who had observed it direct, and there was perhaps no better Witness than a natural Phylosopher, as they tended to be
objective and reliable observers. Williamson had long been a
member of the American Philosophical Society that Franklin
helped found to facilitate the discovery and dissemination of
useful Knowledge. Williamson had served on a Commission that
observed the transits of Venus and Mercury, and he penned an
Essay on Comets that earned international Approbation for its
prescience and originality, though without generating the fantastical Fame of Franklin's Philadelphia Experiment.

The University of Leyden awarded Williamson an honorary Doctorate for his contributions to astronomy. Like Franklin, Williamson was at heart a natural Phylosopher, and they had performed a few Experiments with the electric Fluid together.

Williamson was called into the Cockpit on February 19, 1774, but 22 days after Franklin. Like Franklin, he was treated disrespectful, yet he was not utter humiliate as Franklin was, nor was a coliseum Mob called out as with Franklin. Williamson was not famed enough to warrant such Niceties. Yet he was honest and blunt in the assessment he delivered to the Privy Council, warning them that repression of the American Colonys would provoke Rebellion. Parliament and the crown remained constitutionally incapable of accepting this Truth and sneered at American military prowess. Let the bloody bugger Americans rebel! Britain would gladly prosecute the Insurrection. Redcoats would make fodder of the Ingrates and they would die in Droves until they submitted!

Williamson was one of the few Americans who had lived in disparate regions of the country for prolong'd periods. Finding many different regions admirable, and seeing them grapple with similar problems that were fœderal in character, he developed a fœderalist Outlook and supported a strong fœderal Government.

Like Jemmy, Williamson seemed in desperate need of a Wife, yet his ill Health and gruesome appearance made Matrimony more difficult than talking sense to the British. If he did have children, would they be afflicted by the same ill Health?

When Williamson stood, Franklin saw a friend, albeit not a cluse one, a truly humane natural Phylosopher who had devoted himself to healing men, improving Health, and promulgating

Enlightenment via the Diffusion of Knowledge. Deputies saw a Gentleman who was every inch the gentle Scholar, possessed of a nigh sexist Kindness, and truly horrified by the Brutality of mankind. Being a military Physician during the Revolution seemed to have heightened Williamson's conciliatory bent, perhaps because he had seen the true Cost of conflict while treating the maim'd and dying. He was that rare Deputy who had exerted a cooling Influence upon the Convention, and Deputies peered at him with respect, curious to know what he would say.

Williamson addressed Washington as Mr. President, as procedure required.

"The signing," Williamson said, "should be confined to the letter accompanying the Constitution to Congress. Such a letter might perhaps serve near as well as the Motion proposed and be satisfactory to Gentlemen who dislike the Constitution."

Typical Williamson. The most conciliatory proposal imaginable, to make signing the Constitution irrelevant by forsaking it.

Some Deputies glanced at Blount, who was part of the North Carolina Deputation and seated right next to Williamson. Was Williamson's proposal bourne of principle, or was it meant to induce Blount to sign?

Whatever Williamson's motivations, his proposal was a theoretickal Extreme that elicited quizzical looks from most Deputies. To forsake signing the Constitution was to cheat Deputies of their Fame if it succeeded and their Immortality if it endured. Also, an unsigned Constitution would be attack'd by enemies who would pretend the absence of signatures was a ruse intended to camouflage a want of Support.

"For myself," Williamson said, "I think not a better plan is to be expected and have no scruples against putting my name to it."

Williamson sat.

The Little Lion stood with his usual fleet dextrousity, and addressed Washington as required. Washington's face warmed appreciable and he nodded at the Little Lion. The Little Lion nodded back, less deep than most men did to Washington, and a hint of Hauteur crept into his smile.

Standing, the Little Lion's handsome features positive glowed in the sunlight, which was fearsome bright, morning having absented and it now being after the noon. The Little Lion's eyes seemed bleu'r, as radiant as West Indies water, and his cheeks was rosier, as if rouged. The sunlight also seemed to accentuate the Flawlessness of his complexion. No matter how much one might detest the Little Lion, 'twas difficult not to admire his dev'lish Handsomeness.

Franklin had not seen the Little Lion use a kerchief or wipe his brow, yet no Sweat was visible on his Face. The Little Lion's West Indies upbringing doubtless exposed him to worse heat, and made him imperturbable to it, and his extreme Fitness also probably reduced his propensity to sweat.

Yet even so.

The Little Lion looked right cool. How in the hell could he look so bloody cool? Even the south Gentleman seemed impressed.

"I am anxious," the Little Lion said, "that every Member should sign. A few characters of Consequence who oppose or even refuse to sign the Constitution may do infinite Mischief."

The Little Lion glanced at Blount. And then Gerry. Finally Randolph and Mason.

"Enthusiasm in favour of the Convention may soon subside," the Little Lion said. "Resistance may kindle the latent Sparks which lurk under that Enthusiasm."

The Little Lion peered at Randolph and Mason intent, as if speaking to them personal in a more intimate setting.

"No man's ideas," he said, "are more remote from the Plan than mine are known to be."

Franklin couldn't help but smirk at the agreeable expressions of most Deputies, many of which were tinged with Disgust. Governeur Morris chuckled soft. Early in the Convention, the Little Lion made the ghastly proposal that the President and Senators be elected for Life.

For Life!

Never rotatable out of office, save by Impeachment, no matter how obnoxious they rendered themselves!

The Little Lion's proposal would have made America's leaders similar to the king of England and Lords in the British House of Lords. 'Twas so grotesque and unthinkable an Absurdity that 'twas not even criticized, but rather summarily ignored and not spoken of again.

"Is it possible to deliberate betweenst Anarchy and Convulsion on one side," the Little Lion said, "and the chance of Good to be expected from the plan on the other?"

The Little Lion fixed Randolph and Mason with a hard look, and then sat.

William Blount of North Carolina stood, looking poutyer and porkyer than when seated. Deputies inched forward in their chairs. Blount was among that handful of Deputies who had spoke nary a syllable in debate during the entire Convention, but his occasional commentary in Committee and at nightly Tavern intercourses made it evident he was disinclined to sign. Sweat had soiled Blount's prim powdered face, etching tannish streaks into the pristine white, making him look even more the Dandy, no trifle a Feat. Deputies try'd not to be impertinent, but their glances were nonetheless drawn to these Defilements of the powdering.

"I have declared that I would not sign and would not pledge myself in support of the Plan," Blount said. "But I am relieved by the Form proposed. I will without committing myself to support the Plan attest the fact that 'twas the unanimous act of the States in Convention."

Approval on the faces of Deputies. Even Washington smiled ever so slight, tho' 'twas a stiff and somewhat repulsive gesture owing his false teeth.

Franklin stood, once again using the table as a crutch. Thankfully, the Gout and Stone once again showed mercy.

"I would encourage Gentlemen to discourage the Spirit of Warmth," Franklin said. "This of all days it ought not be rekindled nor countenanced. Let us exhibit Temper. We are here to consult, not contend."

Deputies tapped canes and peered at Franklin with esteem.

Franklin glanced at the Little Lion for the barest moment, then turned his attention to the figurine-faced Edmund Randolph. Randolph's full head of straight brown hair was parted on the side and was short on the top but roamed more free on the sides and rear, concealing most of his ears.

"I am mortified," Franklin said, "that Mister Randolph thought himself alluded to in the remarks I proffered to the Convention this morning. When drawing my Remarks I knew not that any particular member would refuse to affix his name to the Instrument."

Randolph rolled his eyes. Franklin met his glance even but remain'd cordial. Warmth would be a critical Blunder. So would overt Intimidation which demean'd Deputies. If the Little Lion only understood this.

"I must profess a high sense of Obligation to Mister Randolph," Franklin said, "for having brought forward the Plan in the first instance, and for the assistance he has given its progress. I hope that Mister Randolph will yet lay aside his objections. By concurring with his brethren, he will prevent the great Mischief which the refusal of his name may produce."

As Franklin sat, walking sticks and a peg Leg tapped and hands clapped tables, accompanyed by grave expressions, especially on the faces of Jemmy, Tall Boy, and the Little Lion.

Randolph peered at Franklin pointed and then stood. At just under six feet high, Randolph was considered taller than typical, and tho' brawny in terms of physiognomy, he did not seem athletic nor convey physical prowess. Randolph felt like a man that should seem rugged, but he wasn't.

"Signing in the proposed form is the same as signing the Constitution," Randolph said. "The change of form makes no difference with me."

Randolph's chocolate eyes seemed haunted.

"In refusing to sign the Constitution," he said, "I take a step which may be the most awful of my life. But 'tis dictated by my

Conscience, and 'tis not possible for me to hesitate, much less change."

Randolph's voice crackled. The sweat on his forehead seemed to glisten with heightened Vigour and reminded Franklin of dew on a log.

"I must also repeat my persuasion," Randolph said, "that holding out this plan to The People with a final alternative of accepting or rejecting it in toto will produce the Anarchy and civil Convulsions apprehended from the refusal of individuals to sign it."

Randolph sat, grabbed his kerchief off his table, and used it to wipe his Face. The act was contagious. Many Deputies observing Randolph aped him, produced their kerchiefs, and wiped their Faces.

At the leftmost table of the left rear row, at its rightmost Seat, Elbridge Gerry stood, looking thinner, smaller, and graver than typical. Though turned of but 44, he seemed elder, with a spectral Face that could affrighten children. 'Twas more than just his features. Hugh Williamson was perhaps uglier than Gerry, and so perhaps was Franklin, but Williamson exuded Benevolence, and Franklin liked to think he did. Gerry was a Quiz, and at times there was a creepedness about him unintended.

His stutter certain contributed, as did his screwy Squint. Gerry's facial features could also not be acquitted. His face was elongate, and exceeding angular, in a way that detracted from handsomeness rather than imbuing it. As with Hugh Williamson, the portion of the Face behind the cheek Bones was sunk, though this Basin was a greater proportion of the face on Gerry than on Williamson. This was because Gerry's cheek seem'd to extend from just above the ear to the bottom of a long chin in a nigh straight Line, as if his face contained whale Bones. The chin was prominent and reminded Franklin of the end of a thin French Loaf, and overall, Gerry's Face seemed too elongate and the chin too tapered.

Bluish vessels traced out numerate Tributaries beneath the sunk portion of Gerry's face. His eyes were modest deepset with prominent bags, his crow's feet were clawed, and other wrinkles were deeper than typickal, the forehead lines especially. As with Jemmy, the eyebrows seemed to rest on bony ridges, as if Gerry were a clay Sculpture on which brows had been forgotten and added hasty belated, as an after Thought. The long nose had a flat ridge which arced outward from the face gradual but continual, like a Roman Arch.

And there was the domineering forehead. Recessing behind the eyebrow ridges increased its prominency, and it seemed spacious enough to etch a Map of Europe onto. Gerry's white wig puffed out from the sides over the ears but was flat on the top.

In repose, Gerry's Face had an expression which was one of the most singular Franklin had ever seen, yet also one of the most difficult to characterize. Gerry's elongate skull and face, eyebrow ridges, domineering forehead, and sunken cheeks accentuated the peculiar expression of his eyes and mouth, giving the sense of a man trying to ingratiate himself disingenuous or at least of a man not comfortable in his own Skin. Gerry was not such a man, and to judge him so harsh was unjust, but this was none the less his superficial Appearance.

A more optimistic interpretation was that Gerry was wincing perpetual, at times fighting back tears of Pain, and enforcing a slight Smile. Or perhaps he was a squinting slight, perpetual, flexing his Face, a bit sad about his vision Impairment, and his peculiar expression was the result. This would explain the frequent severity of his countenance, and the brooding quality he seemed to possess.

Massachusetts had not seated Samuel Adams or John Adams at Convention, but Elbridge Gerry was perhaps the next worst thing. Like John and Samuel, and most Massachusetts men, Gerry had opposed British attempts to tax the colonys from the moment the French & Indian War ended in 1763. Gerry was a close friend of Samuel Adams and strong influenced by him, which could scarce be reckon'd a vote of confidence in a man's Judgment. Like Samuel Adams, Gerry was not just energetic in fermenting Discontentment with whatever prevalent, but utter tireless, and many Deputies had glum expressions as they glanced at him, perhaps recalling his many oratory Anticks during the Convention.

Yet Gerry was not to be underestimate. He was a man of Sense, integrity, and perseverance, though also a Grumbletonian. Quarrelsome, happiest in Opposition even before the influence of Samuel Adams, he had been of service to the Convention by objecting to every Thing he did not propose. He seemed to vacillate endless between fœderalism and anti-fœderalism, yet was obstinate as an old Mule, defending each new Predilection with vehemence until his opinions turned upon a new Tack.

Gerry's father was a sea Captain who had fled England in 1730 and emigrated to America seeking Liberty and Prosperity. He founded a shipping business in the port city of Marble-head nigh 20 miles northeast of Boston, and eventual became one of the wealthiest merchants in Massachusetts. Elbridge Gerry entered Harvard upon adulthood at the expected age of 14, took his Batchelor's and Master's, and then went to work for the family firm.

When Britain punish'd Boston for The Tea Party by clos-ing its port, Gerry used his family's firm to smuggle goods into Boston, and became an even more outspoken Critick of brit-ish Tyranny. He continued using his firm and mercantile con-nections to supply the Army and outfit Privateers through out The War, and in this regard was an ethical version of Robert Morris, though his Firm was smaller than Morris'. Gerry had earned a prodigious Fortune in The War, yet charged virtual the same rates he did without War, and hadn't profiteered as Robert Morris had. Many Deputies glanced at Gerry and then Morris, contrasting the Honor of the two men seeming. Morris did not flinch under the Scrutiny nor seem the least discomfort by it, even though he probably sensed Deputies' Judgment.

Profiteering was as seductive a Temptation as land Spec-ulation, but Gerry had scrupulous avoided it, which few men in his position would have had the Honor to do. Most men railing against Profiteering was not merchants, and Gerry was conspicuous for being one of the few merchants to condemn the practice publick. During The War he even advocated giving Congress the Power to set Prices, preventing merchants from increasing prices unduly and Profiteering. An unwise policy, ruinous though noble of Intention, and a metaphor for the type of Thinking made Gerry so bloody frustrating.

Gerry had served in the Massachusetts Legislature, and had again made his Integrity manifest by refusing the attempts of Governour John Hancock to appoint him to the state Senate and a county Judgeship. Gerry tartly noted that such Appointments were similar to the British system of Interest that Americans were rebeling against.

Gerry establish'd and presided Marblehead's Committee of Correspondence, the second in America after Boston's, participating in the Patriot communication network that subverted british Authority and acted as an informal American government prior to the convocation of the Continental Congress in 1774. The first Committee of Correspondence was formed in 1764, just a year after the French & Indian War concluded, and nigh immediate after Britain began its attempts to increase Revenue from the Colonys to pay for it. Committees of Correspondence became much more active in the early 1770s as tensions mounted. For nigh a decade, Gerry had laboured tireless organizing Patriots via this committee.

Once Britain closed Boston's port in 1774, War became not just a true possibility, but damn nigh inevitable, and Gerry had been appointed to the local Committee of Safety. He had helped make the prudential Decision to store black Powder and Arms at Concord, inland from the coast where british Ships-of-the-Line enjoyed dominance. Like all tyrannical Governments, the crown was keen sensible that a people could not be oppressed unless first disarmed and render'd defenseless. Britain therefore attempted to seize America's powder Stores, making Muskets as useless as Clubs, and tried to do so in Concord—until Paul Revere raised the Powder Alarm. The Battle to prevent 700 Lobsters from pilfering depots of black Powder in Concord was the first of the Revolution, the literal and metaphorick powder Keg that initiated The War.

Like most Massachuseans who had bore the brunt of british Tyranny, Gerry supported Independency with vehement Warmth during the Congressional debates of 1776, and he signed the Declaration of Independency without hesitation. Yet he was cooler about the Constitution than he had been about Independency.

Much cooler.

Gerry had always opposed energetic central Government, whether British or American, yet he entered the Convention realizing some sort of fœderal Government was needed. He supported a fœderal Government at first, but as it was made ever stronger, ever more national and less fœderal, his Misgivings grew. Much of his vacillation on stances during the Convention resulted from his shifting interpretations of the way propose-ed Clauses would limit or enhance the Sovereignty of state Governments. During debates, Gerry had been vociferous in asserting that States must have significant Controul over the composition of the fœderal Government, and that the fœderal Government ought have exceeding limited Power to circumvent States and act direct upon The People. He had been instrumental in having the Senate electored by State Legislatures, and the President chosen by Electors, as opposed to having them elector'd direct by The People, who he considered a Mob mindless and oft duped.

Like Mason, Gerry was emphatick in his Belief that the Constitution would end in Tyranny unless prefixed with a Declaration of Rights protecting the Natural Rights of The People and the Sovereignty of the States. He would probably never sign the Constitution absent such Declaration of Rights. All Deputies knew it.

Yet few Deputies knew exact what to expect from Gerry. His stutter and squint were easy to rail, and away from Convention, some Deputies did so. Though Gerry's character was inviolate, and at times he was the epitome of Sensibility, in more radical and reactionary moments he could wreak more Havoc than a loose Twenny-Four.

Gerry didn't seem riddled with Angst as Randolph. He stood calm, with a hint of defiance in his eyes

"My situation is one of painful feelings," he said. "As the subject has been finally decided, I feel Embarrassments offering any further observations."

Gerry offered them anyway, causing Governeur Morris to smirk fractional in his roosterish fashion.

Gerry yet again enumerated the Objections that determined him to withhold his name from the Constitution. He disliked the duration and re-eligibility of the Senate, the Power of the House of Representatives to conceal their journals, the Power of Congress over the places of election, the unlimited Power of Congress over their own Compensation, Massachusetts having not a due Share of Representatives allotted her, and the Vice President making Head of the Senate. Gerry abhorred that three fifths of the Blacks were to be represented as if they were Freemen. He feared that the Power over Commerce might beget the establishment of Monopolies.

And cetera.

As Gerry plodded through his Meander, Dictator John looked down at the table and rubbed his forehead vig'rous. Faces and bodies of other Deputies cinched and they also glanced downward or into space. Gerry had voiced these Criticisms innumerate times, both within and without doors, most recent Saturday.

"I could get over all these," Gerry said, "if the rights of the Citizens were not render'd insecure by the by the general Power of the Legislature To make what laws they may please to call Necessary and Proper, To raise Armies and Money without limit, To establish a tribunal without Juries, which will be a Star-chambre as to Civil cases."

Gerry paused. His gaze swept an arc about chambre and he locked eyes with several Deputies momentary.

"Whilst the p-p-plan was depending," Gerry said, "I treated it with all the freedom I thought it deserved. I now feel bound to treat it with respect due to the Act of the Convention."

Gerry's lower lip gyrated erratic for a moment as he stuttered the P in plan. His stutter was slight, but even a slight stutter was a significant impediment to soaring Oratory. So was Gerry's New England cant. New Englanders spoke with a blunt Inflection and a whining Cadence which it was nigh impossible to describe, and 'twas strongest in Massachusetts Men such as Gerry. A stuttered New England cant made even indifferent Oratory nigh impossible, as all who had listened to Gerry could attest.

As Gerry squinted, many Deputies looked away. Gerry squinted more with his right eye that his left, deforming his countenance. His crow's claws were nigh Talons, and seemed so deep Franklin half-expected blood to run out them, the right especially, which was deeper and radiated further outward than the left and reminded Franklin of cracked desert ground.

As always, Franklin was sensible of the ocular Woes that a-stigmatized Gerry. His eyes were probably without Focus to different degrees, in a way no spectacles could aid.

As he had many times during the Convention, Franklin pondered causes and solutions to Gerry's flawed vision. In his mind's eye, Franklin again saw the back of a spoon, and envision'd Gerry's eye lens with such Shape, elongate and elliptic, rather than the proper spherick Shape. Franklin could not be certain this Hypothesis correct, but it felt so, and he had faith in his natural Phylosophy instincts. Was Gerry squinting to enforce his eye into a more spherick Shape that focused proper? With a different shaped spoon in each eye, two different shaped eye lenses each with a different degree of Elongation and Curvature, did Gerry have to squint to differing degrees to make each eye focus? How many years had he spent struggling to train his eye and face muscles to these two different intensities of Squint?

Even now, Gerry seemed to adjust his Squint, clenching the right crow's Claw so tight it might have been clutching an egg. Gerry then relaxed his face and the Claw opened, revealing gash-ed wrinkles that seem'd as deep as dagger Cuts. Franklin nigh expected a quail egg to drop out. The chambre was hot enough that it would probably fry on the floor. Though it also seemed humid enough to poach it.

Franklin removed his double Spectacles and peer'd at their circular lenses. What Gerry probably needed were elongate, non-circular lenses, like a sliver sliced off the outside edge of a long dinner roll at an angle. The corrective thickness of the lenses would have to perfect coincide with the spoon-shaped Deformity of the eye. Even Rittenhouse could not fashion such lenses, presuming the eye could be measured with sufficient precision to determine the exact lens Parameters requisite, which it could not. The approach used with circular Spectacles, of simple amassing lenses of many different focal lengths, peering through them one by one until the best lens was found, and then inserting that lens into spectacles, was inappropriate for Gerry. Franklin nonetheless pictured the spectacles Gerry would require. They would have lenses elongate and non-circular, which would be much larger than common spectacle lenses, probably of different thickness for the left and right eye, and perhaps even of different radius. Such elliptic Spectacles would have to be worn high on the nose, direct a front the eye, in the mode which Caledonia preferenced.

How many decades or centuries would it be, and how many unknowable natural Phylosophy advancements would be requisite, ere such spectacles could be fashioned? Was they even possible? Or just another of the Figments which Franklin's imagination seemed to manufacture in nigh limitless quantums?

"I hope I violate not that respect," Gerry said, "in declaring on this occasion my fears that a Civil War may result from the present crisis of the United States. In Massachusetts particularly I see the danger of this calamitous event."

After Shay's Rebellion, everyone saw the danger of Civil War. Gerry's knack for enumerating the obvious was undiminished. Yet he was from the State where Shay had fermented Anarchy, and Deputies did not easily discount the insights of a Witness to the debacle.

"In my State there are two Parties," Gerry said, "One is devoted to The Democracy, the worst I think of all political Evils."

Many Deputies nodded severe, with rapidity, even those who general disliked Gerry's views or found Massachusetts tiresome. Other Deputies tapped walking sticks. Governeur Morris tapped his peg Leg.

"The other Party is as violent in the opposite extreme," Gerry said. "From the collision of these Factions in opposing and resisting the Constitution, c-c-confusion is greatly to be feared."

Franklin saw exasperated expressions on the faces of many Deputies. It wasn't because Gerry had stuttered the C in confusion. Franklin felt a similar exasperation.

What the bloody hell was one to do with Massachusetts? The state was a ceaseless cauldron of Conflict. It produced most of America's blistering leaders, Old Patriots or Violent Men like John Adams, Samuel Adams, and Gerry. Was there some undiscovered Putrification in the water, fowl, or air of Massachusetts that made its men impetuous? The Tea Party had occurred in Massachusetts, as had the outbreak of war Hostilities at Lexington and Concord, and the first major campaign of The War, Washington's investment and liberation of Boston. As well as Shay's recent Anarchy.

Considering the matter from a more intimate vantage, Franklin had repaired home after serving as Minister to France to find America far less welcoming and appreciative than anticipate, on account of John Adams and Samuel slandering him throughout the Land. The Adams' portrayed Franklin as having been perverted by Francophilia, a Minister who wanted for Industry and dissipated continual, a Libertine more ennued of Fame than advocating vigorous for America. The Lees of Virginia had engaged in similar Backbiting throughout the South, tho''twas that of the Adams that had done the most Injury. The backbiting caused Congress to frustrate Franklin's hope that he might be proffer'd a Grant of some small Tract of Land, and a diplomatick Appointment for his grandson William Temple, as Approbation of his Conduct whilst Minister. Franklin was of a mind to petition Congress with a Sketch of his Services, when he could carve out the time, a contemptible entreatment beneath Dignity, which also ought be beneath consideration, yet one to which he might resort, not out of a desire for Land, but to attain an Appointment for Temple. Franklin felt resentment, and a pinch of Anger, that his Posterity was now cast adrift in the world without employ, in significant measure oweing the Pettyness and Misappraisals of John Adams. Yet expecting Adams not to grew jealous; to not suffer consumption by Shallowing, pretensions, and vanity; to not slander; was like hoping a wasp would not sting. For Adams was a Massachusetts man.

Massachusetts was among the most patriotic States, a repository of the Spirit of '76, the last State from which a non-signee Dissident ought have been expect'd. But Massachusetts being Massachusetts, 'twas of course inevitable that it could not govern its Deputies. Franklin had sent for the Pennsylvania Deputies the day prior and ensured that all members of the Deputation would vote Yea. Could not Mr. Gorham or Mr. King have done the same?

Massachuseans!

The bloody Buggers!

"I think it necessary for this and other reasons," Gerry said, "that the Plan should have been proposed in a more mediating sh-sh-sshhh-shape, in order to abate the heat and opposition of Parties. As it has been passed by the Convention I am persuaded 'twill have a contrary effect."

Gerry's lower lip seemed to freeze momentary as he stuttered the "sh" in shape, drawing it out with a much longer inflection than customary. For once, Deputies seemed to scarce notice the stutter.

They was probably pondering Parties.

Political Factions.

Franklin saw fearful looks on the faces of many Deputies, including Jemmy, Caledonia, and Colonel Mason. In Britain, Whigs and Tories warred with utter Fanaticism, determined to eradicate the other no matter what the Harm to the nation. Before residing in Britain, Franklin had thought the warmth of Parties exaggerate, and was disgusted to find their destructiveness drastic understated.

All Deputies detested political Factions. Most every respectable Gentleman in America did. Parties were profane, like Profiteering, Monarchy, and The Democracy.

The Constitution was purposeful mute about Factions. 'Twas presumed that such Abominations would never be countenanced in America.

Yet Gerry seemed to have many Deputies pondering the fearsome possibility of political Factions corrupting the fœderal Government. The President in peculiar was elected by having each Elector chose the two most eminent Leaders, the one with the most votes becoming President, and the second-most votes becoming Vice President. Electors were presumed to be immune from the Passions of Party, but what if they succumb'd? Would the lack of provisions for Parties in the Constitution condemn America to unintentional mimic Monarchies, with their rampant Coups and Assassinations? Would impeachments become as common as informing upon the State of the Union? Would Americans one day be deranged by the Passions of Party, becoming mere Partizans obsessed with destroying opposition Factions, oblivious to national Needs and the public Good?

"I cannot therefore by signing the Constitution," Gerry said, "pledge myself to abide by it in all events."

Sunlight continued to sear the Deputies mercyless. Some glared at the windows with Irritation. Were they staring straight into the Sun for assurance that a Peeve greater than Gerry existed?

"The proposed form of signing makes no difference with me," Gerry said. "If it were not otherwise apparent, the refusals to sign should never be known from me."

Gerry made a point of not looking at Franklin, and rather focused on the row of Deputies in front of Franklin.

"As to the remarks of that most distinguished Deputy," Gerry said, "I cannot help but view them as levelled at myself and the other Gentlemen who meant not to sign."

Thankfully, many Deputies seemed as irritated as Franklin, and disinclined to even engage Gerry. The Democracy was abominable. Without a new Government, Civil War was probable. What other Revelations would Gerry regale the Convention with? That Parliament corrupt? The sky bleu? Washington honest? Pudding delicious?

Gerry sat, and relaxed his squint.

Some Deputies looked down, including William Few and Abraham Baldwin of Georgia. The vampirish Nicolas Gilman of New Hampshire was clenching his teeth and seemed right warm. He was probably envisioning a lengthy course of debate laden with frivolous Jousting. Deputies were growing resentful of men that were delaying their Intention for purposes ignoble, Deputies from distant States like Georgia and New Hampshire especially, as they had the longest journeys. Thus, I consent, Sir, to this Constitution, the body language of many Deputies seemed to say, because I would absent this bloody Convention and Philadelphia, and retire to my home, my hearth, my wife, my family.

CC stood, Charles Cotesworth Pinckney of South Carolina, an imposing man of Parts, envy'd for his Polish and his Liberalia Studia, his classical liberal Education. CC appeared as what he was: an Aristocrat. He had the stiff posture and Air of an Englishman, and emanated that singular british Arrogancey which so often chafed the non-British.

CC's indigo suit was wrought of fine fabrick but understated, with the crisp English cut and lines considered less vogue in America since the Revolution. Even the Indigo was subdue-ed, not that peacockish Indigo which many Gentlemen of the deep South flaunted, but rather muted with a heavy dose of navy, tending towards a Prussian Blue.

Authoritative Blue.

CC dressed like one of the british Lords whose family had been wealthy for Generations and saw no need to flaunt it. His

Dress bespoke a man who insisted on the finest but stooped not to Ostentation.

CC's chin was clefted by a dimple that seemed to become less pronounced each month as his face a-plumpened, and his chin Fat expanded outward and drooped increasing. Like Washington, CC was tall and large boned, with deceptive lankiness, tho' he was not so tall nor powerful as Washington and also did not emanate a Fearsomeness as Washington. 'Twas difficult to imagine Washington becoming soft and lusty, as CC was inexorable. The midriff of CC's suit seemed to grow tighter by the month, and more roundish.

CC sat a front left of the rightmost table in the rear row, left next to Dictator John, with the south slave States. With sixteen Deputies at five tables, the south States were crowded, and seem'd more like one unifyed Faction rather than five different States, which was certain true when it came to taking any vote that effected Slavery.

As always, CC's junior cousin Charles Pinckney sat left next to him, looking like the entitled Son of some French nobleman. The cousins supported each other in all Things, no matter what the cost. To invest one Pinckney was to battle Both.

Charles Pinckney was another tiny man in the mold of Jemmy and Paterson, and his face reminded Franklin of a ferret. A vain and grandiose Ferret with eyes uncommon intelligent.

Like many Deputies, Franklin couldn't gander Charles Pinckney without thinking of his reputed £3,000 a year, every pence earned on the backs of Slaves. Morris had once given Washington £10,000 to pay his entire Army, and the 46 tons of tea destroyed at The Boston Party, more than 8 Million cups, were valued this same approximate amount. Franklin was one of the wealthy'r Americans with his £2,000 annual Income, and he had attain'd to it only via great Thrift and Enterprize, starting printers through-out America, printing currency for Pennsylvania, and writing and publishing the most popular book in America after the Bible, Poor Richard's Almanack, for decades. To simply be born into the Ownership of seven Plantations which produced £3,000 a year staggered the faculties. Other Deputies such as Robert Morris were wealthier than Charles Pinckney on paper in terms of assets, but in terms of ready Cash, Charles Pinckney was one of the wealthier Deputies.

Or so 'twas reputed. Numerate south Slavers had suffered grievous losses during The War. Many of their Slaves had taken flight, to List a british Army that promised Manumission to all Negroes who acquitted themselves with Valour, or to exploit the chaos wrought by The War and fly North. Many Plantations had been raided by british Forces, staple Crops confiscate as supplies, and some put to the Torch. The South attained income primarily exporting Staples, to Europe especially. As commercial intercourse with Britain had been disrupted by The War, ready markets for south Staples were scarcer. Many a ship brimming with Staples intending for Europe and elsewhere had been sunk or privateer'd, confiscate as a Prize of War by Britain.

And cetera.

Franklin had often heard hazards of his Wealth and income, and that of other north Gentlemen, that were prodigious exaggerate, and he wondered if this was true of Pinckney's £3,000. Pinckney revealt scarce little when pressed. Gentlemen were discreat, about business especially, but many a south Planter was loathe to discuss his finances because they were so deranged. Though many a south Planter presented a façade of Opulencey, their Debts were often grievous plaguy. Perhaps such was the case with Charles Pinckney?

Regardless, Pinckney's income from labour uncompensate was prodigious. 'Twas a curious thing to reckon, for a man of the North accustomed to paying Wages to Labour, and disaccustomed to Slaving. How must it feel, to know dozens or hundreds of persons was a toiling for you remote, nary a Respite, the whole of they output accruing to you? 'Twould be abhorrent to Franklin, yet what of those absent moral Faculty? Deficient moral Faculty at the least? Did not Charles Pinckney, and other Slavers, envision their Slaves toiling can-see to can't-see, enriching them, and derive some sense of Comfort and Satisfaction?

Franklin chided himself, in part. When he owned Slaves had he been absent moral Faculty?

Franklin returned his attention to the larger Pinckney. CC resembled one of the soldiers in the upper-tiers of the British nobility. He looked more the softish gentleman of Leisure than the Warrior. Yet he was the only Deputy besides Washington wearing a sword.

CC was another of those men whose face looked radical different from different vantages, especially different angles or Light. Straight on in dimmer Lighting, his head reminded Franklin of a ham Hock with Jowels, and the dominant nose with its unusual wide ridge commanded one's attention. Yet viewed from an angle in better Light, as now, CC was more noble and æsthetic, with delicate eyes that reminded Franklin of king George's, and precocious lips that seemed perpetual on the verge of a Grin. CC had a full head of greyish-dark hair, worn long over the ears and parted on the side. A wisp of hair on his forehead curled like a breaking Wave.

Few Gentlemen had the advantage of trav'ling to one of the great Universities of Europe for their education, and of making the Grand Tour through France, Italy, and the Continent, to hob and nob with Luminaries, view the art, architecture, and culture of the antient Græcian and Roman civilizations, ruminate upon the roots of Civilization itself, and ponder what Contribution they would make to the perpetuation and advancement of this Heritage. Franklin would have lopped off several toes for such Opportunity, especially after his father could no longer afford to send him to publick School, which he was able to attend for two years only, until turned of 10. Washington could not afford such largesse after his half-brother Lawrence died. Yet CC's family was wealthy enough that he had been so blessed.

CC had been educate at the renowned Westminster School in London, and then at Oxford, where he attended the famed lectures of Sir William Blackstone, one of the most revered legal Professors in History. CC read the Law at the famed Middle Temple Inn of Court, was called to the english Bar, and even rode the british Circuit before his Grand Tour.

CC had interned brief at the Royal Military College at Caen in France. He also study'd Alchemy, chymical Species, and the affinity Table under leading European experts, as well as visiting the best botanical gardens and learning plantarum Species and the use of herbs in Healing. CC had been formal educated as a lawyer, natural Phylosopher, and soldier!

CC's education was right impressive, and he knew it. His oratory had a singular Flourish yet bordered on the arrogant. CC made hyperbolical Proclamations and backed them with Action. Whatever else might be said about him, CC was emphatick in his Views.

CC had every blessing imaginable. His first wife Sarah Middleton had been one of the most handsome Belles in America. She passed in 1784, and in 1786 CC marryed an even more handsome Belle who was also from one of the wealthiest families in Georgia.

CC was revered in the south, yet seemed to be disliked with increasing Vehemence the more north one moved, despite being a staunch Republican and championing a strong fœderal Government. His british Airs were a portion of the reason, but his brazen defence of Slavery horrify'd northerners. CC owned 250 Slaves that made him wealthy and was absolute unapologetic about it. His Liberalia Studia had not penetrated him fully, it seemed. CC and many southerners were perfect willing to support an energetic fœderal Government—so long as Slavery remained off the table. CC had frequent vexed anti-slavery northerners with his Eloquence, often obfuscating by resorting to legal Sophistrys. In debate he could be slipperyer than a muddy Hog.

When CC stood, many Deputies probably saw Slavery. Maybe 'twas just the bright Sunlight, but the Pinckneys seemed a glaring Exemplar of all that was worst about Slavery. Genteel, posturing as men of ethos, while their prosperity was produced by Evil.

Peering at CC seem'd to discomfort Washington ever so slight. There was an odd softness in his eyes and a bit more Irritation than usual in the clenching of his lips as they grouped themselves over his false Teeth. These changes were subtle in the extreme, but Franklin had always been an acute observer.

Unlike Pinckney, Washington had denounced Slavery, and he was trying to finagle a way to manumit his Slaves yet maintain to his Wealth. Impossible, as The General was gradual yet grudging accepting. Denouncing Slavery whilst owning Slaves was the height of Hypocrisy, and Washington could not live with Hypocrisy with the ease of lesser men. Looking at CC, Washington seemed to see a shadow of himself. Was he envisioning the way a Posterity which had eradicated Slavery might condemn the Constitution, the Convention, and most of all its Deputies?

Fear crept into the eyes of George Washington.

Such a rare Thing.

Nothing scared The General.

Save tarnishment of his Reputation. Was he envisioning the way his Weakness and Hypocrisy about Slavery might sully his precious Reputation? Not now, but in Futurity?

Slavery.

Bloody Slavery.

Georgia, South Carolina, North Carolina, Virginia, Maryland. These five States comprising nigh half the American population had been unyielding in their opposition to any investment of Slavery, and Delaware had also often sided with them. In theory, with Voting by States and 13 States in total, there should have been 8 States energetic against Slavery, enough to vote down the 5 slave States when questions were called.

In theory.

With Rogue Island boycotting, New Hampshire absent-ing for months, and New York lacking a quorum due to the absence of its Deputies, there had been 6 anti-slavery States at most times, increasing the relative Power of the slave States in Convention. With at the most 11 States quorumed, the best outcome had been some 6 anti-slavery States against 5 slav-ery States. With Delaware often allying with the 5 slave States upon slave Votes, there had in essence been 6 slavery States and 5 non-slavery States. The slave States had thus been able to prevent the Majority requisite to pass measures that would invest Slavery. The slave States deserved begrudging Praise on such count, having been fastidious in ensuring that all five their number were always seated in Convention with a Quorum.

Yet even if the slaver States could have been outvoted, they had threaten'd to absent the Convention and ally themselves with foreign Powers rather than submit to a fœderal Govern-ment that was energetic on the issue of Slavery.

Franklin again wanted to sigh.

The politicks had been inescapable.

Not just inescapable, a veritable Noose.

And as galling as provisions in the Constitution were, deep south States had pressed for even more energetic Protections of slavery. Possessing sense that eluded many a south Zealot, CC had been instrumental in convincing south States to accept Compromise. Yet he had been equal instrumental in keeping the Constitution mute on the question of making a Fugitive of Slavery or other wise manumitting Slaves.

Franklin glanced about the chambre at the Deputies. White males all. Not a Negro nor a fair Sex present. And few Yeomen or Aprons. What would Futurity say of this?

Deputies who hated Slavery such as Gerry and Governeur Morris seemed troubled as they peered at CC, but they was a trifling Minority. There had been surprizing Acceptance of Slavery by Deputies, even northerners who detested it. No generation could accomplish every Thing, and exploding Slavery had quite simply been beyond their reach. Deputies had come to Philadelphia to create a workable government, not to attempt to cure every human Ill. Slavery might end up being a fatal Blot upon their Character, or a Fissure that engulfed America, but to eradicate it at the Convention while creating a viable government had been utter impossible. Would a Futurity inclined to judge Slavery harsh have any sense of this fact?

Like Franklin, CC's father had served as his Colony's agent to Britain, gathering in Halls and Lobbys to exercise Interest with members of Parliament. CC lived in England with his father during this time, and he was one of the few Deputies who had observed the Corruption of Parliament personal and seemed to truly appreciate its Depth. Upon repairing to America, CC started a successful legal Practice in the city of Charleston. Prior to the Revolution, he was an Attorney General for the crown in the American South. CC had also served in the South Carolina Legislature.

When The War began, CC listed the Army as a Regular and was commissioned Captain. He commanded a specializ'd Force, the South Carolina Grenadiers. Grenadiers were once the troops that hurl'd heavy Grenades which were cannonballs miniature and fuse-ed. Doing so required phenomenal Strength, so Grenadiers were usually the largest and stoutest soldiers in the Army. Grenades had generally become obsolete, yet Grenadiers had remained, and were still the stoutest Companys in any Regiment. Along with the Light Horse, Grenadiers were one of choicest and most prestigious Postings. Grenadiers were the elite assault troops, the Showpiece of most Armies, and entrusted with sensitive tasks such as lifeguarding senior Officers. Having commanded Grenadiers, CC was considered to have extreme Tenacity and Vigour. Like Washington, CC's military record and strategic Competency were dubious, but he evidenced extreme Bravery and inspired fanatickal Loyalty in his men. Like Washington, he believed that Discipline was the Soul of an Army.

CC commanded Grenadiers in the defence of Charleston in 1776, preventing a concert'd amphibious Invasion by British General Sir Henry Clinton. He was thereafter promoted to Colonel and given command of a Regiment. CC fought with Washington at Brandywine and Germantown, earning The General's esteem. He served in Washington's camp and later commanded a Regiment against the British in the Floridas, in a campaign that lost nigh Half its men.

CC's second defence of South Carolina was less successful. In 1779, he commanded a Brigade that attacked Savannah in an attempt to recapture it and suffered grievous Losses. In 1780, CC participated in the failed defence of Charleston, resulting in his capture and imprisonment by the British until 1782, after the end of The War. As CC was the consummate British Gentleman, the British made many Overtures to him during his internment, proffering him Freedom and a Commission in the british Army if he would pledge his old Allegiance. He refused, and cajoled other disheartened prisoners into maintaining Allegiance to America.

Slavery notwithstanding, CC was admirable, and extreme formidable. Washington would nigh certain proffer him a senior Secretariat in the new government. CC seemed a good fit for War or State, and was so able he might have his choice. Yet like Thomas, he loved his Plantation, the tenour of southern Life, and also the Culture and magnificence of the large cities of Europe. It would not surprize Franklin, nor many other observers, if such an iconoclastic man refused high Office and simple partook the Luxury and Leisure of southern Life.

CC prepared to speak. Franklin pictured him standing in Parliament addressing Members and Lords, perhaps even speaking with the king. In a chambre filled with the once-British, CC looked the most British of all.

"We are not likely to gain many Converts," CC said, "by the ambiguity of the proposed form of signing. I think it best to be candid and let the form speak the Substance."

Franklin pursed his lips in Irritation, certain where CC was intending. He had a soldier's mentality. Attack the threat headward. Admirable, but not always practicable. Especially not in politicks.

"If the meaning of the signers is left in Doubt," CC said, "my purpose will not be answer'd."

Washington's eyes hardened like cooling steel. He nodded fractional, yet crisp.

CC glanced around at the Deputies, hand a resting casual on his sword, his expression noble and Gaze expansive. His eyes sudden hardened, like Washington's, tho' they were not nigh as fearsome.

"I would sign the Constitution," CC said, "with a view to support it with all my Influence. I wish to pledge myself accordingly."

Franklin wanted to exhale deep through his nose. This was CC at his best and worst. A blunt creature. Too full of Bravado. If every Deputy view'd signing as pledging unequivocal Support with all their Influence, a dozen or more might reconsider their position. Had the ham Head not considerd why Franklin proposed the second motion of signing by States?

Franklin was careful to quell his Warmth and appear cool. His role was that of The Sage, and he could not fall out of character.

CC sat.

Franklin attempted to stand. The Gout and Stone stabbed him simultaneous. The inside of his kneepan might have been struck by Lightning. Franklin winced, paused mid-movement, gritted his teeth, pressed on the Table, and used it to lift himself up. He remember'd his youth, when his arms were stronger, body healthier, when he had awed fellow British printers by carrying two heavy Presses up numerate Flights of stairs, one in each arm. Long past, those days of titanick Vigour. Now Franklin could scarce piss without crying.

Franklin managed to stand. He wanted to tell Deputies that his Gout was less painful than the remarks of CC. And that Gerry and Randolph were more irritant than a barrow of Stones.

"'Tis too soon to pledge ourselves," Franklin said. "We cannot do so until Congress and our Constituents have approved the plan."

Franklin couldn't have stood any longer even if he had more to say. Brevity was king. President, that is. He sat.

Jared Ingersoll of Pennsylvania stood, another Deputy who had been a Mute during most Debate, but who tended to chart a conservative Tack. The ablest jury Lawyer in Philadelphia, and one of the ablest in America, Ingersoll had a striking Gift for Oratory. If Franklin were ever indicted for Murder, Ingersoll would handle the Defence, with the aide of Caledonia. Most men with Ingersoll's oratory endowments liked to flaunt them, and his unwillingness to show his Parts was something of a Curiosity. Franklin wished Ingersoll's humility had been an examplar that inspired other Deputies to brevity or Silence more frequent, but this expectation was pitiful Naïve at an assembly of lawyers and politicians, most who fancied themselves Sirens.

Ingersoll had a face longer than one of Luther Martin's inebriate Tirades. A deep wrinkle in the middle of Ingersoll's chin was shaped as a downward-facing crescent. Ingersoll pursed his lips in a singular Fashion that reminded Franklin of himself when he was serious or grumpy. Ingersoll had bags under his eyes. His long and somewhat thick nose was rounded like a table edge, widened not at the bottom, and had small nostrils. The hair atop Ingersoll's enormous forehead was fading faster than the East Room drapes. In a few months or years when all the hair on the Pate had fled, the eyebrows would probably be more conspicuous, and the sheer length of the head would doubtless dominate to a disheartening degree, destroying any vestiges of Handsomeness. The bald Ingersoll would probably seem like a Caricature viewed in a Versailles Mirror which distorted width or length.

Franklin couldn't glance at Jared Ingersoll without thinking of his father. They had the same name, but Jared Ingersoll
Sr. had been a notorious Loyalist. When the hated Stamp Act
was passed by the crown in 1765, Ingersoll Sr. became Stamp
Master for Connecticut, the crown Agent responsible for ensuring that all colonists used Paper produced in London that had
an embossed revenue Stamp. Non-stamped Paper produced in
America was made a Fugitive. Stamped paper was much more
expencive than ordinary Paper, and it had to be purchased using
british Pounds Sterling that were dire scarce rather than plenty-
ful colonial paper Scrip. Colonists often had to pay an exorbitant
Præmium to acquire pounds sterling Specie, and then use those
Pounds Sterling to buy exorbitant embossed Paper.

Each time a Colonial put a quill to paper to conduct business
or write a loved one, read a printed pamphlet, newspaper, or legal
document, or even played whist, cribbage, or loo, they would
see the emboss'd Stamp and be reminded of the tyrannical Tax.
In a sheer publick perceptive Sense, a more ill-conceive-ed Tax
which generated more Hostility was difficult to imagine. Until
the Tea Act passed eight years later. Ingersoll's father became
the most despised man in Connecticut, was hung and burned in
Effigy, and was later tarred and feathered, scarring him for life.
Ingersoll had been passive early in the Revolution, torn between
Loyalty to his loyalist father and his belief in the Righteousness
of the American Cause.

Ingersoll had matriculated from Yale, read the Law in Philadelphia, and passed the Bar. When tensions between the Colonys
and crown increased, his father, who lived in London, recommended that his son read the Law at the Middle Temple Inn

of Court and then take the Grand Tour. While on the Grand Tour familiarizing himself with the enlightened Civilizations of Antiquity, Ingersoll become more convinced that America's demands for Natural Rights were just. He spent a year and a half in Paris, called on Franklin, and the two became acquaintances.

By the time Ingersoll repaired home to Philadelphia in 1778, America had declared Independency, and he had chose loyalty to Liberty over loyalty to father. Though many Deputies and Patriots had loyalist Family or friends they had disavowed or disowned, as Franklin had done with his son William, there were few more striking examples of prominent loyalist Family than Ingersoll's father, and he was esteem'd for his Courage in this regard. Some Deputies glancing at Ingersoll nonetheless sprouted wistful or distresst expressions, perhaps reminded of loyalist Family or friends they had forsaken during the Revolution.

Sons was not to be thrown off like coats. Yet William had left Franklin no recourse. Even now, resident in England, William was still an enthusiastic Loyalist, agitating for Britain to renew its War against America.

Franklin didn't like thinking about the Betrayal of his bastard Son.

So he didn't.

Ingersoll was seated a comfortable distance behind the Pennsylvania Deputation, back of his Chair nigh touching the Bar that bisected the chambre. He had sat at the back of the Convention for much of its duration, like a lazy student ducking a teacher. Franklin couldn't help smirking at Ingersoll's detachment, as he had many times during the Convention. Glancing rearward at Ingersoll had been of the rare sources of levity during the tedium and warmth of Debate.

Ingersoll was the personal Attorney to prominent business-men and bankers, as well as the indicted du jour. As a jury Law-yer, he usual spent his days in Court arguing, and had thus been happy to sit silent during Debate. He had been lost in obscurity seeming, hiding in the shadow of the large Pennsylvania Dep-utation, content to let more renown'd Pennsylvanians such as Caledonia and Governeur Morris show their Parts.

Early in the Convention, Ingersoll had advocated revision of the Articles of Confederacy rather than a new Constitution, simply because this was the most legal cautious and defensable interpretation of the Convention's mandate. Since then, he had not spoke a dozen sentences. Ingersoll could have easily been one of the most loquacious Deputies, yet he had spoke only on those rare occasions when he felt some glaring Point had been overlooked by the Convention. Speaking infrequent had the contrary effect to that which Sirens suppose-ed, and had heightened Ingersoll's eminency.

Even heightened, Ingersoll's eminency seemed limited tho-ugh. With so many Gentlemen so extensive read in the Law, it seemed doubtful that Ingersoll would secure a judgeship in the new government, and this would seem to a disuse of his Talents regardless. He seemed best suited as a United States Solicitor, a lawyer who represented the United States in Courts when the need arose, arguing for America. This would make use of his skill as Jurist.

Ever mindful of swaying the Jury, Ingersoll walked to cen-tre aisle before speaking, so the entire Convention would not have to crane their necks rearward or rotate their seats to see him. Though this was the only time he had done so, there was nonetheless a subtle Brilliance to the act, as it would have been impossible for most Deputies who spoke frequent. The Walk to the aisle highlighted the fact that Ingersoll said little but was wise and deserving of Respect when he did condescend to address the Convention.

Ingersoll had somber eyes that seemed to have seen much and take the world serious. There was a Conscientiousness in his gaze and bearing that made clients and jurors trust him. Being Politicians, Deputies enjoyed more Immunity to such Machinations than most, but many were still wooed by Ingersoll as he surveyed the chambre with an expression season'd and shrewd. He simply felt like a man you wanted to believe.

"I do not consider signing a mere Attestation of the fact that the states approved," Ingersoll said. "Nor do I consider it as pledging the signers to support the Constitution at all events. I consider signing a recommendation of what is the most eligible when all things are considered."

As Ingersoll walked back to his seat, Governeur Morris began thumping his peg Leg on the floor. Deputies followed suit with walking sticks and clapped tables. By the time Ingersoll sat, tapping filled the room, the loudest and longest duration of the Convention so far, as if Deputies wanted to preclude further Debate. Wanted the Perspicacity of a humble Deputy who had opposed the creation of a new Constitution initial but had been wise enough to reverse his position to be the final Say.

Silence.

A truly treacherous Silence.

All eyes were on Colonel Mason, the only vociferous Opponent of the Constitution who had spoke not, and far and away
its most æsteemed Enemy.

Mason.

A difficult man to measure.

The intrigued expressions of the Deputies reflected this fact.

Mason was turned of 62, seasoned and wise, Republican to
the Marrow. Seven years Washington's senior, Mason was an
old friend of The General, who often turned to him for education. They were neighbors on the Potowmac River, Mount Vernon Plantation being less than a day's ride from Gunston Hall
Plantation. Mason was as expert in government Phylosophy as
Chancellor Wythe, Caledonia, or Jemmy. Like CC, Mason had
the air of a British aristocrat.

Tho' Mason's chestnut hair had long ago whiten'd, he none
the less reminded Franklin of a petulant child. He was a man
of middling stature, and though not egregious Corpulent, was
soft-bodied, obvious a sedentary Scholar accustomed to good
living. Mason's roundish face was chubb-ed with modest chins.
His nose was attractive yet point-ed, the sort one might expect
on a handsome Witch. Mason seemed French featured, the large
rounded forehead especially, which, while larger than ideal, still
allowed handsomeness, and was not so imposing as on so many
unattractive Deputies.

Mason was irascible and prone to Warmth, and it shewed on
his two dominant facial features, his lips and eyes. His dark eyes
were intense, and usual centred upon the whites like a tea cup
on a saucer, which heightened the sense of Severity they conveyed. Modest deepset, with bags, they seemed to glare perpetual,

constantly on the verge of Irritation. Say some Thing that was foolish or an affront to Liberty or natural Rights, and Mason's eyes would intensify, warm, and burn like embers, condemning with a harsh Intolerance. Mason's feminine lips would also purse tight, like those of some irate sex, and the combination of angry lips and furious eyes gave his face a singular Intensity that was right volcanic.

Deputies had been scorched by Mason's volcanic Invectives all too frequent over the last week and were prepared for another Eruption. Though Mason sat silent, his eyes could have fired a foundry.

Like Franklin, Mason suffered from the Gout, and tho' his Gout was not nigh as severe as Franklin's, he lacked Franklin's humour about it, or any Thing. To Mason's criticks, he was naïve, romanticized Liberty excessive, and was too much of a state man. Yet he was no rash anti-Constitutionalist, like Luther Martin, Mercer, Yates, Lansing, and cetera. Mason had been a zealous advocate of Independency during the Revolution, and most Deputies and Americans categorized him in the highest Echelon of Patriots just below men such as Washington and Franklin.

Mason was brought to bed in Lord Fairfax's County in Virginia, and he spent his childhood on his family's Potowmac River plantation—until his father drowned on the Potowmac when his boat capsized. Mason was then raised by his Uncle John Mercer, a renowned Virginia attorney who was counsel to the Ohio Company of Virginia, which Washington's father Augustine and his beloved half-brother Lawrence founded with Thomas Lee. Lawrence Washington had built Mount Vernon and bequeath'd it to The General.

Mercer had the sort of library that would give Thomas a chubber, and its 1,500 volumes made it one of largest in America, larger than even those at most Universities. Like Jemmy and Thomas, Mason had spent a huge portion of his life, his youth especially, reading and engaged in deep phylosophic contemplation, becoming supreme Enlightened. Like Chancellor Wythe, Caledonia, and Jemmy, Mason had probably read more than a Thousand books on law, history, government, and cetera, and had probably spent at least ten Thousand hours on such reading. Like Chancellor Wythe, Caledonia, and Jimmy, Mason quoted the most eminent Phylosophers throughout history effortless, easily weaving their Wisdom into his oratory. Deputies respected this prowess, and it made Mason imposing.

A childhood spent absent Labour, with leisured access to the writings of most of the great Sages and Scholars in history! Franklin couldn't help but envy such a privileged upbringing. Books was exorbitant for those of indifferent income, costing days of Labour apiece at minimum, and often more than a week's. Most Yeomen or Aprons had but a few books, a Bible, an Almanack, and maybe a single work of Phylosophy or Literature, often religious. Franklin had managed to borrow books from bookseller Apprentices in his youth, but they could usual be borrowed once only, at the most a few times, always had to be returnd the next morning, and were so costly to replace that borrowing them was a significant Favour. Franklin had been forced to read entire books late into the night in one sitting, usual after working can-see to can't-see and then spending time with Deborah and their children. He had sacrificed dear to obtain to

Knowledge which the wealth-born Jemmy, Thomas, Wythe, and cetera, accessed by simply strolling into a study at their leisure.

Franklin started his Library Company to spare others his Ordeal and provide the privilege of books to Aprons and Yeomen. Many Aprons and Yeomans subscribe-ed, subscriptions were used to buy many books, and a junto of Aprons obtain'd access to many more books than any single Apron could ever afford.

Mercer provided Mason the finest Tutors and ensured he was educate at the most elite private Academies. He also allowed Mason to read the Law under him. Mason passed the Bar, practiced law, became a Justice in Lord Fairfax's County Courts, and served in the Virginia Legislature for nigh a decade. When tensions between Britain and America first heightened, Mason helped implement the Non-Importation Agreement, under which America tried to suspend purchase of British wares to harm her for oppressing Natural Rights.

When Britain closed Boston's port in 1774, the Virginia House of Burgesses scheduled a Holiday of fasting, humiliation, and prayer to show Solidarity with Massachusetts. Lord Dunmore, the royal Governour of Virginia, responded by dissolving the House of Burgesses. Burgesses responded by reconvening informal at the nearby Raleigh Tavern, including George Washington. Burgesses decided to draught a Charta which defined their Natural Rights and Constitutional Rights, and they chose Mason to draw it. The resulting Resolves were signed in Lord Fairfax's County by all Burgesses. Though the Resolves emphasized that American colonists were loyal British citizens, they also warned that the Natural Rights and Constitutional Rights of these colonists had to be respected, and that if they were not, colonists would secure them by any mean necessary.

Other counties across America later draughted similar Resolves, but the Fairfax Resolves were the first. The Fairfax Resolves were a precursory Declaration of Independency, albeit on a more limited state and county Level, and 'twas Mason, not Thomas, who had drawn them.

Mason earned fame as a Deputy to the Virginia Convention of 1776. When Colonys declared Independency in 1776, Constitutions designed for British rule became obsolete. Virginia, leader in so many revolutionary actions, was the first Colony to draft a new state Constitution, and Mason was a principal drawer of the Virginia Constitution which became a model for most other ex-Colonys. Mason was most renowned for drawing the Declaration of Rights in the Virginia Constitution. The Declaration of Rights had sixteen Sections which protected the Natural Rights of The People from tyrannick Encroachments by energetic government.

The Virginia Plan, the initial governmental Structure the Convention utilized, drew heavy on the Virginia Constitution which Mason had drawn. The most resonant and famed portions of the Declaration of Independency were regurgitations of Mason's Declaration of Rights and Fairfax Resolves. Mason had been more influencial in draughting the Chartas of the Revolution, the Chartas of Liberty, than any other man.

And yet he would not sign the Constitution! As with Randolph, the way Enemys of the Constitution would fixate on Mason's refusal to sign and distort it to malign the edifice was terrific to contemplate.

Of all the Deputies who opposed the Constitution, Mason seemed the most consonant in his Logic and pure in his Principles. Though Mason acknowledged the need for a more fœderalized Government, he nurtured a pathologic Mistrust of energetic central Government. He had boundless Faith that men as a group could govern themselves, but boundless Cynicism about the corruptibility of individual men, when entrusted with Power especially.

Mason was emphatick that the U.S. Constitution be prefixed with a Declaration of Rights similar to that in Virginia's Constitution, so as to protect natural Rights of The People and Sovereignty of The States. He had proposed such a Declaration five days past, on September 12, Wednesday, during the final bouts of debate. Many Deputies were not opposed to a Declaration of Rights in principle, merely the additional weeks or months of debate it would entail. Many Deputies feared that adding too much to the Constitution might unravel tenuous compromises. As with Slavery, there was much to be said for knowing the limits of one's Reach.

Mason didn't reckon the matter in such Light. To him, an energetic national Government was a betrayal of the Revolution and its ideals. Mason would never sign a U.S. Constitution that had not been prefix'd with a Declaration of Rights. He was more emphatick in this regard than even Gerry. As with Gerry, all Deputies knew it.

Yet all Deputies also expected Mason to stand and speak. To restate the need for a Declaration of Rights. To argue that even with a Declaration of Rights, the new government might become too energetic and violate Natural Rights, in futurity especially. If a Constitution with a Declaration of Rights might beget innovation, one without a Declaration of Rights was certain a derangement!

Still Mason sat, eyes Embers, lips clenched tight, radiating Fury. He was probably thinking that this Vote was a trod down the fateful path to energetic central government. Nigh certain envisioning a Congress passing tyrannical laws that pilfered the Sovereignty of States, taxed The People undue, fermented religious Inquisitions, revoked The People's right to bear Arms, to speak with Liberty, to claim Habeas Corpus, to be free from unlawful Seizures …

Mason's expression grew ever more glum. He seemed to want to stand, yet did not.

Mason was shrewd. And this was not his first Constitutional Convention. His tortured expression reflected the Truth: no oratory would change the outcome of the Vote. He therefore seemed disinclined to fritter his time—or anyone else's—any further.

Mason looked up from the table rapid and glanced at Washington. Washington's eyes softened, filled with tolerance. Mason's body relaxed slight.

Ahhh.

Politicks always was and always would be about Power and Relationships. Washington held the Power. Mason did not. Yet the two men had a Relationship. Was Mason wary of angering his old Friend? Had The General exercised Influence with his old Friend? Promised that he would do every-thing in his Power to ensure that Congress the First proposed a Declaration of Rights?

Some bargain had been struck, at a minimum some Assurance given, and it was clear Mason would not make trouble for his old Friend at the final instant.

"Ere I call the question," Washington said, "does any other Gentleman not wish to be heard?"

Washington waited nigh a full minute, probably to be certain no Deputy could ever pretend that they had not had their grievances voiced.

"With finality," Washington said, "does any other Gentleman not wish to be heard?"

Silence.

Franklin took final measure of the situation.

Some 73 Deputies had been appointed to Convention, with nigh 55 having seated, and 18 not attending. Of the 55 who had seated, 41 were present and 14 absent, and only 7 could be considered inarguable opponents of the Constitution, George Mason, Edmund Randolph, and Elbridge Gerry, all present, as well as John Lansing, Robert Yates, John Mercer, and Luther Martin, all absent. Franklin could not help but think of Luther Martin, who considered the Convention's decision to craft a new Constitution rather than revise the Articles of Confederacy a Coup d'Éstat. Some 7 of 55 opposing the Constitution, nigh 1 in 8, some 13 per cent. Of the 41 Deputies in Convention assembled at present, 3 refused to sign, nigh 1 in 14, some 7 per cent. Such Ciphers tended to conservative, as Franklin seemed to always reckon some additional Deputy who opposed the Constitution. By way of example, Alexander Martin, of North Carolina, who had absented Convention, was no enthusiast of an energetic fœderal Government nor the Constitution, though he had not open opposed it. The same might be reckon'd of a few Deputies who had absented.

All Dissidents present had been given a Voice, even Mason without speaking, and their criticisms of the Constitution were a far from trifles. Randolph feared ratification of the Constitution was impossible, and that Civil War must arise out of the failure to ratify. Mason was certain the Government wrought by the Constitution was an Innovation that would grow Energetic and Tyrannical, even with a Declaration of Rights prefixed, and that a Constitution absent a Declaration of Rights was bloody Madness.

Would these Fears prove to have Foundation? Or would they be lost over time amid the greater success of the Constitution? Perhaps both?

Secretary Jackson called the Vote on Franklin's second Motion, naming States one by one. All voted aye, save South Carolina, which was divided. CC was not granting Quarter on his preference for a more transparent signing method that required unequivocal support by all drawers, and his cousin Charles voted with him. Thus, two of South Carolina's four Deputies favoured Franklin's motion to sign by State, and two opposed it. A tie, neither yea or nay, divided.

Only a simple majority of States were needed to pass a motion, seven of twelve states. Franklin's motion thus passed easy, though the appearance of Unanimity was crucial. Any Deputy later defending the Constitution and the Vote on Franklin's motion could say honest that the Pinckneys dissented out of a desire to support the Constitution more ardent, and that this aside there was Unanimity.

"Major Jackson," Washington said. "Please call parchment the fifth of the Constitution."

Washington descended the dais and proffered parchment the fifth to Jackson. 'Twas large, ditto the size the other four parchments. Jackson stood and held the parchment, as previous.

"In Convention Monday September 17th 1787," Jackson read. "Present The States of New Hampshire, Massachusetts, Connecticut, Mister Hamilton from New York, New Jersey, Pennsylvaniay, Delaware, Maryland, Virginiay, North Carolinay, South Carolinay and Georgiay."

Many Deputies glanced into space morose, scarce listening. The Resolvements had been approved by the Convention previous, and all Deputies knew what they prescribed.

"Resolve-ed," Jackson read, "That the proceeding Constitution be laid before the United States in Congress assembled, and that it is the Opinion of this Convention, that it should afterwards be submitted to a Convention of Delegates, chosen in each State by the People thereof, under the Recommendation of its Legislature, for their Assent and Ratification; and that each Convention assenting to, and ratifying the Same, should give Notice thereof to the United States in Congress assembled."

Franklin wondered about the reception of the Constitution in Congress. The Convention had ignored the Instructions of the Congress, and now presumed to instruct the Congress.

"Resolve-ed," Jackson read, "That 'tis the Opinion of this Convention, that as soon as the Conventions of nine States shall have ratified this Constitution, the United States in Congress assembled should fix a Day on which Electors should be appointed by the States which shall have ratified the same, and a Day on which the Electors should assemble to vote for the President, and the Time and Place for commencing Proceedings under this Constitution. That after such Publication the Electors should be appointed, and the Senators and Representatives elected: That the Electors should meet on the Day fixed for the Election of the President, and should transmit their Votes certified, signed, sealed and directed, as the Constitution requires, to the Secretary of the United States in Congress assembled, that the Senators and Representatives should convene at the Time and Place assigned; that the Senators should appoint a President of the Senate, for the sole Purpose of receiving, opening and counting the Votes for President; and, that after he shall be chosen, the Congress, together with the President, should, without Delay, proceed to execute this Constitution."

Deputies knew such instruction of the Congress would rankle some Members, but 'twas important to disallow Delay of the inauguration of government, which opponents of the Constitution might machinate in a Congress renown'd for its impotency.

Jackson placed parchment the fifth down. The lower half the parchment was empty.

"Major Jackson shall now call the Letter," Washington said.

Washington descended the dais and proffered another smaller, letter-sized parchment to Jackson. Such letter would accompany the present Constitution and be laid with the same before the United States in Congress assembled, when transmitted. The Convention had tasked the Committee of Stile with preparing this draught the week prior, and it had also been approved by the Convention.

Jackson stood and held the letter, which seemed miniscule compared to the large parchments he had been reading.

"In Convention," Jackson read. "September 17, 1787."

Several Deputies peered into the table morose. Dictator John's cheeks expanded, filled with air, and he exhaled slow yet quiet, his eyes growing warmer as his cheeks dissipated.

"Sir," Jackson read. "We have now the honor to submit to the consideration of the United States in Congress assembled, that Constitution which has appeared to us the most adviseable."

The Sir in question would be the President of Congress, Arthur St. Clair of Pennsylvania, a General in the Army during the Revolution. St. Clair was much esteemed by Washington.

"The friends of our country have long seen and desired," Jackson read, "that the power of making war, peace and treaties, that of levying money and regulating commerce, and the correspondent executive and judicial authorities should be fully and effectually vested in the general government of the Union: but the impropriety of delegating such extensive trust to one body of men is evident—Hence results the necessity of a different organization."

Franklin glanced at Governeur Morris, who had drawn the letter, and nodded Approbation. Morris nodded and smiled in his cherubic fashion, exhibiting pleasure at his eloquency.

"'Tis obviously impracticable in the fœderal government of these States," Jackson read, "to secure all rights of independent sovereignty to each, and yet provide for the interest and safety of all—Individuals entering into society, must give up a share of liberty to preserve the rest. The magnitude of the sacrifice must depend as well on situation and circumstance, as on the object to be obtained. 'Tis at all times difficult to draw with precision the line between those rights which must be surrendered, and those which may be reserved; and on the present occasion this difficulty was increased by a difference among the several States as to their situation, extent, habits, and particular interests."

Many a Deputy nodded emphatick.

"In all our deliberations on this subject we kept steadily in our view," Jackson read, "that which appears to us the greatest interest of every true American, the consolidation of our Union, in which is involved our prosperity, felicity, safety, perhaps our national existence. This important consideration, seriously and deeply impressed on our minds, led each State in the Convention to be less rigid on points of inferior magnitude, than might have been otherwise expected; and thus the Constitution, which we now present, is the result of a spirit of amity, and of that mutual deference and concession which the peculiarity of our political situation rendered indispensable."

Franklin peered without the south Windows and was treated to a view within the State House Garden. Trees, luxuriant vegetation, and Promenaders abounded, including a plenitude of the fair Sex. As without the north Windows, Franklin spied the back of a bluecoat militia Sentry who stood to attention. As the north Sentry, the south Sentry seemed right vigilant in præventing anyone from approaching the State House to eavesdrop.

Franklin could not help but fixate upon a Sex in a cochineal gown who promenaded gargantuan Mammaries. They seemed to heave as she went, defying the general motion of her form, afflicting her with continual counterweight. Franklin could spend, and had spent, hours in lewd imaginings of the Sexes that passed without the south Windows within Garden. For this very Reason, he general tried to avoid gandering the Garden when incarcerate the State House on business of import. The distractions to be found could be right consuming.

"That it will meet the full and entire approbation of every State is not perhaps to be expected," Jackson read, "but each will doubtless consider, that had her interest alone been consulted, the consequences might have been particularly disagreeable or injurious to others; that it is liable to as few exceptions as could reasonably have been expected, we hope and believe; that it may promote the lasting welfare of that country so dear to us all, and secure her freedom and happiness, is our most ardent wish."

Many Deputies nodded, some emphatick.

"With great respect," Jackson read, "We have the honor to be, Sir, Your Excellency's most obedient and humble Servants."

Jackson ascended the dais, conveyed parchment the fifth and the letter to Washington, and then returned to his Table and sat.

"If the Resolvements and Letter does not meet the Approbation of any Deputy," Washington said, "they have Licence to speak to the matter now."

Silence.

"The Resolvements and Letter having been approved by a calling of the question prior," Washington said, "and no Deputy proffering additional motions pursuant to them, they shall be coupled to the Constitution and transmitted with it."

Washington recognized Rufus King, who stood, looking right Cæsarish, as always, as if sudden transported to Convention from antient Rome.

"The Journals of the Convention should be either destroyed or deposited in the custody of the President," King said. "If suffered to be made public, a bad use will be made of them by those who wish to prevent the adoption of the Constitution."

This issue, like so many others, had been discussed outside of Convention prior to moving upon.

Caledonia stood, sweat dripping out the edges of his white wig, spectacles high on his nose, measured and compoz'd as always.

"I prefer the second Expedient," Caledonia said in his Scottish burr. "At one time I liked the first best. But as false Suggestions may be propagate it should not be made impossible to contradict them."

"I second such motion," the Little Lion said.

"So moved," Washington said. "That the Journals and other papers of the Convention be put in the hands of the President, under strict secresy, until Congress, if ever formed under the Constitution, adjudicates the matter."

Washington gave Gentlemen a chance to be heard on the question. No Deputy spoke. Washington was the best repository of any Trust.

Secretary Jackson called the Question. All States voted yea, save Maryland, which had been instructed by its Legislature to report back on the proceedings of the Convention and therefore could not vote in Favour of secreting the Journals. The motion passed.

Washington stood.

"What would the Convention have done with the Journals?" he said. "Should Copys be allowed to Deputies if applied for? To those not Deputies?"

Discussion on the question ensued. It was resolved that the Journals and other records remain secret in Washington's possession but subject to the order of the Congress, if ever formed under the Constitution.

Some Deputies possessed Draughts, Copys, and productions by committees and asked Washington how they should dispose them. Washington demanded not such Records, but offered to archive them with the Journals for those Gentleman that desired such repository. Secretary Jackson walked the tables and a number of gentlemen handed Records to him.

"I would remind Gentlemen," Washington said, "that sequestration of Major Jackson's Journal and other records is a Futility if notes of individuals be publicized."

Several Deputies had taken Notes sporadic, and Deputies glanced at these individuals. The Little Lion. James Paterson of New Jersey. James McHenry of Maryland. Colonel Mason. Rufus King of Massachusetts. And of course Jemmy, the only Deputy who had taken Notes continual.

Washington locked eyes with the Little Lion, who nodded. Then Paterson, who nodded. Next McHenry, then Mason, then King, each of who nodded.

Washington stared at Jemmy, who was busy drawing his Notes and saw him not.

Washington waited.

Deputies chuckled.

Jemmy finished drawing, glanced up at Washington, and realized that The General's remarks were intended for him. He was so tiny compared to Washington, almost like a child speaking to its Father. And yet also so meek, so sincere in his Chagrin. Jemmy spoke soft, like a mouse plotting Treason.

"Your Excellency," he said. "Upon my sacred Honor, I would never violate the Secresy."

"An oath I hope all Members will swear," Washington said. "I would not constrain any Gentleman from freely expressing his opinions of this Constitution. Nor drawing from his Convention notes in expressing opinions. But 'tis my earnest desire that all Gentlemen refrain from Publication of their notes."

The instant Washington finished speaking, he strode lithe to the front of the Speaker's table, bent slight, and rotated the Constitution describing a half Circle, that its text was upright to Deputies who approached. As he shuffled through the four parchments of vellum they rustled appreciable. Washington laid the parchments out along the table left to right. There was not enough room on the table for all parchments to be laid side to side. Washington maintain'd ample room on the right for the final parchment, and then fanned the first three parchments on the left, parchment the first atop the two middle parchments. He moved the silver inkstand tray from the front of the table—the back of the table when he was seated behind it—to the rear and placed it near the final parchment.

The inkstand had also been used to execute the Declaration of Independency and was wrought by renowned silversmith Philip Syng, a friend of Franklin and a member of his mutual-improvement club The Junto. The inkstand consisted of a tray which held a pounce shaker, a quill holder, and an inkwell. The tray was ornate silver, like those the wealthy used to serve tea. The shaker, holder, and inkwell were also silver. The shaker and inkwell resembled squat salt shakers and were placed on either side the larger holder, which had a bulb-ed bottom with small holes that three quills of varying sizes were inserted into and protruded from, two black and one white. A rod of silver rose out of the centre of the holder, forming a P-shaped handle that reminded Franklin of a gravy boat. When Washington grabbed this handle to centre the holder on the tray, his massive index and middle fingers filled it so fully they seemed they might be stuck.

Many a Deputy's eye was drawn to the two black swan Quills in the Syngstand, and lingert upon them. Their entire shaft was black. These were the most expensive pen Quill in all the world, black Swans discovering but recent, and known only in New Holland and New Zeeland, at the remotest corner of the globe. Britain alone consumed some twenty Million to thirty Million pens per annum, most imported from Russia. America consumed an unknown quantum of pens, as most were attained local from the prodigious quantum of native Fowl when they moulted, but at least five Million pens consumed per annum, and perhaps as high as ten Million, was a fair Hazard. Yet in all of America and Britain, there were but a few thousand black swan Quills. The black swan Quill was no better than the white swan Quill nor vulgar goose Quill in terms of the quality of its drawing, but its rareification imbued Status. Black swan Quills were often used for Ceremonys, and their inclusion by the Stationer on the final day of Convention was à propos.

Having positioned the Constitution and Syngstand, Washington turned and stood next to the final parchment and table edge, facing the Deputies. Sunlight shadow'd the Bridge of his nose, making it seem flatter than typical, mighty flat, as if planed by a cabinet maker that a procession of toy soldiers could march across it. Sunlight also glistened the Scar on his left cheek, the residual of the Incision for the removement of an abscessed tooth.

As Washington peered out at Deputies, he relaxed his jaw muscles, transforming the appearance of his Face. The corners of his mouth seemed to curl upward fractional. His countenance became benevolent rather than harsh, imbuing him with a subtle Sense of Contentment and Introspection. He might have been standing on his porch at Mount Vernon, hosting guests with a glass of Madeira, cider, or porter in Hand, gazing serene at a sunset talking of crops, canals, colonizing the West.

"I consider our new Constitution as an experiment on the practicability of republican Government," Washington said, "and with what dose of Liberty man can be trusted for his own good."

Washington's jaw muscles retightened, his eyes grew cold, his massive hand clench'd his battle Sword reflexive, and the Soldier men feared returned. Washington emanated Aggression as tangible as the sunlight, Heat, or smell of soot.

Franklin felt what most Deputies surely did: a fearsome sense that Washington wanted to not just harm those who would subvert the American experiment, but dispatch them.

"I remain determined," Washington said, "that the American experiment should have a fair tryal. And I would still lose the last Drop of my Blood in support of it."

Washington's eyes hardened as he spoke the last few words.

Franklin's spine chilled. He couldn't help swallowing, and his throat felt dry sudden. He envisioned some aspirant Tyrant being run through by Washington. The eyes of many Deputies softened with Love. Three tables rightward, CC's eyes grew moist.

Washington bent and picked up a black swan Quill. His black suitcoat stretched taut over his back Muscles as he did so. Franklin was reminded of a horse haunch.

The black swan Quill was appropriate for an oversize signature such as Hancock's upon the Declaration. It seemed large in most hands, but not Washington's.

Washington welled the quill into ink and signed the Instrument. He replaced the quill. Washington then affixed his signature to parchment the fifth of the Constitution, as well as the Letter.

Washington waited a Stretch for the ink to dry and then placed parchment the fifth under the other parchments, but with the upper portion protruding rearward, that it could be observed by Deputies. Washington placed the Letter on the rear left portion of the table.

Washington walked back behind his Table and stood next to his throne a front the signed fourth parchment, shoulders thrown back natural, arms relaxed at his sides, head perfect level and facing outward.

Franklin couldn't help but focus on the Sun on the back of Washington's throne again. Was it a rising or setting?

Deputies formed into a line by States, in the same order Votes had been called throughout the Convention, north to south in geographic Order. New Hampshire first. Then Massachusetts, Connecticut, New York. A line stretched down the centre aisle. States later in the procession remained at their tables.

The wary-eyed John Langdon of New Hampshire was first. The Robert Morris of New Hampshire, he was oft stiled. Standing, Langdon was a large, handsome man, and of a noble carriage. A wealthy merchant from Portsmouth and former President of his State, Langdon's appearance was nonetheless a bit illusory, as he possessed ignoble Vanity, courting popularity with the zeal of a Lover and the constancy of a Martyr. He had been a vig'rous Patriot during the Revolution though, and a supporter of a strong fœderal Government once he finally seated at Convention.

Langdon walked slow left to right in front of the Constitution, inspecting the first three parchments as he went, and then stopped a front parchment the fourth. Washington met Langdon's gaze even. Langdon curtsy'd slight to His Excellency, nodding and bending at the waist. He grabbed the quill, dipped it in the inkwell, held it at an angle, signed the Instrument, replaced the quill, and moved to the right.

Washington was the only Deputy that would sign parchment the fifth of the Constitution or the Letter. Deputies would sign parchment the fourth only.

Nicholas Gilman of Exeter stepped forward. Either his ears was low on his head, or the portion of his head above the ears was excessive. Franklin was never sure which. Gilman's eyebrows arched sharp as they moved outward from the Centre of the Face, and the gap between the upper eyelid and brows increased, imbuing a Singularity. Gilman's pursed lips almost seemed to snarl, even tho' he was not warm. His facial features often made

Franklin think of a Vampire. A genteel Vampire. All that was missing was fangs.

Gilman was from a reputable family but was in Convention because he possess'd a singular Virtue: he had been willing to make the arduous Journey from New Hampshire. Gilman was modest and prudential. There was no Thing brilliant or striking in his Character, but there was something respectable and worthy about him. Though one of the few Deputies of ordinary endowments, he had the Wisdom to realize this, and had general kept Quiet in debates. The few times Gilman had spoke, he championed a strong fœderal Government. The Convention respected Gilman for his humility. If only pompous Buggers like Luther Martin could have evidenced it.

Gilman's brother had been Governour of New Hampshire for more than a decade, and Gilman worked at his family's trading House prior to the Revolution. He listed the Army as a Regular during The War, earned promotion to Captain, and served until the Peace of Paris cemented. Like Hamilton and Mifflin, Gilman was a staff officer valued for his business and organizational Acumen, though had shown Prowess in Combat, especially at Freeman's Farm during the Battle of Saratoga.

Saratoga.

The first great Victory of The War, which made the French believe America could actual best the British. People gave Franklin credit for securing French support, and he deserved it, but all his efforts might have been futile without Saratoga. Saratoga would not have been won without the Valour, Brilliance, and sheer Will of Benedict Arnold, who out-marshaled the British and rallied American troops repeated to ensure Victory.

Thinking of Benedict Arnold, all one could do was sigh. One of the greatest combat Generals of the Revolution, perhaps the greatest. One of the few American Generals comparable to an Alexander, Hannibal, or Cæsar, with that exceeding rare Knack for attaining to Victory under most any condition, even if severe outnumbered. Arnold had been shameless mistreated by America. This excuzed not his Treason, yet Franklin couldn't help but wish that America had shown greater Wisdom, had never disaffected Arnold. He might have been standing behind Nicolas Gilman with the Connecticut Deputation, about to sign the Constitution.

Gilman had suffered at The Forge with Washington's Army during the infamous Winter, and he served in The General's camp for much of the latter part of The War, fighting at Monmouth and Yorktown. Gilman had been a valued Assistant to Colonel Alexander Scammell, Adjutant General of the Army, the chief administrative Officer of the Army.

Serving in this administrative capacity, Gilman had worked intimate with some of the most prominent Heroes of the Revolution, including General Henry Knox, Major General Nathanael Greene, and Baron Friedrich Wilhelm von Steuben. The Prussian von Steuben had been an Aide-de-Camp to Frederick the Great, and he served as Inspector General of the American Army. He had provided the training in European Drill and Discipline that finally allow'd the American Army to meet Redcoats as equals and best them. Tho' fat enough to cripple a clydesdale, Knox was the chief artillery Officer in the Army, one of America's scarce Experts in the nigh arcane specialty of demolishing at Distance. And Nathanael Greene, perhaps Washington's greatest

General, a commander of strategic and tactical Cunning, who also evidenced Obedience to Congress and Civil Authority that other brilliant American Generals lacked. Greene was the man Washington had chose to command if ever felled in Battle—until Congress could have acted to chuse a new Commander. On numerate occasions, Deputies had seen these military Heroes treat Gilman with prodigious Esteem, and this earned Gilman approbation in their eyes.

Gilman moved left to right in front of the Speaker's table, peered at the parchments of the Constitution, and stopped before the fourth and final parchment. He regarded Washington, curtsied, and then signed the instrument. When Washington looked at Gilman it was as a fellow Soldier, with a cordialness and Esteem never shown to non-soldiers, no matter how eminent.

Looking Washington within eyes and making obedience to him was not a pre-arranged Ceremony nor requisite of Procedure. But such was his Stature. To even those long accustom'd to his Person, he was awe some.

Franklin once again envy'd Washington's sheer Manliness. His innate physical Grandeur. His height, his musculature, his strength, the magnanimity of his presence, the Love and Fear he simultaneous inspired, tho' always Love first. George Washington quite simply look'd the part of the storied Leader, and 'twas nigh impossible to stand before him and not feel Admiration. The sheer prowess of his Person was truly awe some.

Massachusetts was next. Queer, not seeing either Adams in its Deputation. Franklin remembered signing the Declaration of Independency in this very chambre eleven years ago, saw John

Adams and Samuel Adams affixing their names to the royal Death Warrant. Franklin saw the younger Adamses as they looked eleven years ago but envisioned them in the Massachusetts Deputation about to sign the Constitution. John less bald, his exposed forehead not yet freckled with age Spots, teeth not yet corroding and yellowish like the pillars of some dilapidate Roman temple, not yet a repugnant, terrific Apparition. Adams probably felt frustrate by his absence from the Convention and would in time surely bemoan it as another Injustice which trapaned him of the Fame he felt entitled.

The ever-likely Nathaniel Gorham of Massachusetts walked left to right, peer'd at the Constitution, shared his moment with The General, curtsied, and signed. Gorham was ignored by most Deputies, who focused on the Massachusetts table where Elbridge Gerry sat alone. The Massachusetts table was at the extreme left of the rear row, increasing the Sense that Gerry was isolate from the Convention.

Signing was a plodding process. Each Deputy seemed to want to take in the Constitution, to have his culminating moment of contemplation and Satisfaction. No Deputy wanted to leave their signature partial dried and have it smeared by the next Deputy who signed, defaming them for all time. Each Deputy thus waited for the ink of their Signature to dry before absenting the dais. Ink usually took a quarter minute to dry compleat, and a half minute or even a minute if one were nice, which was to say fastidious exact, so some delay was requisite if smearing was to be avoided. A blotter could accelerate drying by absorbing ink, but blotters smeart ink upon occasion. With a document this critical, 'twas better to simply be patient. Deputies knew this without telling.

The line rotated left until parallel with the Speaker's table, that Deputies in the rear of the line were left of the first parchment of the Constitution, and moved rightward in front of all parchments as their Turn to sign approached. This allowed them a leisurely View of the engrossment while awaiting their Turn to sign, and kept the line moving, minimizing the previous delay while each Deputy surveyed the Constitution prior to signing.

Rufus King signed next. All he needed was a corona wreath and a toga Prætexta, and he would be ready to Iacta Alea Est and cross the Rubicon. Or would it someday be the Mississippi, Schuylkill, or Potowmac?

"After all our Harrows and tearing at our Vitals," Robert Morris whispered, "the Constitution isn't without a King."

Governour Morris rolled his eyes.

Only two signers from Massachusetts, one of largest and most eminent States. But the Convention had been long, and Massachusetts was some 300 miles distant. She had only sent four Deputies, but Gerry refused to sign and lawyer Caleb Strong had repaired home to tend to his ill Wife.

New Jersey's Deputies vacated their Table and moved to the rear of the line, the left of the line. As they did, the Little Lion approached the Constitution. His step was fleet and graceful, yet also right intimidate. 'Twasn't difficult to imagine the Little Lion turning like a Whirlwind, impaling an Ambuscader before they had time to parry. Or dueling with swords, toying with an opponent arrogant until he no longer amused, and then dispatching him with a single Flourish of the sword so fast 'twas nigh impossible to see.

Washington brightened measurable as the Little Lion approached, that rare Warmth reserved for a chosen few. The Little Lion's curtsy was scarce discernable. Washington smiled ever so slight at it, yet his smile seemed mechanickal, as if his face were operate by clock Gears.

Deputies seemed to veil their Disgust at the Little Lion's impudence. Most with success. Many were probably thinking that by Right, by Procedure, the Little Lion ought not sign the instrument, as New York had not mounted a Quorum and had voted not.

After the Little Lion drew his signature Fugitive, he redipp'd the quill and continued drawing. He rewelled several times, drew several times. Washington leaned in and glanced down, curious. And then smiled approving.

Deputies were also intrigued. Yet no one asked what the Little Lion was drawing.

The state Demarkations, in all problity.

When the Little Lion finished drawing he stood next to the Table rather than gathering with other Deputies below it. Stood on the dais, above the Deputies, like Washington.

Deputies exchanged surpriz'd and disgusted glances. To draw on the engrossed Constitution without even asking permission from Washington! And then stand next to His Excellency, as if his Par. The Little Lion had Brass unrivaled!

The Little Lion saw the resentment in Deputies and simply smirked with cold Arrogancy. Many Deputies was doubtless wishing they had been clever enough to prevent the state

Demarkations, that they could stand on the dais with Washington. Yet most would not have had the Brass even if the thought to prevent had occurred. Or perhaps would have been restrain'd by Humility and Dignity.

Franklin and Governeur Morris exchanged a knowing Glance and allowed fractional grins. 'Twas vintage Hamilton. Preventing before the necessity even occurred to most and out-working even those who laboured incessant. Yet always with alienating Hauteur.

Hamilton's mere presence at Convention was an act of Rebellion and took Brass. Defying the political Powers of his State, especially Governour Clinton, could harm Hamilton's career in New York, even with the patronage of his father-by-law General Schuyler. Hamilton was probably banking on an Appointment when Washington condescended to Executive, a realistic hope, and also seemed to simply believe in the Cause of Constitution.

Yet there was a darker side to Hamilton's courage, independency, resourcefulness, and rebelliousness. Little seemed sacred to the Little Lion, save perhaps his own Ambition. He ignored the instructions of his State as Deputy, of Washington as Aide-de-Camp, agitated the Newburghers, and even advocated a blatant aristocratic and monocratic Government without a scrap of remorse. Was there any Thing the Little Lion would scruple to defy in the name of ambition? Any Thing he was unequivocal loyal to besides Interest?

It seemed not, and such a creature could be bloody dangerous.

Hamilton seemed like a man who might make himself Monarch.

The line was shortening now. Only New Jersey left. Pennsylvania was next.

The fox-faced David Brearly signed. And then the puny William Paterson, just over five feet high. Next was Jonathan Dayton, with his frontiersman Face and Alleghany of a nose. When Dayton moved rightward, no Deputy moved in to take his place.

Hamilton moved in brief, steps as fleet as rapier Ripostes. He dipped the quill, drew again, redipped and redrew several times, and returned to his position next to the table. He was nigh certain drawing the state Demarkations.

The table stood empty and the Constitution sat beckoning. 'Twas but a few yards from where Franklin sat, but might as well have been in Charleston. Franklin had equal chance of walking either distance unassisted.

Damn the bloody Gout!

Curse the bugger of a Stone!

The longer Franklin stared down the aisle, the more gaping the distance seemed. Better not to dally.

Without doors, Washington had offer'd to transport the Instrument to Franklin's table for signing. Franklin refused, an act of unadulterate Stubbornness and Pride.

Franklin saw Deputies watching him expectant, showing the same Love they had Washington, though not as intense on most faces, and absent on some. Franklin stood, and then leaned immediate into his walking stick as the Gout and Stone ravaged him. He felt as if thousands of tiny water moccasins were within bladder and joints, curled Fangs drawn like daggers, biting him again and again and again and again without cessation. The dizziness was surely the result of their Venom.

Franklin saw the table drifting away with rapidity, growing more distant until it blurred. The aisle to the Constitution seemed infinite, like ocean stretching to the horizon.

Franklin managed a few steps. And then slumped onto his walking stick like a sack of roots. On Franklin's left, Caledonia grabbed his arm, help'd him hobble forward.

Step by agonizing step, the Constitution drew nearer.

Franklin felt some Thing massive to his right. He put his arm around it, leaned in. It felt steady, reassuring, a veritable Pillar.

The raspy voice of Washington pierced Franklin's pain.

"If you would allow me the Honor," Washington said to Caledonia, "I shall assist Doctor Franklin."

Caledonia stepped aside and curtsy'd.

"Your Excellency," he said.

Franklin was 5'10" high, a respectable height, but Washington was nigh half a foot higher, which made him imposing. His brawny neck seemed to resent the cloath which encircled it. To Franklin, the neckcloath seemed like a scarf wrapped about a log. A Mississippi of a jugular exited the neckcloath. Washington's skin was ashen even though his face unpowdered. Light Pockmarks speckled his face, remnants of the Smallpox.

Franklin marveled at Washington's gigantic Bones and Joints. His feet and hands were gargantuan, perhaps the largest Franklin had ever seen, and his legs and arms were extraordinary long. Washington's mammoth Skeletature camouflaged his muscularity. When Franklin viewed Washington's entire body from a distance, as when he was standing upon the dais, the predominant impression was lankiness, yet up close any lone limb was burly.

Washington's potent presence was the result of his powerful Physique and harsh face, yet it also transcended mere physical stature. Always Franklin had felt in Washington a fundamental Gravity, a turbulent emotional nature that was not easy govern'd, and most of all innate Aggression, a flickering inner Violence that could be ignited and channeled to the brutal necessities of War.

Washington was terrific. Franklin knew Washington would never harm him but was nonetheless affrighted when in such close proximity. The same basic feeling one had when close to a Lion or Tiger, even if caged or suppose-ed trained or tamed.

Franklin put all his weight into Washington, like a child clutching its parent. Washington's arm was draped around Franklin's back, and with each step Franklin felt Washington's bicep bulge. Washington then lifted Franklin, moved forward, and lowered him slow with surprizing delicacy.

Flex of the arm, bicep balled into the back, lift, move forward, lower slow, bicep unballed. Repeat. Franklin measured movement by the rhythmic pressure of Washington's bicep against him. Step by less-agonizing step, the Constitution drew closer.

At last Franklin stood before the Constitution. Washington made certain Franklin had a secure grip on the Table, and then stepped aside respectful.

"My gratitude," Franklin said, "to the world's bravest Crutch."

Deputies smiled, and some chuckled, eyes filled with Love.

Washington curtsied deep to Franklin, with extreme Respect, the deepest curtsy anyone had offered thus far, and also the most graceful.

The five parchments of the Constitution consumed the table. The vellum was much less rectangular than writing paper, more squarish, about two feet wide, the length about half a foot greater than the width. For once the bright Sunlight was beneficial. It made the drawing on the Constitution easy'r to discern, though Franklin still had to use his double Spectacles. On parchment the first, "We the People" was written in the upper left in a massive gothic Script. The rest of the Constitution was a procession of exceptional neat calligraphic writing. Row upon row upon row upon row, flowing endless, broke up only by leftward indentations for new Clauses, and rightward spaces where the ends of clauses filled not an entire row. Centred gothic "Article" headings with antient Numerals, in the Roman stile, were interspersed, but as the Constitution was broke up into but seven Articles, these were sparse.

On parchment the first, nigh atop, and leftward, Franklin saw a "the" inserted in Article I Section 2, Clause the First. It read, "and the Electors in each State shall have Qualifications requisite for Electors of the most numerous Branch of the State Legislature." A "the" had been inserted above and between "have" and "Qualifications" that it read, "have the Qualifications."

Franklin examined the Amendation by Jackson. About a quarter length down the parchment, on the immediate beginning of a line, "forty Thousand" had been drawn in a calligraphic Script. Jackson had erazed the "for" in forty but left the "ty" and then drew "thir" as a replacement. The erazure was not perfect—no erazure could be—and the background was smudged. The "thir" Jackson had drawn was also darker and in a different Hand than the drawing of Jacob Shallus. The smudged background,

ABOVE: Parchment the First of the engrossed Constitution of Government executed by Deputies in Convention
assembled, Sepetember 17, 1787.

darker ink, and incongruous Hand made the Amendment right conspicuous.

Farther down parchment the first, nigh the middle of its height, and leftward, Franklin saw "is tried" inserted in Article I Section 3, Clause the Fift—nay, the Sixth, Clause the Sixth. It read, "When the President of the United States, the Chief Justice shall preside:" The words "is tried" had been inserted above and between "States," and "the" that it read, "When the President of United States is tried, the Chief Justice shall preside:"

Nigh the bottom of parchment the second, leftward but tending towards middle of horizontal, Franklin saw "the" inserted in Article I Section 10, Clause the Second. It read, "No State shall, without the Consent of Congress, lay any Imposts or Duties on Imports or Exports," A "the" had been inserted above and between "of" and "Congress" that it read, "Consent of the Congress,"

Franklin had inspected the Engrossment after Shallus compleated it, so was not enthralled with its novelty as many Deputies. He had nonetheless expected a feeling of Ceremony, but there was only a consuming sense that an Ordeal was finally over.

Franklin slid down the table and stood before the fourth and final parchment. The last three Articles filled the upper third, Article V, Article VI, Article VII, and then the final words of the Constitution, "The Ratification of the Conventions of nine States, shall be sufficient for the Establishment of this Constitution between the States so ratifying the Same."

Direct below the final Article and Clause of the Constitution, the text was broke into two columns, the left filling about a third the width, the right about two thirds. The narrow left column was typical reserve-ed for errata and attestations by the Secretary or other Witness, while the right column contain'd the Date and a Closing which preceded the signatures.

Though the left column for errata was at present blank, Jackson would have to attest three errata totalling four omitted words, the two instancys of "the" and also the words "is tried." Four words of errata in some Thousands of words of Copy. Jacob Shallus, Assistant Clerk of the Pennsylvania Assembly, had begun engrossing Saturday night immediate after the Convention adjourned, and had scarce slept until the Convention convoked hours ago. Drawing with a quill was grueling Work. Shallus' fingers was probably still aching! Yet the Script was lovely and true, the errata scarce. Shallus had earned his $30, his 30 Spaniard Dollars, equivalent to some 11 weeks Wages for a labourer absent trade, craft, or other skill.

Franklin wondered how futurity would judge the Convention. What topics never discussed in Convention would seem glaring omissions to Posterity, perhaps even censorable? What Clauses would Futurity be appalled by? What portions would it consider perspicacious, ingenious, or revolutionary, if any? Yet again Franklin asked himself if the Convention had truly crafted a Constitution prescient enough to endure.

The right column next to the errata began with an oversize gothic "done." Franklin read the words, "done in Convention by the Unanimous Consent of the States present the Seventeenth Day of September in the Year of our Lord one thousand seven hundred and Eighty seven and of the Independance of the United States of America the Twelfth." Immediate after the "Twelfth" was an oversize gothic "In witness." Franklin read the words, "In witness whereof We have hereunto subscribed our Names,"

Franklin was glad that his Motion on the mode of signing had passed. If not, "Consent of the States present" might have been another erratum which required last-moment erazure and amendation. Shallus had spellt Independance in the least common mode, with an A. Though there was no formal Rule, Franklin might have preferenced an E.

The Twelfth year of American Independance. Eleven years, two months, and two weeks since they had executed the Declaration of Independency. Would there be a Twentieth year? A Fiftieth year? A five Hundredth year of the Independance of the United States of America? Or even the Existence of the United States of America, independant or otherwise?

Direct below the closing, on the extreme right of the vellum, The General had signed, "G. Washington, President and Deputy from Virginia."

The indispensable signature, right certain.

Washington's signature and the Integrity it manifested would make most Americans liable to support the Constitution, no matter what it said. Without the sanction of Washington's name, few Americans would support the Constitution, no matter what it said.

Franklin knew that his signature was the second most crucial. The concert of Washington and Franklin's signatures would give Americans who understood not the Constitution's phylosophical nuances confidence in its Integrity and make the Charta nigh unassailable.

Franklin corrected himself.

Less assailable.

Franklin glanced at the Letter on the upper left of the table, saw Washington's signature upon it, and felt immediate Comfort. On parchment the fifth, the instructions and Resolvements on how Congress should dispose of the Constitution, Washington had signed unlevel, his text sloping slight upward. Washington drew, "By the Unanimous Order of the Convention." Below, he had signed abbreviate, "Go Washington, Presidit."

Franklin could imagine Members of Congress desirous of maligning the Constitution energetic, or of ignoring its Instructions. The signature of Washington on the instruments would give them prodigious Pause and deter many from Machination.

Franklin returned his focus to parchment the fourth. Under Washington, Deputies had signed one below the other in a long column, the left portions of the first letter of each Signature general aligned. State names were written left of the signatures in Hamilton's script, which was messyer than that of Shallus as he was no Scribe. Rogue Island was galling absent from Hamilton's enumeration of States, which irked Franklin, as there was no true Unanimity without her.

Brackets expanding rightward from the state names were used to group the Deputies, though the signatures did not line up precise with the brackets, especially in the case of Connecticut, whose signatures dipped below the bracket. Hamilton was the only signee without a bracket. Three periods extended from the words "New York" to his signature. Franklin wondered if the Little Lion had drawn the state names and brackets sole to ensure New York included, that he could sign and cement himself into history. A more scrupulous man might have omitted

New York, as it had mounted no quorum and had affirm'd not the Constitution. Had the Little Lion intercoursed the matter with Washington in advance and attained Approval?

Probably nay.

Nigh certain nay.

Superficial, to the Ignorant, the inclusion of a New York bracket would impart a fallacious Sense that it had positived the Constitution, thereby enhancing the Illusion of unanimity. Franklin could not object this, even if it but a machination in service of Hamilton's Impetuousness and Vanity. Was Washington perhaps of the same mind?

There was no empty bracket for Rogue Island tho'. Such conspicuous proof of absence of Unanimity might have been the only Thing more galling than Rogue Island's absencey, even though this probably would have been the most honest, the indifferent honest, presentation.

Franklin remembered John Hancock's striking Signature on the Declaration of Independency. Deputies had signed haphazard all over that instrument, not in rows by States, and Hancock drew his large Signature in the centre just below the text. It had thick portions of lines intermixed with thin, a difficult Effect to achieve with a quill as its Angle to the paper had to be altered while still moving it. Hancock's letters had drooping Curls at the bottom that resembled elongate Tears. Such flourish. Hancock was in ill Health and less than exubrant about a central Government, so had seated not the Convention. No signature as stilish as Hancock's was to be found on the Constitution, though many Deputies still had to sign. Franklin liked to remain optimistic.

On the lower right, just below the New Jersey bracket and signatures, and extending to the very bottom of the parchment, Hamilton had drawn a huge bracket and labeled it "Pensylvania." Spellt with one N.

Franklin wanted to chuckle. Such was the Little Lion. Gifted. But not so gifted as he suppose-ed.

"Pennsylvaniay have two Ns," Franklin said to Hamilton.

"Apologies, Good Doctor," Hamilton said.

Hamilton offered not to correct his erratum. He looked especially Little Lionish despite his infant face and blue eyes. Franklin imagined Hamilton with a lion tail he used to grab the quill and sign the Constitution. After he'd swatted all the Flies.

Washington did not order Hamilton to correct the erratum. It was impracticable to litter the document with trivial changes. In cases of true Significancy only, would amendments be made. Pensylvania would remain misspelled in the Constitution for all time.

Franklin was wise enough to know which details not to fret. He did not let the erratum or Hamilton's impetuousness diminish his Satisfaction. The empty Pennsylvania bracket awaited his signature. It seemed so inviting!

Franklin bent. He reached for the black swan Quill, felt the tickle of the swan feather on his fingers, grabbed the fire-harden'd Tip, wished as he had numerant times that quill Tips were bigger, smoother, easier to grip and use. At least with a mere signature the quill would not have to be dipped repeated, as with longer drawing.

Franklin dipp'd the quill.

And then paused.

He had written so many words in his life. Millions. And yet these Words, so meaningless in an absolute grammatickal sense, were apt to be his most important and most remembered.

His signature.

His mere signature.

Yet was not a signature the Incarnation of a man, the Encapsulation of all he had worked for, fought for, stood for? And was not the Constitution the incarnation of what all Americans had worked for, fought for, stood for, of the cooperation and unity Franklin had toiled tireless for his entire life?

Men working together could attain to more than ever possible singly. This was the basic Premise of Civilization. Cooperation was the fundamental action that raised man out of a State of Nature. A State of Savagery. And now all States, all People in America would co-operate to a much greater degree, to the benefit of all Americans, living and unbirthed, and probably all mankind.

E Pluribus Unum, indeed. Out of Many, One, indeed. Never had Franklin's motto of the Revolution seem'd more apt.

Franklin felt a Serenity in the chambre, in himself and among Deputies. Such a contrary feeling than the Fear during the signing of the Declaration of Independency, an act which had made every Deputy in the chambre a Fugitive subject to Quartering. Defiance had also been in the air that day, the warmth inevitable when Deputies pondered the Tyranny they had been subject to and their Rebellion against it.

Yet they had hung together, and escaped Hangings separate. Providence smiled, and now there was only Joy. A joy greater than Franklin felt signing the Alliance with France which

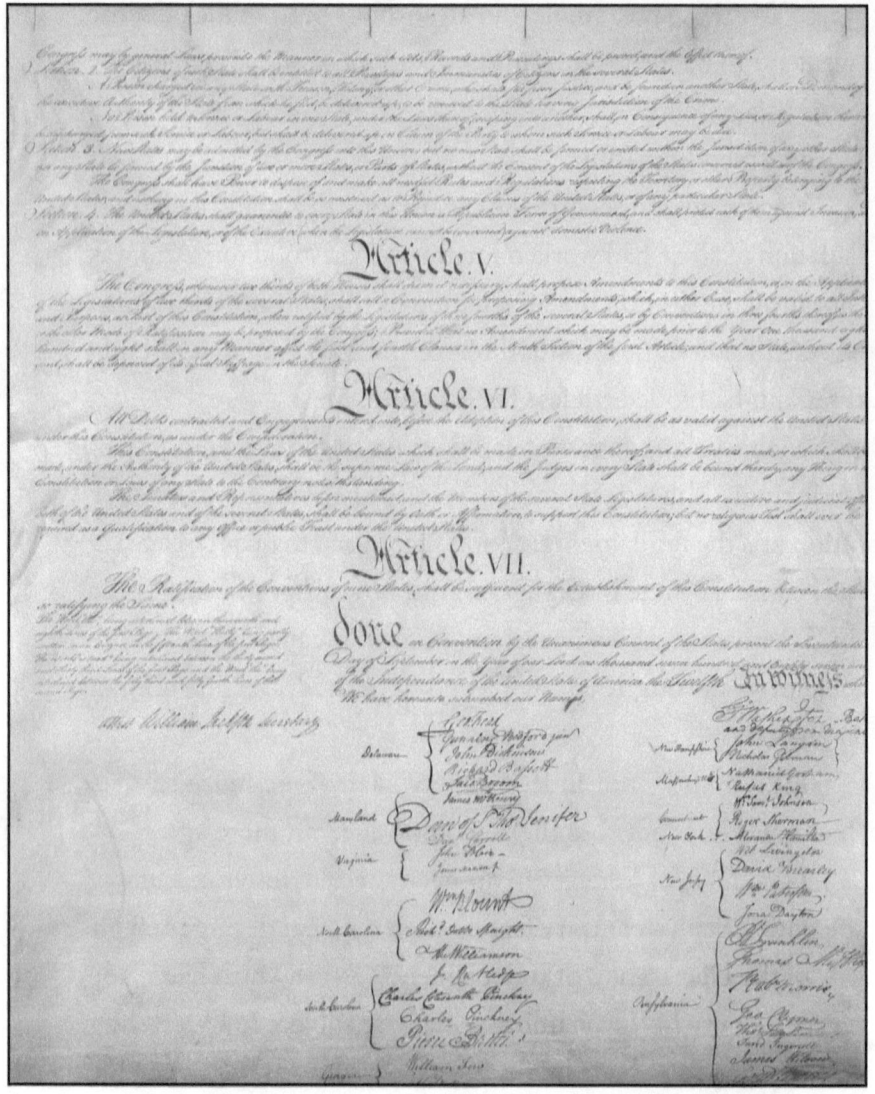

ABOVE: Parchment the Fourth of the engrossed Constitution of Government executed by Deputies in Convention assembled, Sepetember 17, 1787.

brought the first real hope of Victory in The War. A joy which transcended that he felt signing the Treaty of Paris which ended The War formal and secured Peace with Britain.

The Declaration, Alliance, Peace, and Constitution. Only Franklin had direct brokered them all. And he knew unequivocal that this Constitution was if not the most difficult to attain of the Achievements, certainly the most significant of them, as it was the Culmination of them.

Franklin enjoyed shaping world events. He wondered about his Wisdom. If he were still chandling, would the man in his Place have fared so excellent well?

The momentous events that had transpired in the East Room flashed through Franklin's mind with rapidity. The years of meetings of the Continental Congress. Young Washington appointing Commander of the Army by the Congress. The Vote for Independency and the signing of the Declaration of Independency. The signing of the Articles of Confederacy, which Franklin missed serving as Minister to France, yet had heard described in intimate detail and could envision. And now, finally, the Constitution!

Franklin scrawled his signature onto the vellum. The Gout and Stone flared, but the pain seemed somehow distant. Franklin heard the scratching of quill on parchment, but it too seemed somehow distant.

Franklin felt Exultation when saw his signature affix'd to the Instrument, and it heighten'd when he pondered the Principles it sanctioned. Liberty for all, secured by a large Republic that was but the second in human history and the first in nigh 1,700 years!

Franklin felt wetness on his cheeks. He rubbed them, examined his fingers.

Tears.

Was he weeping?

Actual weeping?

By Providence, he was.

Whilst he waited for the ink to set, Franklin picked up the large silver shaker and sprinkled it into his hand. Coarse tannish particles of Pounce fell onto his fingers and through them. The sand-like Pounce made Franklin think of the Sands of Time and caused him to once again ponder the permanency of the Constitution.

Franklin wiped the Pounce from his hands, the Tears from his cheeks, and glanced at his Signature one last time. He smiled and looked to Washington, who acknowledged his Joy with a warm glance, less stilted because 'twas smileless and emanate from the eyes. The General then helped Franklin back to his table, balling his bicep into his back rhythmickal as before.

As Franklin sat, he had the inescapable sense that this was his last momentous Contribution to the nation he so loved. Franklin felt gratifyed, yet also strange hollow. He wondered if the outcome of this day would have been different without his speech.

Probably not.

But he would never know.

In truth, it didn't matter, and thinking it was vain.

Franklin continued thinking it none the less.

The other Pennsylvania Deputies lined up and began signing. Being the host State, Pennsylvania had the largest Deputation, two thirds as numerant as those of all States that had already signed. Still seduced by state Pride, Franklin took satisfaction in the prominence of Pennsylvania Deputies, especially the Morrises, Caledonia, Mifflin, and Ingersoll. 'Twas no act of bias to call Pennsylvania's Deputation the most esteem'd of the Convention. Only the Virginia Deputation might be considered Peer.

Governeur Morris was the most conspicuous of the crowd of Pennsylvanians Deputies owing his peg Leg. He was at the rear of the line on its utmost left, and as always, he oscillated ever-so-slight when standing. Morris held his thick cane on the same side of his body as his peg Leg, and seeing both touch the floor next to Morris' lone foot, Franklin felt a pronounced sense of artificiality, as if he were viewing the bottom of a Table rather than a person.

Whilst Pennsylvanians signed, Delaware Deputies moved to the back of the line. The remaining Deputies would probably sign in a new column on the instrument, left of the rightward column which contain'd Pennsylvania at the bottom. Would those viewing the Constitution at a later date erroneous presume that the States in the left column had signed before States in the right?

Washington continued to regard each Deputy before they signed. He was cordial to all Deputies, warm to but a few. All Deputies curtsied to His Excellency with varying degrees of deference, as their personal Eminence or Reverence for Washington dictated, though all curtsys save the Little Lion's was the deeper sort indicative of significant Esteem.

Deputies remained standing and congregated after signing, tho' mindful of procedure and not wanting to be rude, they seemed disinclined to intercourse. They simply stood back in the central aisle and watched the Constitution fill with signatures.

Governeur Morris planted his peg Leg firm before signing, causing a single wooden clack to reverberate, as if a sentry with a halberd had sudden stood at attention. Morris bent prodigious at the waist as he signed to compensate for the want of bend in his peg Leg. After signing, he was the only Deputy that stood not with the crowd. He returned to the Pennsylvania table and sat with Franklin, looking more the Cherub than roosterish. Franklin and Governeur Morris shared a contented glance—until Morris' stomach interrupted with a succession of bawdy Gurgles.

Deputies chuckled. 'Twas past three o'clock. Dinner time.

The bird-faced George Read of Delaware drew his signature and then showed a letter to Washington. Why did Read's face always remind Franklin of Thomas? They didn't look remarkable similar, but Read had the same long Face, thin nose, ruddy cheeks, and expression of relentless Optimism. Read's letter was from John Dickinson, and it authorized Read to sign the Constitution for Dickinson.

Eleven years ago in Congress, Dickinson had been the most energetic Cool Devil, or reasoned opponent of Independency. Cool Devils such as Dickinson and Caledonia had infuriated advocates of Independency such as John Adams. Dickinson had been a resident of Pennsylvania at the time and a member of the Pennsylvania Deputation. A unanimous Vote for Independency had been attained to only when Franklin and others induced Dickinson to absent himself on the final July 2 vote, and he refused to sign the Declaration of Independency.

More than a decade later, Franklin had again machinated to conjure an Illusion of Unanimity for a critical vote. He smiled wistful. How seldom things changed.

Dickinson single-handed had damn nigh prevented adoption of the Declaration of Independency. Dickinson's obstinate refusal to positive the Declaration, and his willingness to enforce the belief of the minority upon the Majority and drag America to ruin with him, as if he his own personal Senate, had injured his Esteem grievous. Having forsaken his chance to sign the Declaration of Independency had perhaps made Dickinson more cognizant of the need to sign the Constitution. Dickinson believed in the Constitution, but the absence of his signature on both the Declaration and Constitution might be the fatal Fell to his diminished Reputation, with Posterity especially.

Washington read Dickinson's letter, approved it with a nod, and handed it back to Read. Richard Bassett, the Methodist, was gracious enough to let Read back into line and he became the only Deputy to sign twice. In future years, would other absent Deputies with no signature lament their want of Dickinsonian foresight and wish they had employed a Proxy?

Franklin couldn't help allowing a fractional smirk when the conniving-eyed James McHenry of Maryland signed. Despite his resentment of Franklin's speech, he seemed to have been wooed by it. Maryland's two other Deputies, Daniel of St. Thomas Jennifer, and Daniel Carroll, also signed.

Virginia's signing was perhaps the most curious. The largest State, with a situation direct south of Pennsylvania making travel to the Convention practicable, it had boasted one of the largest Deputations, yet had only two Deputies in line to sign, John Blair and Jemmy.

It seemed a bit queer not to have Washington in line with the Virginia Deputation, as he had sat with them in the Committee of Whole for much of the Convention. Washington was a Power unto himself, however, more dominant than any State, and his Segregation seemed a fitting Emblem of his Transcendence.

The absence of Thomas in the Virginia Deputation was also glaring. What would he have said of the Constitution were he present?

Chancellor Wythe had repaired to Virginia to nurse his ailing wife. Edmund Randolph and Colonel Mason sat at the Virginia table, still unwilling to give the Constitution the sanction of their names. Could Wythe the Wise have persuaded Randolph to sign? Not unthinkable. Yet a far from probable.

Elbridge Gerry was still seated at the Massachusetts table at the extreme left of the rear row. Perhaps Randolph and Mason had more Fortitude than Gerry, but they seemed more comfortable than him. All three Dissidents nonetheless remained grim. Especially the pouty-faced, irascible Mason, whose expression was so despondent he might have been envisioning the collapse of Civilization and a return to Barbary for humankind.

Washington was a foot higher than the diminutive Jemmy, who looked puny standing a front of him, like some lad who had snuck into the Convention. Except Jemmy was far too grave to be a lad. Had he laughed or lampooned even in youth? Or had he matriculated out his mother reading Locke's Second Treatise of Government with a furrowed brow? The dichotomy in the musculatures of Washington and Jemmy made the contrast between them even more severe. Washington's eyes and expression softened when he looked at Jemmy, and he conveyed warmth.

Jemmy signed, and surprizingly scurried not back to his table to take notes. He stood with the crowd of Deputies, and though he still seemed of the lowest stature, he no longer looked like a child owing the low stature of other Deputies such as Paterson.

The Deputies from North Carolina, South Carolina, and Georgia strolled to the line together, as if a single State. Their walks were as leisurely as a drawl and accentuate by the exaggerate Pivot of their walking sticks. They might have been strolling through a garden with cool Drinks in their hands.

North Carolina signed, and then South Carolina, including the pair of Pinckneys. CC curtsied extreme deep to Washington, a curtsy of exceptional Grace, and then glared at the Little Lion pointed. The Little Lion grinned with Hauteur. CC signed. And then the miniscule Charles Pickney. Next Dictator John. Then Pierce Butler.

There were only two Deputies remaining in line, from the last state, Georgia. As they moved closer to the Constitution, expectation built, a tangible sense of Finality.

William Few signed. His face reminded Franklin of a Ram. Finally, the last Deputy, Abraham Baldwin, he of the windswept hair and sourpuss lips.

There were 41 Deputies present and 38 had signed the instrument, not including Dickinson's proxy signature. Mason, Randolph, and Gerry refused to give the Constitution the sanction of their names.

Secretary Jackson was last. After asking Washington permission, he brought his chair to the front of the table and sat direct in front of the Constitution.

Jackson reviewed the entire document careful again, line by line, noting each Amendation or Erratum and drawing it upon a separate piece of paper. He then compared this paper to a different paper, probably that provided by Shallus documenting his Errata. Jackson then copied his paper notes, enumerating the Errata and Amendation on the lower left portion of parchment the fourth.

'Twas a bit curious that Washington had not enforced Jackson to draw the Errata and Amendation prior to the signing by Deputies, that they might observe all alterations before giving the Charta the sanction of their name. In most executions in most Assemblies, this was the mode. The Secretary would document all Errata and Amendations, Deputies would affix their signatures, and then the Secretary would sign last, attesting the Validity of the Copy and the execution, and that he had witnessed all a signing. Washington had perhaps wanted to avoid a lengthy delay prior to signing, during which Deputies might revizit their Doubts and decide not to sign. Whatever Washington's motivation, 'twas not a glaring deviation, nor cause for concern.

Whilst Jackson wrought his documentary, several Deputies approached Franklin's table, David Brearly among them. The afternoon Sun was exceeding bright where Brearly stood. He peered upward without window, direct into it rather than a-squinting like most other Deputies. Franklin was once again gazing at the Sun carved into the back of Washington's throne.

"As above, so below," Brearly said.

"As east, so West?" Franklin said.

"Perhaps we ought explore the West ere presuming," Brearly said.

"Or perhaps explore the Heavens ere presuming."

Brearly chuckled.

"Touché, Doctor Franklin."

Silence reigned for a spell.

Brearly continued to stare straight into the Light.

"Novus Ordo Seclorum," he said.

This was Latin, which translated as New Order for the Ages.

"Are your eyes not seared?" Rufus King said to Brearly.

"Though it can burn or even blind," Brearly said, "we must all seek the Light."

"We have," Franklin said.

Brearly turned away from the Light and focused on Franklin with a bemused Smile. His gaze held great Intensity.

"Indeed, Doctor Franklin," Brearly said. "Indeed, we have."

Brearly stood next to Franklin, peered at the carved Sun upon Washington's throne, and sought a different Light. Other Deputies did the same.

"Painters find it difficult in their art," Franklin said, "to distinguish a rising from a setting Sun. Often and often in the course of the Session, and the vicisitudes of my hopes and fears as to its issue, I looked at the Sun on the President's throne without being able to tell whether 'twas rising or setting."

Franklin spoke loud, which for him was still right soft. Most Deputies eyed the Sun carved on the back of Washington's throne. Even Washington.

Jackson returned his chair to his table. He stood and signed parchments the fourth and fifth, to attest, and as he did Hamilton absented the dais.

"But now at length," Franklin said, "I have the Happiness to know that it is a rising and not a setting Sun."

It was done. The American nation was established, Liberty secured for multitudes living and unbirthed. The crowd of Deputies percolated with satisfaction, optimistic that America was a rising and would seek the Light. A few Deputies hugged and conveyed manly Love for each other. Some wiped tears away discreet. Others sprouted serene Smiles.

Eyes turned to the table, the cherished Constitution upon it, and finally the belove-ed Hero who stood on the dais bathed in Light.

George Washington.

Alone.

Above the fray.

Watching over Convention, and America, as always.

Franklin felt a familiar comfourt.

As long as Washington was present, America was safe.

"Mister Fry," Washington said to the Door-Keep. "Summon Mister Weaver if you please."

Fry was still standing motionless at attention, like a Golem. He animated, opened the doors, closed them behind him, and re-entered a few moments later with Mr. Weaver at his side, again closing the doors behind him.

Weaver was squat, muscled, and had wary eyes that roved. He wore a sword, two flintlock pistols, and a small seven-inch dagger that he kept murderous sharp. Weaver had served in the

First Volunteer Corps of Pennsylvania during the Revolution and was the Sergeant-at-Arms of the Pennsylvania Assembly. He curtsyed extreme deep, with flourish.

"Your Excellency," he said. "Your most humble and obedient servant."

"I pray the City Tavern has prevented the relishes," Washington said. "Inform Mister Moyston that the Deputies will soon stand in need of refreshment."

"Aye, Your Excellency."

"Also acquaint Messieurs Dunlap and Claypoole that we have put a period to it and that Secretary Jackson shall call forthwith to present amendations to the Constitution of Government. The thirty Thousand amendation shall necessitate a fresh Striking, and the remainders of the prior Striking of Saturday are to be disposed. Messieurs Dunlap and Claypoole is at Liberty to call on myself, Secretary Jackson, or Doctor Franklin at any hour to expedite the Striking. As many Deputies intend to coaches in the morrow, 'twould be munificient if the first copys struck could be furnished at their lodgings forthwith."

By the morrow, Washington signify'd a few hours after midnight, when coaches oft departed.

"Aye, Your Excellency," Weaver said. "I'll deliver the fresh struck Copys to all Deputies personal. One per Deputy?"

"Four per Deputy. Secretary Jackson shall provide you a roll of each Deputy and their lodging. You may call on him at the City Tavern."

"Aye, Your Excellency."

"Doctor Franklin," Washington said. "I would draw on your typing Expertise, if you please. Can we expect the struck Copys compleated ere the morrow?"

Messieurs Dunlap and Claypoole had spent Saturday evening and the Sabbath setting the Type, manual affixing the entire text of the Constitution to composing Sticks one letter at a time, along with Spacing, and then galleying and forming them to the Press. Dunlap and Claypoole stood ready to strike copys of the Constitution for sale to the Publick, and so had retained their type Setting rather than hellboxing it. Though they had probably hoped no fresh Striking of the Convention requisite, they would at the least be pleased that the Amendations but minor. Major amendations might lengthen a single Row of type, causing words on one Row to have to be reset on the sequel Row, thereby causing the following Row to have to be reset, and cetera, often necessitating resetting of an entire Page of type, and if numerate amendations, numerate Pages or all Pages. Skilled printers such as Messieurs Dunlap and Claypoole would not have set the type undue compact, and would have left an empty Row or two at the bottom of each page, that a lengthening of the Type on one page would not spill to the sequel Page and necessitate a resetting of all Pages. The minor Amendations requisite could be made rapid and the striking of Copys commence nigh immediate, though Messieurs Dunlap and Claypoole might perform a resetting after striking for the Convention, that the more voluminous and wide transmitted Striking for the Publick be perfect, and reflect well upon them.

Deputies knew all this. What they knew not is how fast copys could be struck. Franklin having been a Printer, he was consulting.

"How many Copys would you have struck?" Franklin said.

"Some five Hundred," Washington said.

"With parchment the fifth of Resolvements and the Letter each a separate page, as in the fresh struck Charta of today?"

"Aye, Doctor."

"You would not absent the Resolvements and Letter pages from the Striking to expedite?"

"Nay."

"If a printer possess Competency," Franklin said, "and Messieurs Dunlap and Claypoole do, three to four Spreads can be struck per minute, or some two Hundred per hour. Five Hundred struck copys of a single Spread of two pages would require some two and a half Hours. All six Pages, all three Spreads, would require some seven and a half Hours. Additional time would be requisite to change the Presses for each Page, to reset the Type adding the Amendations and correcting Errata, and for printers to respite themselves. The process is also more plodding by the light of chandle and would gravitate towards three Copys struck per minute. Such a tantivy is grievous fatiguing, however, and as with musket Exercise, nigh impossible to maintain to. This is especially true if a striking done with care and an eye for quality, as Messieurs Dunlap and Claypoole are habituate, which can slow the Striking to a plod. I would forecast nine or ten hours to compleat."

"Nigh one or two in the morrow," Washington said. "Not rapidity enough."

"Employment of multiple presses would allow the striking of several Spreads concurrent," Franklin said. "I cannot speak to this potentiality. I had heard tell that Messieurs Dunlap and Claypoole had two Presses, but also that one was age-ed and now defunct. Whether it might be brought back from pasture and suffice for a single striking, I shan't hazard."

"Presume the dernier Resort of but one Press," Washington said.

"If each Deputy is to have four Copys," Franklin said, "then some two Hundred ample. Two strikings might be employed, one of two Hundred and a second of three Hundred. This would slow the Striking, as the plates would have to be changed twice. But the first striking of two Hundred would be compleat in just over three hours at best, four hours more probable, five in the dernier Resort."

"Eight or nine of the clock this evening," Washington said.

He peered at Weaver.

"Messieurs Dunlap and Claypoole," Washington said, "are to employ multiple Presses if practicable and strike two Hundred immediate regardless. The three Hundred is to be a second striking."

"Aye, Your Excellency."

Deputies nodded with approval. They would be accosted by the curious upon repairing home. And while journeying home, at inns, when waylaid by the curious on roads, and cetera. Embarking without a finalyzed copy of the Constitution simply would not suffice, even though it would probably be published by most Papers before many Deputies even vacated Pennsylvania. Having a formal Copy to present each House of the Legislatures, as well as Executives, while also keeping a Copy personal, was prudential and good manners.

"Out of remainder after aforesaid Copys allocate for Deputies," Washington said, "you shall reserve two Copys for each Member of the Pennsylvaniay Assembly, Executive Council, and supreme Court, which you shall furnish to each Body."

"Doctor Franklin is to have six Copys?" Weaver said.

"Merit he not them?"

Weaver stiffened. His expression became contrite.

"Aye, Your Excellency," he said. "I meant no offence."

"I shall have seven as well," Washington said.

"Aye, Your Excellency."

"All Deputies may also request additional Copys, as they please, which shall be furnished prior to any Publication. All other Remainders shall be intrusted to Doctor Franklin, against any unforeseen Exigencys, and to make utility of as he deems prudencial."

"Aye, Your Excellency."

"You may proceed, Mister Weaver."

Weaver curtsied, turnt, and strode towards the exit.

"Mister Weaver?"

Weaver stopped, turnt, and faced Washington. He curtsied again.

"Your Excellency?"

"The relishes first."

"Aye, Your Excellency."

Weaver curtsied again. As he headed without doors and Fry secured them behind him, Deputies tapped their walking sticks. Some chuckled.

"Here, here," someone said. "Relishes first."

Ever sensible of the proper allotment of Ceremony, Washington allowed the Deputies to savor the Signing for a stretch. He then return'd to his throne behind the Speaker's table. Washington remained standing. He waited for all Deputies to seat themselves and for silence to return.

"I would ask," Washington said, "that we remember the contribution of Gentlemen who assisted this Convention but could not be present to affix their signatures to the Instrument." Washington held up a piece of paper and read from it. "Chancellor Wythe, may Providence bless his departed Wife. Mister Strong, may Providence also aide his ill Wife. Mister Houston, may Providence restore his ill Health. Mister Lansing, Mister Martin, Mister Mercer, Mister Yates."

Franklin could not help but smirk at Washington's political Savvy. Chancellor Wythe, Strong, and Houston were mention'd first out of compassion for the ailments they or their wives suffered. Then the four Dissidents not present, as an act of Conciliation, a show of Respect for opponents that would need wooing if the Constitution was to ratify. Washington also used alphabetized ranking, probably to prevent any savour of Favouritism. Many Deputies seemed to make an observation similar to Franklin's, either smiling fractional or increasing the frank admiration in their eyes.

"Mister Davie," Washington read, "Mister Dickenson, Mister Houstoun, Mister Ellsworth, Governour Martin, Mister McClurg, and Major Pierce."

This was all Deputies not present who had attended the Convention. Washington let silence linger, to honour the Absent.

"The Constitution of the United States of Americay has received the unanimous assent of eleven States," Washington said, "as well as Colonel Hamilton from New York."

Washington waited a long moment.

Silence.

"Major Jackson," Washington said.

Jackson stood and faced Washington with a stern military bearing.

"Your Excellency," he said.

"You shall take possession of this Constitution. You shall transmit it to the Congress in New York in the morrow, engrossed and fully executed. You shall make adequate Provision for Defence of yourself and your cargo. The Constitution sha'n't absent your sight nor your person for even an instant."

Jackson beamed, his thoughts a transparencey. Washington could have had one of the dozens of Deputies intending to Congress in the morrow transmit the Constitution to it. Instead he would have the Honor!

Franklin could not help but feel jealous that Temple deny'd such Honor.

"Aye, Your Excellency," Jackson said. "Upon my sacred Honor, nothing shall prevent its safe transmission."

There was that steel in Jackson's voice and bearing that only hardened Veterans seemed to possess. As Jackson gathered up the five parchments of the Constitution and the Letter and rolled them into a tight bundle, Franklin had to grudging concede that he was perhaps a better choice for Secretary than Temple.

"You shall also convey the Constitution to Messieurs Dunlap and Claypoole immediate upon Adjournment," Washington said. "I put it twice, that there be no scruple of my Instruction. The Constitution sha'n't absent your sight nor person."

"Aye, General."

Jackson saluted Washington, a crisp Salute, elbow locked, palm facing outward, touching his forehead where the indent of a cocked hat would be, had he been wearing one.

Washington had Jackson call the roll and ascertain each Deputy's place of Boarding, for furnishment of struck Copys. Several Deputies requested a half dozen additional Copys or more, which was also duly recorded. So many Deputies requested such a prodigious quantum of additional Copys that Washington had Jackson re-call the roll and ascertain which Deputies was intending early in the morrow on coaches, that they could receive struck Copys first.

Washington had Jackson account the total Copys requisite, nigh 400, as well as those requisite by Deputies intending coaches early in the morrow, nigh 300. Washington instructed Jackson to have Messieurs Dunlap and Claypoole strike 300 Copys immediate, with 200 in a second Striking. Washington also had Franklin recompute the time to strike 300 Copys, to ensure compleation against Coaches departing.

Washington accounted the Dispences of the Convention. They would be transmitted to the Congress, which had no way to pay them, save by drawing upon Credit. Deputies appointed by the several States were not compensate by the Convention nor the fœderal Congress, not even for expences, nor had Pennsylvania charged Rent for use of the State House. Major Jackson would be paid for service as Secretariat, at the contracted salary of $2,600 per annum, pro rata for nigh four Months, which was $866.80.

Jackson's eyes dilated with Lust as his stipend was read to Convention. 'Twas a handsome sum, right certain, equivalent to nigh six Annums of wages for a Labourer absent trade, craft, or other skill. The expressions of some Deputies cinched, as the sum was nigh a Fugitive considering how scant Jackson's notes. Other Deputies glanced at Jemmy, still scribing Pro Bono Publico without renumeration, whilst Jackson sat idle. Franklin resisted the urge to make sarcastic enquiry of how many pence per word Jackson had been paid, and again felt resentment that Temple had not been appointed.

Washington continued accounting Dispences. Joseph Fry, the Door-Keep, was owed a salary of $400 per annum, pro rata for nigh four Months, which was $133.30, nigh an Annum of wages for a Labourer absent trade, craft, or other skill. Nicholas Weaver, the Messenger, was owed a salary of $300 per annum, pro rata for nigh four Months, which was $100, nigh nine Months of wages for a Labourer. Washington also accounted what owed the Stationer.

Washington computed the sums owed Messieurs Dunlap and Claypoole, for previous Strikings including the Committee of Detail Report and Committee of Stile Report, as well as the present Strikings of the final Charta. The Convention was fortunate that Messieurs Dunlap and Claypoole charged a fixed price per Copy, allowing simple ciphering of altered quantums. Ever methodical, Washington scrupled to tender the Bill for the

Strikings until they compleat, though he would transmit the matter to the Congress that they might renumerate.

"The Strikings not with standing," Washington said, "that ought be all expences, which accompt to fifteen hundred and eighty six dollars."

"Excepting our slave Labour," Governeur Morris said. "Tho' we are nigh Manumit."

Deputies chuckled. Even some of the South.

Washington frowned. Was he thinking of his looming Internment as Executive? His own Slaves and Reputation? Irritate that Governeur had not asked to be recognized before speaking?

Washington gave Gentlemen license to speak on the question. None took license. Washington closed the question. He called for a vote of Deputies approving the accounting and the billing of the sum of $1,586 to the Congress, as well as all Strikings, the final dispences incurred by Deputies in Convention assembled.

The positiving of the measure was rapid and unanimate.

"We can but hope," Washington said, "that the Congress, The People, and our Posterity reckon this a prudencial Expenditure."

A request was made to Washington for a calling of all Amendations and Errata not in the struck Copy, in case Deputies was unable to attain a fresh struck Copy prior to intention homeward. Washington ordered Jackson to provide such corrections.

"The Word, 'the', being interlined between the seventh and eighth lines of the first Page," Jackson read. "The Word 'Thirty' being partly written on an Erazure in the fiftee—"

"Major Jackson," Dictator John said. "Excuze my interruption, sir. But do read more plodding. We have struck Copys, not the engrossment. The pages and lines on the struck Copys differs from those on the engrossment."

Jackson's apologetic expression was one of impotent earnestness. He referenced a struck Copy and provided reckonings the Deputies could make utility of. Most Deputies amendated their struck Copy meticulous, save some Pennsylvania Deputies who were certain to attain the finalyzed struck Copy, and a few such as Washington who intended leisurely in the morrow.

Thomas Fitzsimons asked to be heard and requested permission to present the Constitution to the Pennsylvania Assembly, still in session above stairs. Washington agreed, upon adjournment, but warned Fitzsimons not to dally, as Jackson needed to expedite the Charta to Messieurs Dunlap and Claypoole.

Washington waited patient, suffering a long Silence, in case any other requests surfaced.

None did.

"Final requests for the Chair or the Secretary?" Washington said.

Silence.

"I hereby remove the injunction of Secrecy," Washington said. "I commend the Honor of Gentlemen who adhered to it so scrupulous, keeping the publick ignorant of these proceedings. Without such Honor and Ignorancey, this Constitution 'twould've been impossible."

The Honor evidenced by Deputies in keeping the publick Ignorant of the proceedings bordered on miraculous. Everyone knew it.

"This Convention," Washington said, "is now adjournt Sine Die."

"Sine Die" was Latin, without day. No readjournment date was set for the Convention.

Jemmy scribbled for a few moments and then plopped his quill into its Stand. He rubbed his weary pen Hand with the other, opened and closed his fingers repeated, and exhaled deep. Deputies chuckled. And then stood for Washington's exit, as Procedure required.

"Mister Fry," Washington said. "Without doors, if you please."

Fry obeyed and proceeded to open the chambre doors.

"The business being thus closed," Washington said, "I would encourage all gentlemen to adjourn to the City Tavern and dine with me forthwith. After such a long internment, it seems only proper that we take a cordial Leave of each other."

Washington gathered his notes, donned his cock-ed hat, and traversed the central aisle. Bloody hell, did he have long shanks. Having spent years in the forest, Washington strode as a Savage and seemed to almost flow over the ground. His muscled thighs flexed his breeches rhythmic as he passed by Franklin, and his lithe gait gobbled distance. Washington's expression was pleasant and grew more pleasant as he passed the Bar, moved without doors, and absented Convention.

FOUR

After Washington absented, Deputies trickl'd out. Most still seemed elated, but some appeared more serious, seemed to have already turned their minds to home, family, and business, and the arduous Travel that would have to be suffered in the morrow.

As Deputies passed, Franklin glimpsed wigs, cocked hats, dark shoes most a-buckled, and knee-high stock drawers nigh all of white silk. Also suitcoats that draped half the length the thigh minimum in most cases, of multitudinous hues, many bright, to flaunt wealth and be crack stiled, but also bring a bit of Chear to life. Heel-ed shoes perturbated upon floor, creating another Cacophony of clacking, the loudest yet, as if a cavalcade of horses within chambre contre-dansing.

Some Deputies paused to intercourse Franklin. Others curt-syed their heads at Franklin as they passed him, and then the Bar. As the name Bar suggested, 'twas a barrier which barred the public from entering the working area of a Courtroom or Assemblyroom. In mediæval times, barring furniture was a formidable physical Barrier analogous to a castle wall, which thwarted violent attempts to intervene in Trials or Legislatures. As with the mace, the modern Bar was more ceremonial than functional, a crotch-high, balustraded parapet that wouldn't stymy an investment by grammar school'rs.

The Bar none the less had significancy. Earning the Privilege to work in a courtroom, to pass through the Bar from the public area into the working area, was a momentous Accomplishment for any man. Franklin had never passed the Bar in a legal Sense, had never read the Law and was not a lawyer, but he had done so in a political Sense, no less significant an Accomplishment for a man born as humble, some would say as low, as he.

Seeing the bar never failed to remind Franklin that serving the Publick was a sacred Honor. He had strove to never abuse this Trust. Whatever errors he had made from want of Wisdom, and there were many, he had never wanted for Virtue when serving the public. Franklin hoped that American leaders present and posterity would show the same Virtue when serving the public Thing.

The instant Franklin formulated the Thought, he chided himself. The American Republic would become prodigious corrupt'd, as all other nations, empires, and governments in history had. 'Twas not a question of if, but at what time. The Republic would become corrupt because The People would, and leaders elevate from amongst them must then also be corrupt.

Franklin pictured a Congress of futurity. Its members would scurry passed the Bar with nary an inkling of its significancy, obsessed by Jobbing and Interest. Worse yet, the Congress of some corrupt future America might have no Bar at all, symbolic of leaders with no Conscience or moral Sense at all. Such leaders would be mere Beasts who jobbed for Interest or catered to the capricious whims of Mobs.

Perhaps America would remain uncorrupted longer than its Predecessors. Perhaps this longevity could induce other nations to make government a public Thing. Or perhaps all government was doomed to denigrate owing the intrinsic Depravity of the human Animal.

William Few and John Dayton approached. Few strolled with leisure, as was the southern habit. Dayton seemed like a leash-ed dog chomping to walk faster, but governed himself to Few's pace. Franklin was disfortunate enough to once again be presented the disattractive side vantage of Dayton and the crags of his Allegheny nose.

"I cannot help but recall the Despondency of latter June," Few said to Dayton, "when the Convention had serious thoughts of adjourning without doing anything and all human efforts seemed to fail."

"An awful and critical moment," Dayton said.

"Aye," Few said. "If the Convention had then adjourned, the dissolution of the union of the States was inevitable. This consideration no doubt had its Weight in reconciling clashing Opinions and Interests."

The Bar contain'd a central gate with two doors that was hinged on two enlarge-ed and elevate rectangular balusters. The gates swung inward towards the dais and tables, suffering easy entry, but when exiting, the gates had to be pulled towards one and held open while walking through, which Few and Dayton did.

"This plan of Constitution," Few said to Dayton, "is formed on principles which do not altogether please anybody, but 'twas the most expedient that could be devised and agreed to."

"This may be one of the last Tryals," Dayton said, "to be afforded to this or any other country, whether the people have ability to govern themselves or must in all cases submit to receive a Master of their own or others chusing."

"I do apprehend the Supremacy," a Deputy to Franklin's right said, "of the Power t—"

A cacophony of Voices had filled the chambre, making it difficult to isolate the single and ascertain who had spoke. Deputies were also turning and moving while intercoursing, causing their intercourse to become indiscernate.

"—rder to counterbalance the evil predictions of its Enemies," Dayton said, "the favorers of the new government may be led to utter extravagant Prophecies. The many may give into the Belief and suffer their expectations to be unreasonably raised. Expectations not to be gratified. Their disappointment may furnish the first ground of Discontent and giv—"

Direct right of Franklin, Governeur Morris stood. Franklin saw not the movement, yet felt a towering presence at his right, and heard Morris' peg Leg clack as it contacted the floor.

Robert Morris also stood. His corpulence made Franklin think of an otter or Seal. The seal that Franklin pictured wore a cravat which slid down its neck repeated, causing it an expression of Consternation. Franklin wondered what derogations Deputies conceived when they observed him.

"I'm bloody gutfoundered," Governeur Morris said.

"Breakfast you not?" Robert Morris said.

He pronounced breakfast in the typickal manner, as two separate words spoken with more rapidity than usual, break that it rhimed with rake, and fast. Break fast.

"A pittance," Governeur said. "But a small Beer, a bread and Butter, a few nibbles of salt Fish, and some cheeses."

This would have been at 9 am approximate, perhaps early'r, but not before sunup. Most Americans ate but two meals daily. They broke their fast soon after can-see and dinnered early-to-middling afternoon. The more prosp'rous might also have a lighter repast in the evening, supper, soon after can't-see when the day's labour ended.

"My stomach worm gnaws as well," Robert Morris said. "I had but hoecakes garnish'd with pork Strap and Virginiay hamsteak, taken with a Bracer and a cup of Bohea."

Franklin wanted to laugh. Hoecakes with pork Strips and ham Steak a far from a light repast.

"I entertained the Delusion," Governeur said, "that the business would proceed with Dispatch and we would retire to the City Tavern timely."

"Expedition," Robert Morris said, "'tis not a speciality of this Assembly."

"Nor any Assembly," Franklin said.

The Morrises chuckled.

Misery wanted for society, so Mason and Gerry walked towards the Bar together. They made a curious coupling owing Mason's corpulence and Gerry's gauntness, tho' both men had aristocratic carriages.

Mason appear'd in exceeding ill Humour. Not just warm. Right rage-ed. He stopped, turnt, and glared at the Constitution of Government with disgust. Secretary Jackson held the rolled Charta reverent in both hands. He and Thomas Fitzsimons were transmitting it to the Assembly convoked above stairs and thus walking towards the doorway at the far northeast corner of the chambre, where the stairwell was resident.

"There is no Declaration of Rights," Mason said to Gerry. "In the House of Representatives there is not the Substance but the Shadow only of Representation."

By this, Mason signify'd the smallness of the number of Representatives, in proportion to the Multitude of population.

"The Senate have the Power of altering all Money-Bills," Mason said, "in conjunction with the President of the United States, although they are not Representatives of the People or amenable to them. The Senate being one complete Branch of the Legislature will destroy any Balance in the Government and enable them to accomplish what Usurpations they please upon the Rights and Liberties of the People."

"I pine my Ann," Gerry said.

"We all pine our familys," Mason said. "Tho' were my wife as ripe as Lady Gerry, I would pine her more a-certain. The Judiciary of the United States is so constructed and extended as to absorb and destroy the Judiciaries of the several States. This shall render Law as tedious, intricate and expensive, and Justice as unattainable by a great Part of the Community, as in England. And enabling the Rich to oppress and ruin the Poor."

"I pine Ann's Irish brogue. The conceit of her smirk. The aroma of Lavender in her perfume. The warmth of h—"

"I had not the Gratification of transporting my wife to Phila-delphiay for much of the Convention," Mason said, "as you. The President of the United States has no constitutional Council, a thing unknown in any safe and regular Government. He will therefore be unsupported by proper Information and Advice and will generally be directed by Minions and Favorites. Or he will become a Tool to the Senate. Or a Council of State will grow out of the principal Officers of the great Departments, the worst and most dangerous of all Ingredients for such a Council in a free Country."

"I trust to Washington," Gerry said.

"And when His Excellency expires?"

"I pray such day be long delayed."

"As we all. But lest you fancy His Excellency immortal, as some Græcian God, such day shall none the less hearken."

Gerry said something but stuttered, making him impossi-ble to understand. Franklin also failed to hear the beginning of Mason's retort.

"—ence also sprung that unnecessary and dangerous Offi-cer the Vice-President, who for want of other Employment is made President of the Senate, thereby dangerously blending the executive and legislative Powers, besides always giving to some one of the States an unnecessary and unjust Pre-eminence over the others."

"I l-l-long for my goose-ed mattress," Gerry said.

"We all lust for our beds," Mason said, "And warm Wives within them. The President of the United States has the unre-strained Power of granting Pardon for Treason. Which may be sometimes exercised to screen from Punishment those whom he had secretly instigated to commit the Crime and thereby prevent a Discovery of his own Guilt."

"What suppose your grandchildren at this instancy?" Gerry said.

"Their studies," Mason said, "if they would avoid the Switch."

"Have thy slaves whip them?" Franklin said.

Mason scowled at Franklin.

"I am not in the humour for your lampoons, Doctor."

Franklin met Mason's gaze even.

"Lampoons, like Armys, seek not the assent of the ambuscaded. Be merry, Colonel Mason. All shall be well."

Mason scowled deeper and turnt away. Deputies walked around him rather than engage his Fury. Mason winced, and gript his stomach, a common Complaint he evidenced in times of distress.

"By declaring all Treaties supreme Laws of the Land," Mason said to Gerry, "the Executive and the Senate have in many Cases an exclusive Power of Legislation. Which might have been avoided by proper Distinctions with Respect to Treaties and requiring the Assent of the House of Representatives, where it could be done with Safety."

A few Deputies glared at Mason as they detoured him. Mason stood unrepentant, impeding traffick like a turd on a walkway.

"By requiring only a Majority to make all commercial and navigation Laws," Mason said, "the five Southern States will be ruined. Their Produce and Circumstances are totally different from that of the eight Northern and Eastern States. Rigid and premature Regulations may be made as will enable the Merchants of the Northern and Eastern States not only to demand an exhorbitant Freight, but to monopolize the Purchase of the Commodities at their own Price. Requiring two thirds of the Members present in both Houses would have produced mutual Moderation, promoted the general Interest, and removed an insuperable Objection to the Adoption of the Government."

Gerry's expression grew glum.

"Under their own Construction of the general Clause at the End of the enumerated Powers," Mason said, "the Congress may grant Monopolies in Trade and Commerce, constitute new Crimes, inflict unusual and severe Punishments, and extend their Powers as far as they shall think proper. The State Legislatures have no Security for the Powers now presumed to remain to them, or the People for their Rights."

The general clause at the end of the enumerated Powers decreed that Congress shall have Power To make all Laws which shall be necessary and proper for carrying into Execution the foregoing Powers, and all other Powers vested by the Constitution in the Government of the United States, or in any Department or Officer thereof.

Necessary and proper.

Few Deputies seemed fearful of this clause.

Ought they be?

Gerry glanced at the chambre door as if it a beguiling Belle.

Mason clutched at his kneepan and winced.

"Zounds!" he said. "Bloody a-curse-ed damn Gout. In me knee withal. Absolute buggers."

Mason stood straight, evidencing tenderness, as if he a horse with a crack'd hoove. His face pinched with Pain as he worked his knee gentle, gradual, by letting the leg hang in the socket and the joint dangle errant. Franklin knew of experience that this a gentle way to manumit the gout within knee.

Pain evacuated Mason's expression sudden. He sighed long and deep, and then placed weight upon both legs again.

"There is no Declaration of any kind for preserving the Liberty of the Press," Mason said. "Or the Tryal by jury in civil Causes. Nor against the Danger of standing Armys in time of Peace. The State Legislatures are restrained from laying Export Duties on their own Produce."

Dictator John approached. He observed Deputies detouring Mason, and peered at them curious, as if the action absurd.

"Please, sir," Dictator John said to Mason. "Cease your ejaculations. The Constitution shall be ratify'd. Now come partake of dinner, lest Mister Gerry bludgeon you as the only surety of respite. And if you must ejaculate on the Constitution to the disgust of all, do so without aisle."

Mason stepped aside and stood just without aisle. He again pillored the absence of a Council of State or Privy Council attached to the Executive, to monitor and check abuses of power.

Dictator John strode by, affixing Mason with a glare that was right caustick.

Gerry looked at the rear of Dictator John and took a halting half step, as if to follow him, but it stutter'd. Gerry moved without the aisle, next to Mason.

Dictator John passed the bar, passed without doors, and absented Convention.

"Both the general Legislature and the State Legislature are expressly prohibited making ex post facto Laws," Mason said, "though there never was nor can be a Legislature but must and will make such Laws, when necessity and the public Safety require them."

The Gout flared and Franklin was consumed by agony for a span indeterminate.

"—ereafter be a Breach of all the Constitutions in the Union," Mason said, "and afford Precedents for other Innovations."

Franklin discerned not the meaning of the truncate thought. He wondered if Mason were growing insensible in his Objections, or if the unheard portion would have provided illumination. Probably the latter. Mason was a far from insensible. Many of his criticisms had Validity. Most, in point of fact.

Gerry's eyes had evacuated and was fixated straight ahead into nothingness. He might have been learning Latin or receiving a lecture from his wife. Though Lady Gerry was so handsome no man was Fool enough to unnafix his Gaze, no matter how tedious the intercourse.

"The general Legislature is restrained from prohibiting the further Importation of Slaves for twenty odd years," Mason said, "though such Importations render the United States weaker, more vulnerable, and less capable of Defence."

"Manumit your Slaves, sir," Governeur Morris said, "if Slavery's weakening of Americay anguishes you so furious."

A few Deputies chuckled. All was of the North.

"Manumission in unity would alter the national Character but scant," Mason said.

"It would respite us the odium of your Hypocrisy," Governeur said.

Mason turned and faced the chambre expansive, as if the Convention were still convoked and Washington still chairing at the throne. He spoke louder, though was still cool and reasoned.

"This government will commence in a moderate Aristocracy," Mason said. "It is at present impossible to foresee whether it will, in it's Operation, produce a Monarchy or a corrupt oppr-essive Aristocracy. It will most probably vibrate some years between the two, and then terminate in the one or the other."

"You have my profound gratitude," Governeur said, "And that of all Deputies, I hazard. For adjoining such Cheer to the celebratory."

Some Deputies chuckled. Others smirked.

Mason entered the aisle and passed the bar. Gerry joined him. Mason continued enumerating his Objections to the Constitution of Government. He gave the Sense of a man who was just gaining impetus and could continue in such vein for hours.

Governeur Morris laughed as Mason and Gerry passed without doors and absented Convention.

"I fear," Governeur said, "that Mister Gerry is consigned to a tedious walk."

"Mister Gerry have but himself to accompt," Franklin said. "He could have averted such Tedium by affixing his signature to the Instrument."

"Who would Colonel Mason have harangued thence?"

"Mister Randolph," Franklin said.

The totem-faced Randolph was walking by and shook his head emphatick.

"Such threat," he said, "might have induced me to affix my signature to the instrument."

Deputies laughed.

"His Excellency's final evening in Philadelphiay shall be right splendid," Robert Morris said. "My chef is preparing a light supper. Salt Fish, encrusted with Brazil nuts ground exceeding fine. Snap beans sauced in Bristol Milk and Bavaria Mustard, almonds shaved so thin they curl."

Washington evidenced a fondness for salt Fish and nuts. Especially Brazile nuts, which was hard as jewels. Washington had lost his teeth in measure by cracking Braziles on them. Or cracking his teeth on Braziles, to reckon the matter proper.

George Clymer approached. His hair was in recession and his thin yet consuming nose reminded Franklin of a crack'd hatchet. Clymer's face was severe, aristocratic, with an excess of forehead and ample chin.

"Can His Excellency not chew nuts upon occasion if slow and cautious?" Clymer said.

"Not whole nuts," Morris said. "And certain not Braziles. Thus the encrust ground exceeding fine. This suffers his His Excellency to savour a Delicacy he has long been deprived."

"Right considerate," Clymer said. "And right ingenius."

Franklin stifled irritation. He disliked sycophancy. When Franklin thought of ingenius, he pictured the new contrived steamboat of Finch, who had exhibited it to Deputies on the second-to-last Wednesday in August. Or the telescopy of Rittenhouse. Or John Pringle's Experiments on Septic and Antiseptic Substances. Or the prose of Thomas.

Daniel Jenifer sauntered by with James McHenry. McHenry went without wig and his hair clung tight to his head in tiny Curls. Even in repose his face seemed petulant. Jenifer had a softish manner, a buttery Face that somehow evaded Corpulence, and a lower lip that tended to jut as if a child pouting or swollen from a Brawl.

"It shall be right pleasant to intend to Annapolis," Jenifer said. "Stepney hearkens, and I have pressing business at Port Tobacco."

Stepney was Jenifer's plantation on the outskirts of Annapolis.

"A lot of Negros due?" McHenry said.

"I have sworn never to purchase or sell another Negro," Jenifer said. "And to manumit my Negros upon my death, after a Stretch."

"You will want for the income. Your traffick in Colour is lucrative."

"Indeed. But when a man comes to his End he thinks of else but Wealth."

"How long a stretch ere manumission?" McHenry said.

"I would bequeath my inheritor time to effect Reformation of plantation operations. To a new mode absent dependency upon Negros."

"What mode?"

"I haven't the scantest notion how to survive a plantation absent Negros," Jenifer said. "Elseways I would have manumitted long previous."

Franklin doubted this. So did Governeur Morris, who scowled.

"Might your inheirit not simply procure replacement Negros?" McHenry said.

"I shall 'tleast and at last have manumitted mine," Jenifer said. "Should I stand before the Author of our Being and be asked to account, I may earn some measure of Mercy."

"I rather doubt such," Governeur said.

Jenifer pursed his lips sanguine.

"I apprehend you correct, Sir," he said.

Jenifer and McHenry turned left into the aisle and approached the Bar.

"What stretch envision you," McHenry said, "ere manumission effected?"

"I feel as if intercoursing my solicitor," Jenifer said. "Mister Morris sets a fine table."

"The finest," McHenry said. "He sparest no dispence."

"Tho' his courses tend to rich and buttered."

"My Chef is French, Mister Saint Thomas," Morris said to Jenifer. "Plus de beurre!"

Morris pressed his two longest fingers to his thumb and raised his hand into the air as he uttered the French phrase. He laughed.

Governeur Morris and Caledonia join'd their employer in laughter, but it seemed enforced.

It occurr'd to Franklin that more beurre also incurred more chins. He pictured the French chef rendering a sculpture of Morris out of butter. 'Twas perhaps the only material whose texture did Morris' chins justice.

"Manumission is rendered simpler," McHenry said to Jenifer, "by you never having taken a wife."

"Most things are rendered simpler," Governeur said, "by not taking a wife."

"Contracting The Syphilis?" Franklin said.

Governeur laughed.

"When shall you take a wife?" Clymer said to Governeur.

"I strive for one a month," Governeur said. "At the minimum."

Prodigious laughter. Tho' some Deputies frowned.

Jenifer and McHenry passed the Bar. They paused to take in the chambre one last time and stood silent for a long moment.

"Shall you host one of your sumptuous Festivitys ere winter?" McHenry said.

"I hope to," Jenifer said. "But it may take a stretch to repair my affairs to a state of Order. And I grow olde. Many nights I find myself a-longing for scant more than my Hearth and a bumper of Bordeaux."

"Grow you not at times lonely? Ach for a wife?"

Jenifer shrugged.

"Liberty 'tis not without price," he said. "I lavish'd its benefits and find it unmanly to snivel at the accounting. Tho' in earnest I w—"

Jenifer and McHenry strolled towards the door and Franklin could no longer discern their intercourse. The same was not true of Robert Morris, misfortunately.

"A steak and kidney pie," Morris said, "with a butter crust, fresh mortared Nutmegg, and the sweete—"

"Steak and kidney pie?" Hamilton said.

"Steak and kidney pie," Morris said.

"Why a steak and kidney pie?" Hamilton said.

"His Excellency is right fond of steak and kidney pie," Morris said.

"Not an hour ere retirement," Hamilton said. "And I proffer thanks for the Revelation. I had never supped with His Excellency."

Morris' eyes narrowed ever so slight.

No merchant nor man of business nor Aspiration could afford to incur the wrath of Robert Morris. Hamilton curtsied with envyable grace.

"Your humble servant," he said. "I meant no discourtesy. But a steak and kidney pie a bit rich for supper, would you not say?"

"I would not have you say what I say," Morris said. "Or not say. I am not His Excellency."

"Nay, sir," Hamilton said. "You are not."

There was a Hint of insolence in the Little Lion's tone. But just a Hint. Morris' eyes narrowed and he peered at Hamilton intence, trying to discern if he was insubordinating. Morris shrugged, as if deciding Hamilton warranted not such nicety. His glance became dismissive.

"Nothing is too rich for His Excellency," Morris said. "If we scrap it to the Hounds, 'tis but a Trifle. I would rather discard a hundred Guineas of relishes than have His Excellency want for a morsel."

Franklin resisted the urge to roll his eyes.

"Hounds in Versailles feast not so well," he said. "They shall be laid up like hibernateing Bears. Or dragging their bellies about like a spinster's duggs."

Everyone laughed.

"Bequeath the remnants of your feast to the Poor?" Franklin said.

Morris shook his head, or more proper his chins, which seemed like Sails flailing to catch wind.

"The Hounds," Morris said.

"Why not the Poor?" Franklin said.

"Hounds evidence more Industry."

"Is the kidney of the pie," Franklin said, "that of Peasants?"

Morris' expression became droll and a trifle irritate.

The Little Lion smirked fractional.

"Also a Fish Muddle," Morris said, "with mussels, prawns, skallops, cubed shad flesh, and cetera, seasoned with tarragon, pepper, sweet herbs, and cetera, fresh from the Indies. Garnished with fresh ovened French bread. Authentick French bread, to be sure, as my Chef is French. Had I mentioned that my chef is French?"

"You may have," Hamilton said. "Upon occasion."

His tone was conspicuous devoid of sarckasm.

"Not the impostor loaves that masquerade on Market Street devoured greedy by the Ignorant and packs of Poor," Morris said. "Proper French loaves."

Governeur Morris, Caledonia, and Hamilton nodded earnest, as if Robert Morris were Montesquieu and discoursing upon segregated Powers.

Franklin wondered if Morris recollected that Franklin had bought "impostor loaves" when first arriving in Philadelphia. He had been one of the "packs of Poor." Tho' he agreed that French loaves shamed Philadelphia's.

"My wife longst ago attained the receipt for Lady Washington's whisky cake," Morris said, "which shall be bak't to honour her absencey. My confectioner is also baking a tipsy cake. And gâteau au chocolat."

"Cherry pie?" Hamilton said. "His Excellency is most fond of cher—"

"Don't be thick," Morris said. "Obviously there is a cherry pie. With cherries of Morrisville."

Morrisville.

The very name made Franklin want to groan. Morris owned one of the largest and most opulent mansions in Philadelphia but felt that a three Hundred acre estate without city was also requisite. The Morrisville mansion was atop a commanding hill with a dictatorial view of the Delaware River. It had its own powerplant, compriz'd of a small damn and waterwheels. Also perhaps the finest greens House in all of America, where Morris grew an astounding variety of tropickals and citrus.

Morrisville.

Not Monticello. Not Mount Vernon. Nor Montpelier nor Stepney. Not an artizan Name, nor one honouring another, as Washington's brother Lawrence had in naming his plantation after Admiral Vernon.

Morrisville was in fact but a Hamlet a cross the Delaware from Trenton, near Colvin's Ferry. 'Twas scarce populous enough to be reckon'd even a Hamlet, and had no formal incorporation nor name, yet Robert Morris was habitual in designating it Morrisville.

There was some Thing defective inside a man, when he had need to brandish his name so brazen and crass. Franklin had much named after him, even a propose-ed State, and derived prodigious satisfaction thereof, but others had suggested such

Homage. Franklin would never have proffered it himself, nor campaigned, even by insinuation. Had Morris any sense how pitiful this propensity? How vulgar? How vain? How oppugnant?

If he had, would he care?

Nay on all counts, in all problity.

Morris continued his labor'ous description of the supper menu, as if determined to craft a culinary imitation of Mason's Objections. There were to be pumpkin Chips, pickled cucumbers, and pickled nuts. Pickling rendered the nuts soft.

"Soft enough that His Excellency might chew them?" Clymer said.

"Tender as a boilt egg," Morris said.

Franklin wondered if Washington would enjoy such delicacy. The flavor was perhaps irrelevant. At minimum, the curiousity was something he would not countenance in publick, as eating queer foods distinctive soft made his false teeth manifest in a manner he felt undignified and embaressing. The ability to enjoy such delicacy in Privy was probably what signify'd most.

Morris continued his dissipations. His chef was rendering a fresh catsup, though attaining the mushrooms that were the sole ingredient, save spices, had been right arduous.

"It need not be said," Morris said, "that I demanded mushrooms from Porto Bello."

These was the finest but exceeding rare, and exorbitant. Few could afford them. Most that could cooked them for eating rather than employing them to render Catsup.

"My chef also rendered a butter of nuts, from a mixing of nuts."

"How is that effected?" Clymer said.

"Mortar and pestle," Morris said. "After roasting the nuts. Tho' we have requisition'd a hand Mill from the Continent."

"Truely a kin of butter?" Clymer said.

"Tending more to a lard or Ointment," Morris said. "Unless served heated. But right tastey."

"And right curious," Clymer said. "Your chef invented the dish?

"'Tis a prediliction of the Savages of the lower Americays," Morris said.

"As with the Cacao?" Clymer said.

"Aye," Morris said. "I heard Spaniards account of butter of nut and paid one who had observed it rendering to recount to my chef. He rendered the receipt as best he could. The Experiment is ongoing."

When Robert Morris said the word Experiment, Governeur Morris glanced at Franklin, observed the mild pursing of his lips, and smiled fractional.

"Is butter of nut a garnishment of vegetables and meats?" Clymer said. "The foundation of novel mother sauces? As with butter?"

"Nay," Robert Morris said. "Less universal in application. But 'tis right tastey on bread. As the butter of nut must be heated to spread with ease, and only with difficulty even then, my chef has taken to roasting the bread so as to stiffen it that it takes easyer."

"This must have taken numerate trials," Clymer said.

"We have discarded enough bread and butter of nut in our Experiments," Morris said, "to feed half the bloody hounds in Americay."

"I would fancy a Marmalade upon the butter of nut upon the roasted bread," Franklin said.

"An intriguing notion," Morris said. "Would you dine with me the coming week, I could have my chef prepare Marmalades of your fancy. Or if the Gout and Stone render you immobile and you're desirous of flaunting your new dining room, I could have my chef prepare a meal at your home and instruct your cook the receipt."

"That is gracious," Franklin said. "I shall call upon you."

"At your leisure," Morris said, "I am yours."

Morris answered Clymer's other enquiries about the butter of nut. The crux of the intercourse was that Morris' chef floundered finding an ingredient to fold with the nut butter so as to render it thinner and more pliant. Every incorporation Morris could conceive had been attempted, including Water, honey, molasses, melted bear lard, oils, different nut Species, and cetera, but none answered the Need.

"Have you not," Franklin said, "incorporate butter of milk with the butter of nut?"

Morris' face froze.

"Nay," he said.

Deputies chuckled.

"'Twould seem a nigh perfect solution," Morris said.

"Perhaps meritious of experiment," Franklin said, "at the least."

"How could I fail to consider something so manifest?" Morris said.

Franklin had manners enough to leave the question unanswered.

"You might also seat a butter of nut warm before a hearth, but not hot, nor heated above fire. You might then skim the oil atop and add this to a separate rendering of butter of nut as a thinner. Or perhaps render the delicacy only in summer."

"Have you ever render'd a butter of nut?" Clymer said.

"Nay," Franklin said.

"Then how know ye there be oil of nut that will clarify?" Morris said.

Franklin shrugged.

"How knows a bird to migrate?" he said. "Or a Hound to lick its Vitals?"

Gentlemen chuckled.

"His Excellency might transport the butter of Brazile to Mount Vernon if he fancies it," Morris said.

"Might it not gum his false Teeth?" Franklin said.

Morris' face froze.

"I hadn't considered such," he said.

Franklin remembered a Hound he had seen given a butter of nut by a Spaniard fresh into port, who doubtless knew the outcome and was lampooning the curious owner. The Spaniard fed the Hound a prodigious Gob. It fancy'd the nut Butter initial, but then worked its mouth energetic as the butter of nut gummed it, becoming right furious. Franklin pictured Washington eating Morris' nut butter and working his false Teeth energetic, like the Hound. Except that his false Teeth had springs and were mechanickal and might be gummed to Ruin. And Washington furious was more dangerous than any Hound.

"His Excellency," Morris said, "may be undesirous of the butter of Brazile."

"I would dine upon relishes rather than intercourse of them," Governeur said. "Have we postponed ample?"

"A stretch still," Morris said. "When accosted by the Mobile Vulgus without doors, I would be delinquent to City Tavern and draw upon such pretext to retire to it."

Mobile Vulgus was Latin, which translated loose as The Fickle Crowd.

Franklin disliked all derogations of the common Folk and could not help but scowl. Robert Morris observed Franklin's displeasure but redress'd it not.

"If the throng even half that which gather'd for the Declaration of Independency," Clymer said, "repair to City Tavern may be nigh impossible."

"No bloody Ceremony nor reading as with the Declaration of Independency," Morris said. "Thank Providence for that."

Gentlemen nodded emphatick.

Morris recommenced his Cavalcade of Gluttony, describing the Sweetmeats of his supper in excruciate detail.

His Braggadocio was right tiresome.

Franklin disattuned Morris and thought of his Mulberry Tree. He envision'd himself sitting serene under it in Solitude, and then fixated on the vision, as if meditating.

Franklin eventual focused on his surroundings again. South Deputies at tables right of Pennsylvania's continued to absent. Amongst them was Pierce Butler of South Carolina, and Hugh Williamson and William Blount of North Carolina. Gandering the Dandyish Blount made Franklin want to whistle Yankee Doodle, while the crow-faced Williamson made him want to glance at any Thing else. Butler had the aristocratic aire of a genteel planter and savoured of Arrogancey. He was exquisite dressed, with a fine wig powdered gen'rous, a handsome Stock—neck Cravat—of embroidered silk that seemed damn nigh Æthereal, and ornate gold Lace inlaid his coat and waistcoat.

"Discount is good pay," Blount said. "Yet no invention nor industry nor labour even requisite. Employ Negroes."

South Gentlemen chuckled.

Franklin was baffled as to why, as he had arrive-ed tardy to an intercourse whose subject he knew not.

"Such attitude, sir," Governeur said to Blount, "'tis why the South will never beget invention nor manufactures."

Blount remained right cool and smiled knowing, as if humouring a child.

"The South wants for neither," he said.

Walking sticks in the south Congregation tapped.

"Here, here," someone said.

"Pile upon thyselves in citys," Blount said. "Like Roches trapped in a trunk. Defile water and forest, land and malaria, with the ill-sented Dung of your shambles, tanners, and manufacturys. We recoil and laugh from a far in the Eden of the South."

"Adam," Governeur said, "owned no Slaves."

"He ought have," Butler said.

"To harvest the contraband Fruit?" Franklin said.

Southern Deputies laughed. And many of the North. Governeur Morris scowled.

"I never smell this city nor breathe its malaria again," Blount said, "I shall count myself blesst."

Franklin wanted to tell Blount that Philadelphia sharet the same sentiment about hosting him again.

Richard Spaight, also of North Carolina, approached. Turned of but 29, he was the third youngest Deputy, and but one of four Deputies not turned of 30. Spaight was earnest, had spoke but sparing in Convention, yet had been fastidious in attendance. His coffee suit was plain but respectable.

"What a vile city," Spaight said.

"Shitehole incarnate," Blount said.

Blount pronounced Shite in the common mode, that it rhymed with Light.

"Some Half-Wits would have Philadelphiay the fœderal Capital," Butler said. "The whole government might succumb to pleurisy, the bloody flux, or the putrid sore throat."

Franklin was careful to keep his expression indifferent, but also thought it prudent to tack the conversation upon a different course.

"A question of Curiousity not contention," he said to Butler. "If you please."

"Aye, Good Doctor?"

"You have never a-contemplated building a factory and employing Slaves?"

"Not on your bloody life."

Other southern Deputies shook their heads emphatick.

"Impracticable," Spaight said. "Grievous impracticable."

"Why?" Franklin said.

"Negroes break every Thing delicate or complex," Spaight said.

"And most any Thing hearty and simple," Butler said.

"And pilfer what they don't despoil," Spaight said.

"Bloody thieves," Butler said.

Some southern Deputies chuckled. Others nodded.

"My consolation," Governeur Morris said, "for your mistreatment by your Slaves."

Some southern Gentlemen smirked. Others seemed to chew their cheeks to keep from laughing at Morris.

"Manufactures," Spaight said, "are at odds with the tenor of southern Life and would pervert it irreperable."

"The South shall continue to import manufactures," Blount said. "Reaping the attendant Benefits without the requisite Defilement, which we gladly cede to the North and East."

"If Tall Boy is done pilloring Slavery," Butler said, "I believe relishes await."

The eyes of all south Deputies affixed Governeur Morris.

"Well, Tall Boy?" Butler said. "No more dissipations upon the ills of Negroes?"

"Blacks," Governeur said, "Not negroes."

"Negroes," Butler said.

"Blacks," Governeur said.

"Negroes," Butler said.

"Blacks," Governeur said. "And the ill is Slavery."

"We south Deputies find your ejaculations upon Negroes so profound and illuminate," Butler said, "we should all willing absent dinner to partake them."

A few south Deputies smirked.

So did Governeur Morris.

"I should rather regulate Commerce," he said.

The smirks of south Deputies vanished. Save Butler's.

"A pity you haven't time for a Sermon," Butler said to Governeur. "Moral disquisitions from America's most notorious

Libertine is so very refreshing. Another day, then? I hope we shan't find you too busy despoiling Philadelphiay's wives and effecting profligate ruination of Marriages to lecture we simple southern Folk about our Depravity."

Butler spoke the words "simple southern Folk" with an exaggerate Carolina twang.

"May thy Slaves revolt," Governeur said, "and dangle you."

"Thou art a Slave," Butler said. "To thy Roger. Before regulating Commerce, first regulate thyself."

Nigh all the south Deputies a smirked.

"Bed a betroth-ed of the South, Tall Boy," Butler said, "you'll find husbands demanding Satisfaction. And the Law none too anxious to prosecute your Dispatcher."

Governeur curtsied with his head. But his eyes was Embers. Butler met his glare even.

"Another day then, Tall Boy?"

"Another day indeed," Governeur said.

The south Deputies returned rightward to their tables to gather their possessions. They continued what seemed to be their prior intercourse as they did.

"Bloody murd'rous summer," Butler said. "Four months of close Confinement injured my health much."

He exhalt deep.

"I would like to fancy the sacrifice worthy," Butler said. "We closed the business Committed to Us, but how well We have succeeded is left for other Letterd Men to determine."

"Though I signed the instrument," Blount said, "I am not in sentiment with my Colleagues. As I have before said, I still think we shall ultimately end not many Years as separate and distinct Governments perfectly independent of each other."

"If we end as separate and distinct Governments," Franklin said, "Mister Butler ought be Minister Plenipotentiary to the North."

Nigh everyone in the chambre chuckled. Even Butler.

"If that be your sentiment," Spaight said to Blount, "why sign the instrument?"

"Would you rather I hadn't?"

Spaight chuckled.

"Nay," he said.

"The Constitution with all its imperfections is the only thing at this critical time that can rescue the states from civil discord and foreign contempt," Butler said. "It reflects naturally our circumstances, the too little disposition of most of the states to submit to any government. If it meets with the approbation of the States, I shall feel myself fully recompensed for my share of the trouble."

"Shall it meet with the approbation of the States?" Spaight said.

"I prefer giving my consent to a trial of the Constitution in question with all its deficiencies," Butler said, "to what appears to me the inevitable alternative. That there are parts of it I like not you well know, but still I prefer a trial of it to seeing the Gordian knot cut, the instrument having within itself a power of Amendment. The Knot of Union in my judgment Will be no more if this Constitution is rejected."

"Shall the Constitution be rejected?" Spaight said.

"The Convention saw I think justly," Butler said, "the Critical Situation of the United States. Slighted from abroad and tottering on the brink of Confusion at home. 'Twas wise to bring forward such a system as bids fairest for general Approbation and adoption so as to be brought soon into operation."

"You have a constitutional incapacity," Spaight said, "of answering a query direct."

"Apologies, Sir," Butler said. "'Tis nigh impossible not to cogitate. The Constitution I think will be adopted. Though it has some few opponents, where is that Work of man that pleases everybody?"

The glances of Butler, Blount, and Spaight gravitated to the throne where Washington had sat. Franklin had the momentary yet fearsome sense that with Washington not present, America was not safe. The Fear struck him as if Lightning.

The conglomerate of Butler, Blount, Spaight, and Williamson stood in reflective silence.

"We had Clashing Interests to reconcile," Butler said, "Some strong prejudices to encounter. The same spirit that brought settlers to a certain Quarter of this Country is still alive in it. The system of government conceived results from a spirit of Accomodation to different Interests. It is not the most perfect one that the Deputies cou'd devise had we a Country better adapted for the reception of it than Americay is at this day, or perhaps ever will be."

Another span of silence from Butler, Blount, and Spaight, and continuing silence from Williamson, whose nose so grotesque it seemed almost to caw.

At last Butler sighed deep.

"Pains and attention were not spared," he said, "to form such a Constitution as would preserve to the individual as large a share of natural Rights as could be left consistent with the good of the whole. And yet ..."

Butler expelt air again.

"It is a great Extent of Territory to be under One free Government," he said. "The manners and modes of thinking of the Inhabitants differing near as much as in different Nations of Europe. If we can secure tranquillity at Home, and respect from abroad, they will be great points gain'd."

"There's no man of reflection," Spaight said, "who has maturely considered what must and will result from the weakness of our present fœderal Government, and the tyrannical and unjust proceedings of most of the State governments, but must sincerely wish for a strong and efficient National Government."

"There's a fulsome plenytude of such men," Butler said. "Messieurs Mason, Randolph, and Gerry amongst them. Torrents of such men shall parade and agitate when Ratification undertaken."

"Ratification," Spaight said, "'tis mighty more arduous than suppose-ed."

"Only Fools fancy ratification a trifle," Blount said.

"We shall at some time or other have a King," Hugh Williamson said, "though I wished no precaution omitted that would postpone the event as long as possible. I still preference the insurance of a President ineligible a second time."

"Nay, Sir," Robert Morris said. "His Excellency ought serve during good Behaviour."

Deputies glanced at the empty throne again. Franklin again felt a shock of Fear, the sense that with Washington not present America in peril.

"After all our Endeavours," Butler said, "our System of Government is little better than matter of Experiment. Much must depend on the morals and manners of the People at large. In a large and wide Extended Empire, let the System be ever so perfect, good Order and Obedience must nonetheless greatly depend on the Patriotism of the Citizen."

"Indeed, Sir," Williamson said.

Butler, Blount, Spaight, and Williamson turnt, began walking, and approached the Bar.

"I had sworn to mail a Copy of the result of Our deliberations to Mister Butler in Britain," Butler said, "but this Constitution of Government not worth the expence of postage."

Mr. Butler in Britain was Weedon Butler, a relative of Pierce.

The south Gentlemen stopped in the aisle and savoured the chambre one final time. They then swung the bargate towards them and passed the bar.

"I pray the blind Piles revive not on my journey homeward," Blount said.

Blind piles was hæmorrhoids that bled not. The absence of bleeding exacerbated swelling and made them prodigious excruciate. Blount's blind Piles, and the diarrhœa resultant, had prohibited him trav'ling to Philadelphia and taking his seat in Convention, until nigh the end of June.

"One physick," Blount said, "wanted to pierce my anus withinst to drain the blind Piles, as they would not resolve."

Butler and Spaight sprouted expressions of horrour.

"Bleed you from withinst?" Butler said. "You didn't submit such Quackery?"

"Nay," Blount said. "Tho' I gave it earnest consideration as the Pain encamped and invested."

Williamson smirked prodigious.

"Rather John Adams or Governour Clinton elevate to President," Butler said, "then let a physick bleed me from withinst the arse."

Williamson laughed, a rarity given his innate gravity.

"You make sport of my Agony?" Blount said.

"Nay," Williamson said. "As a physick, I am always somewhat amuzed by the reticence of males to suffer any Thing within Rectum, even when a physickal necessitude to alleviate Disease."

Blount chuckled.

"My blind piles Complaint is hardly called Sickness," he said. "But it is undoubted the most painful teasing Complaint that I have ever experienced. It enforc'd great Use for what I have none of when in pain, namely Patience."

"You have scant Patience when not in pain," Butler said.

"Indeed," Blount said, "I would be a right disagreeable travel compatriot should the blind Piles revive."

"Complainst too grievous," Butler said, "we may bleed you without."

Blount laughed.

"I can but pray," he said, "that the blind Piles re—"

Franklin could no longer discern the intercourse.

"Mister Butler," Governeur whispered, "is a blind Pile."

Morris, Governeur, Ingersoll, and cetera, all chuckled.

Blount was almost without doors. Governeur glared at him with Enmity.

"Misaccount another three hundred Thousand," Governeur whispered.

Blount listed the Army during the Revolution and had been Paymaster to General Horatio Gates. At the Battle of Camden, wherest Gates defeated, Blount lost 300,000 of paper Money that he had requisitioned for soldiers' Pay. 'Twas never accounted.

"To evacuate such sum amidst Battle would be right cunning," Ingersoll said.

"And right brazen," Hamilton said.

"Bloody dastard bastard bugger prigger probly pilfered it for his land Peculations," Governeur said.

"Would suprize me not the least," Robert Morris said, "though I would not presume absent Evidence."

If Blount had pilfer'd the 300 Thousand, Franklin hoped he'd spent it rapid. Paper money being emitted in ruinous Quantums during The War, causing its value to depreciate, the 300 Thousand was worth Less than a Thousand by war's end in 1783, nigh certain, and might not have been valued at a Hundred by 1785.

Butler, Blount, Spaight, and Williamson craned their heads rearward at Governeur Morris as they moved without doors. They laughed hearty. Except Williamson. At last they moved without doors and vanished from View.

Silence reigned, and a sense of Fatigue and Frustration. Agitations upon Slavery were a rut they had retrod ad nauseum in Convention assembled, and without Convention, over the last third a year.

Morris, Governeur, Ingersoll, Hamilton, and cetera, resumed their intercourse along a more frivolous tack. Franklin disattuned the intercourse.

For the thousandth time, Franklin asked himself how to put the electric Fluid to practicable use for the benefit of mankind?

Some mode or apparatus of artificial electric Fluid seemed requisite. A mode more potential and durable than a lone Leyden Jar or even Batteries of them. Franklin saw the electric Fire in a bottle, frolicking energetic, like a puppy proffered ten cups of Hyson. Frothy blue tentacles of Lightning, untamed, galloping the plains free.

What then?

What bloody then?

How to break the Stallion that was the electric Fluid? Saddle it and yoke it to useful Work?

Franklin ruminated and ruminated and ruminated, but deduced no remedy.

"—s almost as vain to expect permanency from Democracy," Governeur said, "as to construct a palace on the surface of the sea."

"All Republican government is radically defective," Hamilton said. "The Constitution will prove a shilly shally Thing of mere milk and water. It cannot last. It is only good as a step to something better. But I shall labour to prop the frail and worthless fabric."

"Especially," Governeur said, "if His Excellency stands in need of a Secre—"

Might the electric Fluid begot by the steam engine of Watt? Waterworks in Britain and the Continent were powered by such engines. As was Mr. Fitch's boat. Perseverance indeed.

Franklin could not but help but envision ball-ed Lightning. 'Twas exceeding rare, yet of nigh indefinite Duration, by the mode of Spin. Lightning when spun might attain to what eluded the Hound, namely to catch its Tail.

Formed into a ring, spinning, ball-ed Lightning seemed to draw electric Fluid from its surroundings, thereby replenishing itself nigh continual. It dissipated not as the Lightning when striking the Ground, or the electric Fluid within the Leyden Jar

Franklin pictured ball-ed Lightning in a bottle, spinning furious rapid, a long conductor Rod, a lightning Rod, penetrating its centre, the depth of Protrusion determining the quantity of electric Fluid syphoned.

By such mode might the electric Fluid be yoked as a mule and made to do useful Work? What mi—

The percussion of a musket Shot aroused Franklin him from his rumination. The Shot sounded some blocks away, though still within city. The fire of Arms within city was cause not for alarm. No Deputy within chambre evidenced Concern, and most did not even pause their intercourse.

"—ad wanted to dismiss a Balloon ere supper," Robert Morris said, "decorated as the flag so symbolic of the ascension of Americay. It would carry under it a large Lanthorn with inscriptions on its Sides."

"You jape us," Ingersoll said. "A Balloon?"

His eyes was wide with Wonder. All Deputies in vicinity of Morris were enamoured.

The Balloon Invention had captured the fancy of the Publick. Franklin had observed one of the first species of such aerostatic Experiment, in France in 1783, in the Bois de Boulogne, at the conclusion of negotiations of the Treaty of Peace with Britain. Hollow Globes of England Oiled Silk were impregnated with a Solution of Gum elastic in Lintseed Oil, and then filled with permanent inflammable Air. Though the Balloon Experiment had been replicate by Men of Science and mechanic Dexterity throughout the world, such men were sparse, and the dispence prodigious. Few balloons had arose, and few people had thus seen a Balloon, much less one populate by a man. As yet there had been no verifitable flight of a Balloon within America.

"Much Lustre would have accrued to Americay," Morris said, "had I dismiss'd its first Balloon the day the Constitution of Government executed."

"And to you," Hamilton said.

Morris allowed a smile.

"And Philadelphiay," Ingersoll said. "Why was such Miracle not undertaken? Did the contrivance prove insurmount?"

Morris shook his head. And his chins.

"'Tis a thing not to be quacked," he said.

"Right sure nay," Ingersoll said.

"In time," Morris said, "with the aid of the Good Doctor and other natural Phylosophers and Mechanicks of repute, success ought be had."

"A dearth of funds was certain not a Bar," Ingersoll said.

Morris allowed a wider smile. Hauteur crept in.

"Certain not," he said. "'Twas thought His Excellency would not want such a crowd as the Spectacle might elicit."

Morris had probably reckon'd correct, at least in portion. Washington wanted no Spectacles at his place of residency. However, he would probably have countenanced a Crowd for a chance to view a Wonder such as a man flying. Or even a Balloon Invention levitating unpopulate.

Alas, ascending as the birds—and most important staying levitate—was more arduous than Morris reckoned. As Balloon Inventions were filled with air but once upon ground, by a Fire lit upon it and under Balloon, their Gravitation when the air within Balloon dissipated or cooled often defy'd regulation. Balloon Inventions wrought by dabblers or pretenders had been reported to gravitate fearsome rapid, with Velocity which exceeded the most forceful charriage Crash.

Franklin doubted Morris could have dismissed a Balloon, or would ever, unless he imported a balloon virtuoso such as Mr. Montgolfier, Mr. Charles, or the Robert Brothers. Such virtuosos would nigh certain intend to America eventual regardless, touring the whole of the nation and dismissing Balloons for crowds or towns who would pay to observe the Wonder. Franklin would lay Wager that the first Balloon Invention dismissed in America would be by this mode, not the pretensions of Robert Morris.

Franklin wondered, in time, if Balloons or more advanced modes of Flight might make utility of the electric Fluid?

Electric Fire, ball-ed as a spool of yarn, spinning within a glass jar. With a conducting rod protruding into its centre, syphoning, drawing out the electric Flu—

Nay, not a conducting rod, which might but diffuze the ball-ed Lightning or even explode it. A conductor within a glass rod?

Even then, the ball-ed Lightning must be created and corral'd. Franklin knew from Experiment that this was difficult and dangerous, and frequent fatal.

Franklin had the sense that he approached the Remedy, in measure, but still missed the mark a far.

Some conductor without the glass jar rather than within? External yet presented near. It would absorb the electric Fluid freely, as the conductor atop the Kite had, and as the knucle presented near the Key had. Electric Fire might then stream out plentyfull, be yoked to Work, an—

"—ay Doctor Franklin?"

Governeur Morris was waving his hand afront of Franklin's face.

Franklin chuckled.

"Aye," he said.

The Morrises, Little Lion, and Ingersoll chuckled.

"Electricity is a subject that still affords me Pleasure," Franklin said, "tho' of late I ha'n't much attended to it."

"We shall grant the Phylosopher his solitude," Robert Morris said. "What other Inventions of benefit to humanity might matriculate from you, had we but sense enough to parole you to Privy?"

"A right vexing dilemma," Governeur said. "Had we granted Doctor Franklin sufficiency of time for his natural Phylosophy, we might have many Wonderments, yet not our Liberty."

Decades spent not in political Offices, political Gaols, but in natural Phylosophy pursuits. 'Twas an alluring thought. Yet Franklin had derived much satisfaction shaping events on a world stage and might have felt a void acute were he less multifaceted and a natural Phylosopher only. His political appointments had facilitated his access to leading natural Phylosophers as well, which had augmented his learning prodigious.

The last of the deep-south Deputies strode by Franklin, once again pivoting their canes as they went, strides still as leisurely as southern Drawls. William Few and Abraham Baldwin of Georgia were in intense discussion, expressed worry over the agitations of the Creek Indians in their State, and were desperate for news from the Packet. The Creeks were under the Delusion that the territory of Georgia was properly theirs and were proving right recalcitrant.

The pair of Pinckneys nodded respectful to Franklin as they passed and tipped the fronts of their triangulate cocked hats. Franklin nodded and smiled back. Charles was prattling his politicks incessant to CC, and Franklin made Pains not to hear.

When the Pinckneys neared the doors, and were about to move without them, Charles Pinckney paused and said something to CC. CC reply'd and his voice reverberated throughout chambre.

"Dawdle not," CC said, "I would repair to City Tavern with all possible Expedition."

The ferret-faced Charles Pinckney returned to his table, moving upstream against the North Deputies who were in the midst of vacation. Pinckney's low stature was accentuate when in motion, making him seem almost a child among adults. His eyes was dark calculate, pupil and iris nigh the same Colour, saucers of Cunning and Hauteur which suggested a bottomless Vanity.

Pinckney seemed to think he had left some Thing at his table, but upon searching, found nought. He shrugged, returned to the aisle, seem'd ready to pass the Bar, but then saw Jemmy alone and approached him.

"Are you not abundant convinced," Pinckney said to Jemmy, "that the theoretical Nonsense of an election of the members of Congress by the people is clearly and practically wrong?"

Jemmy's smile was nigh a Wince.

He shrugged.

"Are you not full convinced," Pinckney said, "that the Senate ought at least to be double their number to make them of consequence? To prevent their falling into the same insignificance that the state Senates have merely from their smallness?"

"I foredain the opposite effect," Jemmy said.

Franklin could not help but chuckle. Jemmy was of a low stature, and thus perhaps prone to favour the gravity of smallness. Pinckney was one of the few Deputies of as low a stature as Jemmy. Two dwarfs debating the virtue of smallness.

"Yet is it not fulsome manifest," Pinckney said, "that th—"

"Please do not think me impolitick," Jemmy said, "but I have no time for Debate. I must tend my Notes."

Pinckney frowned, but curtsied.

Franklin wonderd if Pinckney had but contrived to have forgotten some Thing, as pretence to invest Jemmy and others.

Rufus King was passing, reminding Franklin of a paunch-ed Julius Cæsar as always, and Pinckney latched to him, walking in stride. Pinckney had to take more Strides than King to pace him.

"I always preferred the election of the Executive by the Legislature to that of the people," Pinckney said. "I will now venture to pronounce that the mode which you and Mister Madison and some others so thorough contended for and ultimately carried is the greatest Blot in the constitution."

"Venture to pronounce later," King said. "To some other ear."

"In surety, sir," Pinckney said, "you would not dispute but that the Congre—"

"A wood Pecker proturbating the Drum of my ear," King said, "would be less a Torment than your imbecilic ejaculations."

Franklin chuckled and saw Jemmy do similar. The legendary Massachusetts tact. Plied to useful ends for once. Franklin thought of John Adams in France, nigh unwinding years of Diplomacy in minutes with similar curtness, and his chuckle diminished appreciable.

King passed the Bar, strode faster, pulled away from Charles Pinckney, and cocked his hat to CC as he went without doors. Charles Pinckney rejoined CC and they went without doors together.

Franklin glanced about chambre. Not a single south Deputy remained, save Jemmy. Jemmy's back was turn'd to them, seated, and he seemed engrossed in his Notes, oblivious of all else. A troop of light Horse might trot by and scarce disturb him. Jemmy's plantation Montpelier comprehended thousands of acres and he employed nigh a hundred Slaves, but Franklin knew Jemmy would nonetheless have the Constitution ratified.

"You ought not threaten south Deputies with regulation of Commerce," Franklin whispered to Governeur, "lest you plantation seeds of Discord that sprout high as turkie wheat."

Turkie wheat was maize.

"Aye, Good Doctor," Governeur said.

"We all know your Agitations against Slavers fountain from a reverence of Natural Rights," Franklin said, "but this Constitution of Government shall be murderous enough to ratify without you making every Planter of the south petrify'd for the Security of they Slaves."

"Indeed," Jemmy whispered.

Governeur seemed half cherub half rooster. He nodded solemn, as if a scolded child.

"Be cool," Franklin whispered. "A veritable cool Devil. Never suffer Slavers to make you Warm nor govern you by yoking your Passions."

Governeur curtsied deep to Franklin, with flourish and grace that was impressive, given his peg Leg.

"Upon my sacred Honor, Doctor," Governeur said, "I shan't agitate Slavers again until the Constitution of Government ratify'd."

Standing behind Governeur, Robert Morris smirked a bit. Governeur was nigh certain sincere in his Oath, but all who knew him marvelled at his absence of self Government. Governeur remained turbulent in his Passions and they exercised the vilest Despotism over him.

"A thousand undressings of Slavers shan't alter they Disposition," Ingersoll said, "for 'tis bottom'd on Interest. I cannot honest pretend that was the whole of my Wealth wrought by Slaving, which was thought the natural Order since man first civilized, and was scarce execrated until but recent, I would be zealous for Manumission."

Gentleman nodded approbation. 'Twas easy to see why Ingersoll the finest tryal Lawyer in Philadelphia and possibly America. To him, all men was Jurors, and he was perspicacious in assaying what swayed them.

"I apprehend," Ingersoll said, "that Slavery shall be exploded in Americay by the Sword only."

"Yet the Sword must always be the dernier Resort," Franklin said. "We have greater chance of exploding Slavery marry'd with Slavers in a single Government, over which we exercize some Dominion, than having them a nation Foreign, unify'd in defence of Slavery, over which we exercize Dominion not."

"Aye," Ingersoll whispered. "The time to invest Slavery is after the Constitution ratify'd and the south States lured into the folde."

Franklin whispered prodigious soft.

"If the Sword it must be," he said, "Providence hath smiled. Wars are won in the Supply as much as the Fighting. We ought count ourselves fortunate the South hath not the Brainpan to erect modern Manufactures, not even of Arms."

The last vestiges of Warmth seemed to ebb out of Governeur, like a hearth at twilight.

"I would dissipate upon Slavery no more," Franklin said. "This day ought be a Celebratory."

"Here here," Ingersoll said.

"If His Excellency not exalted by your supper," Franklin said to Robert Morris, "shall you serve up your Life in the manner of Vatel?"

Hamilton smirked immediate, but then seemed to bite the inside of his cheeks and govern his smile. Ingersoll was incapable of mustering Hamilton's self Government, and chuckled a bit. Only Governeur had Brass enough to laugh outright.

"Many backbiters demean my Culinary," Robert Morris said. "Even my bosom friends. I credit you for saying within doors before my Face what others say without to my Arse."

Morris glanced at the smirks gentlemen wore.

"I shall never beg Pardon for partaking life's fineries," he said, "which I have rightful earn-ed. Nor is my motive vainity nor luxurie as Backbiters suppose. His Excellency is the only man in whose Presence I feel any Awe. I thus spare no dispence in bringing him what Comforts within my Powers."

Gentlemen nodded approving.

"All that remains to us," Governeur said, "is to manumit Doctor Franklin."

The Little Lion pass'd by, cool as always, fleet and Trim, movements quick and graceful. Robert Morris was at his side, chins a-jiggling, prattling on about iced Creams parloured upon a Balloon he would own in futurity. Ingersoll strode with Governeur Morris, and both men curtsied at the neck to Franklin. He curtsied back, at the neck.

Soon only Roger Sherman, Jemmy, and Franklin remain'd. As always, Sherman was the reverse of Grace. There was not a more striking contrast to beautiful action than the motions of his hands. Franklin could never discern precise why, but much blame lay with the slender forearms, as of a Sex, the bony wrists, and the digits uncommon long and slender, inches longer than common, and so bony they seem'd as if absent Flesh and of an Apparition.

Sherman glanced around the chambre, savouring it one final time. He conveyed contentment, yet even in repose his face seem'd severe, in large measure because of the deep frown

Fissures at the edges of his mouth, though the cavernous eyes with darkened bags could not be absolved.

"I may never stand withinst this chambre again," Sherman said.

"I shall alas stand withinst the morrow," Franklin said.

At such time the Pennsylvania Assembly would reclaim its Quarters. Being President of the Executive Council and head of the State Deputation to the Fœderal Convention, Franklin had to report to the Assembly on the Convention and Constitution of Government.

"Shall you stand for Office?" Franklin said.

"I shall serve if call'd," Sherman said.

"You'll be electored to the fœderal House or Senate by Connecticut nigh certain," Franklin said. "Whether you stand or nay."

"Perchance," Sherman said.

Silence for nigh a minute.

"Many a Deputy may stand withinst this chambre again," Franklin said, "if Philadelphiay chozen Capital."

"Interim Capital perhaps," Sherman said. "Tho' I still scruple to think I shall stand withinst again."

Sherman smiled at Franklin, but it so disattractive a smile—nigh a Snarl—that Franklin felt revulsion. He exercised self Government and enforced an indifferent expression.

Sherman offered to help Franklin to his Sedan, but Franklin refused and glanced at Jemmy. Ever wise and gracious, Sherman discerned, curtsy'd, and absented. Seeing him shamble towards the door, and pass without it, Franklin saw twinges of the loose, shackling Air of Thomas, though none of Thomas' grace nor the Exuberance he typickal conveyed.

Jemmy scurry'd down the aisle, carrying his notes like a fragile Treasure. His step was quick and bouncing, and imparted the sense that he as energetic as the government he champion'd.

At closer vantage, Jemmy was not what he appeared from a far nor a rear. His stilish suit was blue and buff, with ruffles a breast and sleeve. Jemmy carryed some muscle upon his frame and wore the suit well. His complexion was ruddy, as Thomas', absent the pale Pallor of a Scholar cooped constant. Though no Quixote, Jemmy cut a respectable Figure.

Jemmy paused before Franklin, peered at him with kind yet severe blue eyes. With Charles Pinckney, Franklin felt he was seeing a tiny dwarf-ed adult, but Jemmy seemed a child that had age-ed premature. A nervous child who had perhaps knucled the sugar Chest or pilfer'd sweetmeats.

"Pleased with your Archive?" Franklin said.

"My researches into the History of the most distinguished Confederacies you well know," Jemmy said, "Particularly those of antiquity. I found deficiency in record of the process, the principles, the reasons, and the anticipations which prevailed in the formation of most Confederacies."

Jemmy had explained this rationale for his Notes to Franklin numerate times over the last third a year, using nigh the exact same words in each instance. Franklin had long since renounced attempts at correcting Jemmy when redundant. Jemmy's didacticism stemmed not from Hauteur nor Stupidity, as with most men who behaved so, but rather from his exorbitant fastidiousness.

"This determined me to preserve as far as I could," Jemmy said, "an exact account of what passed in the Convention whilst executing its Trust."

Jemmy had a soft Voice, like Thomas. Even a few feet away, he was uneasy to hear.

"Posterity deserves an authentic exhibition," Jemmy said, "of the objects, the opinions, and the reasonings from which the new System of Government received its peculiar structure and organization. I hope I have renderd a valued contribution to the fund of materials for the History of the Constitution. For on this Constitution will be staked the happiness of a young people great even now in its infancy, and possibly the cause of Liberty throught the world."

Even spoken a seventh or eighth instance, it remained a sobering thought. Franklin let it hang in the air a moment, like a Balloon.

"I commend your diligence, Mister Madison," Franklin said. "I don't believe you absented a day of the Convention."

"I absented no more than a casual fraction of an hour in any day," Jemmy said.

Even this did not do Jemmy's labour justice. When the Convention recessed July 3 and July 4 that Deputies might partake Celebrations of the anniversary of Independency, Jemmy forsook leisure and laboured on his Notes. When the Convention stood in recess for ten days at the end of July and beginning of August, that the Committee of Detail might render the first draught of the Constitution, other Deputies not on the Committee fish'd, or respited, or flew home to their families. Jemmy laboured on his Notes—and doubtless brooded much, as seemed his habit.

Jemmy might well be the only Deputy who had labour'd every day without exception since the Convention convoked.

Franklin wondered what Jemmy even did for leisure. Since he had never seen Jemmy engage in leisure, save for taking the Exercise many an afternoon, he had no inkling. Franklin had met Jemmy upon occasion prior to the Convention, but the Encounters were cursory, and they had not served in the Congress concurrent, as was the case of Jemmy and other Pennsylvania Deputies. The Convention was Franklin's first protracted society with Jemmy, though his reputation for Nicety and Earnesty preceded him. Thomas also sung Jemmy's praises as he did few others. Franklin wondered if greater familiarity would reveal Jemmy in repose. Or was he constitutional incapable of respiting or partaking of Enjoyment?

"You have fathered the Constitution of Government," Franklin said, "as sure as any man."

Jemmy shook his head curt and emphatick.

"Nay," he said. "The Constitution of Government too remote from my core Principles to be reckon'd my childe. Nor I its Father."

"Might we not at the least say you've sired a Bastard?"

Jemmy's sigh was more of a Groan.

Franklin could not help but laugh, and rather ferocious at that.

"The Notes are a Drudgery," Jemmy said. "The labour has nigh kill'd me."

"They that draw the Quill, Perish by the Quill."

Jemmy frowned.

"Must you always lampoon, Doctor Franklin?"

"Ever you lampoon, Mister Madison?"

"Not Liberty."

"What then?"

"Nor a moment such as this."

"When then?"

Jemmy's frown grew more severe.

Franklin laughed.

"Your betrothment to your scholarship is unrivaled, Mister Madison. And that is no lampoon."

"If posterity offers Huzza, that is gratitude sufficient."

"'Twill be tempting," Franklin said, "to alter your Record in coming years. As transpiring history makes pronouncements here seem foolish."

"I shall endeavor to resist such temptation."

"You are accustomed not to looking foolish," Franklin said.

"Is anyone?"

"Me."

Jemmy chuckled.

"Few are as wise as you, Good Doctor. Or as humble."

"An Oath to endeavor," Franklin said, "is not an Oath to alter not."

Jemmy smiled. His eyes twinkled. The frostbite scar on his nose seemed to glisten. And it occurred to Franklin that even children could be cunning.

"Should you succumb Temptation and attempt to paint us wiser than we are," Franklin said, "history may be perverted irreparable."

Jemmy bristled.

"Few revere History more than I," he said. "And I trust you will feed enough of your convention Speeches to the Papers to prevent a total perversion."

Franklin allowed a slight smirk.

"We all value Reputation," he said. "With posterity especially. But I and other Deputies are not in sole possession of the Convention's only Record."

"His Excellency is in possession of the Record."

Franklin pursed his lips.

"Jackson's scribblings are feeble as against your Notes. As you bloody well know. Humour an old man. A friend. Remember this conversation in coming years when vainity strikes."

Jemmy curtsied respectful, a quick partial curtsy appropriate during conversation. He bent forward at the waist fractional, accentuated the effect with a simultaneous crane of his head, paused momentary, and then snapped back to his upright posture like the Bow of a violin.

"When the fœderal Government becomes more energetick than you can conceive," Franklin said, "your Sermons to Convention about designing it more energetick will appear foolish."

"I'll be long inhumed," Jemmy said, "ere the fœderal Government ever becomes so energetick."

"Nay," Franklin said.

Jemmy froze and fixed Franklin with an intense expression. Franklin felt as if he'd just explained Rogering to an incredulous child turned of eight.

"I pray you wrong," Jemmy said.

"I oft am."

Jemmy's expression tighten'd. Franklin's humility seemed to make him more nervous. Perhaps because 'twas the antithesis of Jemmy's arrogance?

"When much of what you espoused in Convention proves wrong," Franklin said, "and much of what you condemn'd in Convention is proven effecious, think of a future scholar at a future American Convention in desperate need of Truth. Resist the Temptation to enhance the appearance of your Prescience."

Jemmy looked more serious than typical. And right troubled. Had he truly been so arrogant as to fancy his Views infallible?

"My original query," Franklin said. "Are you happy with your Record?"

"To not leave such a Record would be unconscionable Malfeasance."

"But are you pleased with it?"

"I am pleased I have left it. Or shall leave it. Upon my passing."

Franklin pursed his lips.

"You can be most vexing, Mister Madison."

"'Twas not my intention."

"I rather think it was."

Jemmy chuckled.

"How fares Mister Jefferson?" Franklin said.

"Mistress Cosway would not consent to residency at Monticello."

This was antiquate news from the year prior, which friends in France had already reported. The death of Thomas' wife five years prior had nigh destroyed him. In agreeing to succeed Franklin as Minister Plenipotentiary to France, Thomas hoped in part to escape the tormenting Memories resident at Monticello.

Thomas had at least sighted high. Maria Cosway was one of the handsomest Sexes on the whole of the Continent. Princes pursued her. Her husband was a Dandy who resemblet a monkey, and he was indiscrim'nant in his Infidelities. Cosway loved him not at all, but was in need of his Purse, and his Prestige to fill her parlour.

"Mistress Cosway fancies Europe," Franklin said. "And the lavishes of a Multitude of Suitors. She would hang herself in a fortnight in the Confines of Monticello."

Jemmy chuckled ever so slight, but then his expression became grave.

"I entertain doubt," he said, "that Mister Jefferson will ever make Love again."

"I have long sensed such," Franklin said.

"To have a Friend who so illuminates the world find so sparse his Joy," Jemmy said.

"Take Hope," Franklin said. "Love can stryke when least the expectation. As the Lightning."

Jemmy seemed unconvinced.

"My fondest Wish," he said, "is that Mister Jefferson find domestic Felicity once last."

"My fondest Wish," Franklin said, "is that you find it once first."

Jemmy sighed deep.

"Must you always lampoon, Doctor?"

Franklin laughed.

"'Tis no Lampoon."

"Mister Jefferson," Jemmy said, "would have Americay apply a Loan in Holland to the discharge of the pay due the foreign Officers."

"The last Loan which Mister Adams negotiate?"

"Nay," Jemmy said. "The balance of that will be wanted for the Interest due in Holland."

Franklin pursed his lips.

"I fear all the income here will not save our Credit in Europe from further wounds," Jemmy said. "I doubt the present Government can be kept alive through the ensuing year or until the new one may take its place."

"The countenance of matters is rarely as dour as you perceive," Franklin said. "The Constitution's compleation and complexion will induce one last bout of Credit from Europe. Insurance against losses on previous Loans, if nay else."

"You know the tenour of Europe better than I," Jemmy said. "I pray you correct. But the last Loan in Holland, and that alone, saved the United States from Bankruptcy in Europe."

"Aye know."

"That loan was obtained from a belief that a Constitution would be certainly, speedily, quietly, and finally established. And by that means put America into a permanent capacity to discharge with Honor and Punctuality all her engagements."

"Aye know," Franklin said. "Though not so expeditious a mean as the Financiers of the Continent might hope, the end is none the less approached."

"His Excellency condescending the Presidency," Jemmy said, "would quiet Concerns from this Quarter."

"From every Quarter," Franklin said.

"If His Excellency should refuse to condescend …"

Jemmy mightn't have been graver was the Grym Reaper about to scythe him.

"Ruin despite all else," he said.

"Then perhaps The People ought campaign him to condescend," Franklin said.

"Will he condescend?" Jemmy said.

"You inform me?"

Jemmy chuckled.

"You shall mail Mister Jefferson his Notes on the Convention?" Franklin said.

Jemmy pursed his lips.

"Must you always lampoon?"

"I had thought your Notes for Mister Jefferson," Franklin said. "Posterity being ancillary."

"I shan't indignify with Retort," Jemmy said. "Mister Jefferson is curious, to be sure, and I have sworn to post to the Packet immediate once the Secrecy lifted. I intended for the August Packet, but the Convention again proved incapable of expedition. I pray Commodore Jones still in port."

Commodore Jones was John Paul Jones. Though the Secrecy lifted, correspondence among senior leaders was not for the common packet, which was oft spied. Commodore Jones could be trusted to secure Mail, deliver it unmolested, or destroy it other wise.

Even then, Jemmy would certain not mail his original Notes, but rather a draught summation of them only. His original Draught was at present the only Copy, and 'twould take Jemmy or some other scribes days or weeks to copy the Notes compleat.

'Twas doubtful Jemmy would entrust the Notes to any Copier, save perhaps Thomas himself, and probably not even Thomas.

Jemmy would copy his Notes himself, nigh certain. Franklin could not quell the image of Jemmy making amendations as he copyed, revising History as he went. Not out of Malice, yet with malicious Effect nonetheless. If Jemmy had not time to copy his Notes for some years, which was probable as he would nigh certain be listed to champion Ratification and enter that Fray, an imperfect memory might augment amendations and Distortions. Imperfect memory as well as Vanity.

Jemmy removed his cocked hat and scratched at the top of his head. Franklin half expected a squeaking sound. Jemmy was balding right rapid, and habitual in combing the thinning hairs that had not yet evacuated straight downward and frontward. The effect was decided infashionable at best, and at worst proper oppugnant or comick, usual tending to the latter because Jemmy's low stature made the crown of his head visible. All vestiges of Stile and Handsomeness imparted by Jemmy's suit, eyes, and well-knit Figure were destroyed by his hair.

Most men afflicted such resorted to the wig, but Jemmy did not. 'Twas said he look'd ridiculous in a wig, owing his small stature. A wife would see a man without his wig in any event—before she betrothed.

Jemmy replaced his hat.

"What have we wrought at last?" he said. "I cannot help but ponder."

Franklin shrugged.

"Time shall render its Verdict," he said. "When it sees fit."

"I hazard an opinion," Jemmy said, "that the plan should it be adopted will neither effectually answer its national object nor prevent the local Mischiefs which every where excite Disgusts against the state governments."

Franklin shrugged. He had wonder'd what stretch it would be before Jemmy harped on the absence of a fœderal Negative upon state Laws, as well as the absence of a Council of Revision.

"The future increase of population if the Union should be permanent," Jemmy said, "will render the number of Representatives excessive."

"On this we concur," Franklin said. "Though not in the Senate."

"Whatever Reason might have existed for the equality of suffrage when the Union was a fœderal one among sovereign States," Jemmy said, "it must cease when a national Government should be put into the place."

"On this we also concur," Franklin said.

"Uniformity of state Suffrage alas ceases not," Jemmy said. "Shan't expire with the Articles of Confederacy as proper."

"Nothing must," Franklin said, "unless it would."

"Would you truly have a Senate not?" Jemmy said.

"Truly," Franklin said.

"The Senate," Jemmy said, "is the great Anchor of the Government."

"Anchors sink ships as well as steady them," Franklin said. "And no other anchor requisite when government bottomed upon The People."

Jemmy shook his head.

"I would have a Senate," he said.

"You have one," Franklin said. "Let us see how you fancy it."

"I can never fancy a Senate in the present Form. Its Representation ought be apportioned to Population, not uniformed."

"Not to be," Franklin said. "Had you choice betweenst a uniformed Senate or no Senate, what preference ye?"

Jemmy shook his head and expelt.

"Right unfortunate," he said, "that the little States made an equality in the Senate a sine qua non."

Sine qua non was Latin, which translated literal, meant without which not. A sine qua non was an absolute essential aspect of a thing.

"Not unfortunate to them," Franklin said.

"A constitutional Negative on the laws of the States seems necessary," Jemmy said, "to secure individuals against encroachments on their Rights."

Franklin laughed.

Jemmy's mouthline remaint as flat as the horizon.

Franklin laughed harder.

"'Tis nigh impossible to intercourse you," Franklin said, "absent your Refrain for a fœderal Negative upon state Laws and a Council of Revision."

"I reprize the measures," Jemmy said, "for that they are indispensible to good Government. A fœderal Negative upon the laws of States most especially."

"Nay," Franklin said. "You err and have transupposed."

"Nay," Jemmy said. "The mutability of the laws of the States is found to be a serious Evil. The injustice of them has been so frequent and so flagrant as to alarm the most stedfast friends of Republicanism."

"Not in Pennsylvaniay," Franklin said.

"In Pennsylvaniay especially," Jemmy said.

"Nay," Franklin said. "Regardless, your Remedy to the mutability of state Laws is fœderal Laws that may prove nigh immutable?"

"Not immutable," Jemmy said. "The People are at Liberty to effect Reform as they pleasure."

"Unless Tyranny be anchored."

"I am persuaded I do not err in pronouncing," Jemmy said, "that the Evils issuing from State sources contributed more to that uneasiness which produced the Convention than those which accrued to our national character. Evils issuing from state sources have prepared the public Mind for a general Reform, moreso than inadequacy of the Confederation to its immediate objects."

"Encroachments of the Rights of The People may emanate from the fœderal Government," Franklin said. "A negative upon the Laws of the States may enforce Tyranny rather than rampart it as you would supposit."

"You tend to the Radickal in your politicks," Jemmy said. "Such tendency encreasing as you age."

"You tend to the Naïve," Franklin said. "If trusting Government to The People be radickal, I plea guilty."

"You intrust The People too much."

"You intrust them insufficient."

"It remains to be enquired," Jemmy said, "whether a Majority having any common Interest or feeling any common Passion will find sufficient motives to restrain them from oppressing the Minority. If two individ—"

In the northeast corner of the chambre, Major Jackson and Thomas Fitzsimmons descended from above stairs and exited the door to the stairwell. They had compleated their transmission of the Constitution of Government to the Pennsylvania Assembly. Major Jackson carry'd the executed Constitution of Government, which was rolled and lashed about centre.

The moment Jemmy heard the clacking of Jackon and Fitzsimmons' shoes upon floor, he silented. Jackson and Fitzsimmons spoke not to each other, nor Jemmy, but rather made strait for the west door, probably more out of a desire to expedite to City Tavern than to grant Jemmy privy. They passed the Bar, giving Franklin but the most perfunctory curtsies of the head, and then went without doors.

"If two individuals are under the biass of interest or Enmity against a third," Jemmy said, "the rights of the latter could never be safely referred to the majority of the three. Will two Thousand individuals be less apt to oppress one Thousand, or two hundred Thousand less apt to oppress one hundred Thousand?"

"The problem of history," Franklin said. "is of the one Thousand oppressing the Millions."

"I am not insensible to this penchant," Jemmy said. "The great desideratum in Government is so to modify the Sovereignty as that it may be sufficient neutral between different parts of the Society to controul one part from invading the Rights of another, and at the same time sufficiently controuled itself from setting up an interest adverse to that of the entire Society."

"I apprehend," Franklin said, "that you may find the fœderal Government ample adverse without granting it a Negative upon the Laws of the States."

"There's less danger of Encroachment from the General Government than from the State Governments," Jemmy said.

"Nay," Franklin said.

"The mischief from Encroachments will be less fatal if made by the General Government," Jemmy said, "than if made by the State Governments."

"Nay," Franklin said.

"All the examples of other Confederacies," Jemmy said, "prove the greater tendency in such systems to Anarchy than to tyranny. To a disobedience of the members than to usurpations of the fœderal head."

"Even was the Historys definite," Franklin said, "such sha'n't be the tendency of Americay."

Jemmy froze. Fear dilated his eyes. He peered at Franklin with prodigious intensity for a stretch. Fear eventually draint from his eyes.

"I too look to the Historiums for guidance," Franklin said. "But I would not have their Examples constitute a straitjacket."

"Guards are more necessary against encroachments of the State Governments on the General Government," Jemmy said, "than of the latter on the former."

"Nay," Franklin said.

"Shall you utter a syllable besides Nay?" Jemmy said.

"Nay," Franklin said.

Jemmy's expression became even more vexed and serious.

"Without a General Government negative upon State Laws," he said, "a check in the whole over the parts, our system involves the evil of Imperia in Imperio."

Imperia in Imperio was Latin, which literal translated, meant powers within power. In this case, state government Powers nested within fœderal government Power.

"Fœderal and state Powers co-equal" Franklin said, "perhaps not the Chimæra you reckon."

"In most Confederacies of history, one such Power supreme. They ought not be blended, and certain not made a Peer."

"By your reckon. State and fœderal Power might co-exist, co-equal, a dual Sovereignty, without ruin."

Jemmy shook his head.

"We constructed them co-equal not of a Design, but pandering to political Interest."

"Accord from states disassembled, from the Parts," Franklin said, "not so easy as you suppose."

"Disaccord is my fear."

"Not mine," Franklin said.

"Your betrothment to The Democracy," Jemmy said, "colours all views."

"Betrothment to The People," Franklin said. "But Aye."

"Experience in all the States has evinced a powerful tendency in the Legislature to absorb all Power into its Vortex," Jemmy said.

"Not in Pennsylvaniay."

"Also in Pennsylvaniay."

"Nay," Franklin said.

"Aye," Jemmy said. "The Vortex of the Legislature is the real source of danger to the American Constitutions, and the General Government. It necessitates giving every defensive Authority to the other departments that is consistent with republican Principles."

"Nay," Franklin said. "Nay, nay, nay, nay."

"The Executive and a convenient number of the National Judiciary," Jemmy said, "ought to compose a Council of Revision with authority to examine every act of the National Legislature before it shall operate. Dissent of the said Council should amount to a rejection un—"

"Mister Madison, Sir," Franklin said. "Please pardon my intercession. I esteem you prodigious. But I would not retrod the entirety of the Convention at its adjournment."

"Apologies, Good Doctor," Jemmy said, "for playing the Pinckney."

"Theorizing a government 'tis one matter," Franklin said, "implementing it efficacious quite another. I being the Elder, please grant me the final word, if of no other cause than to humour my Vainity."

Jemmy curtsied, but his eyes rebeled.

"I tended towards the Naïve when less season'd," Franklin said. "As you. And tended to think myself wiser than all others. As you. Such is the provenance of youth. I pray you be wary in innovating our national Government energetick. For I apprehend that in short interim you may find it more Consolidated and Energetick than you might prefer."

Jemmy's eyes animated, and agitated, yet he kept silent.

Franklin again wondered at the defects of the Constitution of Government. Jemmy had been emphatick the Executive should be electored by Congress for much of the Convention, and then altered his thinking abrupt in middling July. The 17th had it been? How many other structures of government which Jemmy advocated so staunch and zealous, with such profusity, might be Errata? In a year or decade or score, would Jemmy reverse course on national Supremacy, admitting himself in Erratum? 'Twas damn worrisome to have someone who had asserted such a decisive Influence on the Convention find their Judgement so wanting. Yet in fairness, much of what Jemmy advocated had been perspicacious and wise.

"Ratification must now command our attention," Franklin said. "What hear you fromst Virginiay and other quarters?"

"Reports and Conjectures abound concerning the nature of the Plan," Jemmy said. "The public however is certainly in the dark with regard to it. We are, alas, equal in the dark as to the reception which may be given to it on its Publication."

"Have you snift The People's inkling?" Franklin said.

"All the prepossessions are on the right side," Jemmy said, "but it may well be expected that certain characters will wage War against any reform whatever."

Franklin could not but help think of Samuel Adams. And Patrick Henry. The Violent Men. The tearers down. There would be many.

"My own idea," Jemmy said, "is that the public mind will now or in a very little time receive any Thing that promises stability to the public Councils and security to private Rights. No regard ought to be had to local Prejudices or temporary Considerations."

"I am not enquiring what ought be," Franklin said, "but what is at current and shall be."

Jemmy shrugged.

"If the present moment be lost," he said, "it is hard to say what may be our Fate."

"And the Old Dominion?" Franklin said.

"Information from Virginiay is far from being agreeable," Jemmy said. "In many parts of the Country the drouth has been extremely injurious to the Corn. I fear, tho' I have no certain information, that Orange and Albemarle share in the distress."

Most Americans was Yeomen, farmers tilling they own land. In the South especially. A drouth that killt crops, or even stunted them, signify'd Impoverishment widespread.

"The People of the Old Dominion also are said to be generally discontented," Jemmy said. "A paper Emission is again a topic among them. So is an instalment of all debts in some places and the making property a Tender in others."

This state of affairs did not suprize Franklin. Such problems were present in most States. There was insufficient quantity of the circulating Medium, insufficient quantity of Money in existence, to conduct all Commerce. The solutions generally advocate were an emission of paper Money to increase the quantity of circulating Medium to a level sufficient to conduct all commerce; the instalment of Debts, their deferment into payments at later intervals; and allowing property to function as a Tender, a means of payment or money, even if specie payment specify'd in a contract.

While Franklin tended to favour Emissions in such Cases, he also felt disease at the government interceding in private Contracts negotiate freely, altering the mode of payment ex post facto. 'Twas a dangerous precedent.

"The drouth aggravates such Convulsions," Franklin said, "nigh certain. Like pissing in a wasp's nest."

"Aye," Jemmy said.

"Virginiay might secure a paper Emission," Franklin said, "with backing of Land."

"Effected at present," Jemmy said, "by a mode indirect."

"'Tis better effected," Franklin said, "by a mode direct."

"Perhaps," Jemmy said. "Your printing of Emissions and your enquiries into paper Currency have made you profund in the arcane Craft. I shan't disputate on a subject you evidence such Faculty. Nor lay claim that the Old Dominion's policy optimate. I have no more Power to command the Virginiay Assembly to prudential measures than the Convention. 'Tisn't the time to dissipate upon paper Money."

"Or negativing State Laws or Councils of Revisions."

Jemmy frowned morose.

"The Taxes are another source of discontent," he said. "The weight of them is complained of and the abuses in collecting them still more so. In several Counties the prisons and Court Houses and Clerks offices have been willfully burnt. In Green Briar the course of Justice has been mutinously stopped, and associations entered into against the payment of Taxes."

Franklin was insurprized. Such Spectacles had been repeated throughout America. States had levied higher Taxes to try and honour The War Debt, and to fund the expences of Government which the crown had bourne previous. Had commerce not been crippled, and drouths not marauded, such Taxes might have been much less onerous, though perhaps still not countenanced.

"Are you alarmed not?" Jemmy said.

"Nay," Franklin said.

"How can you be alarmed not?"

 Franklin shrugged.

"Stones a'n't to be bled," he said. "What expect you of The People when chusing betweenst Taxes and Squalor?"

"'Tis not the choice."

"For multitudes of Yeomans and Aprons, 'tis express the Choice. Would you have their familys starve that Taxes paid or a Loan honoured?"

"Would you have Creditors defrauded as a System? Government dissolve-ed for want of Funding?"

"Nay," Franklin said. "Nor did I misapprehend such would result. I am not given to Gloom and apprehend not a general Anarchy."

"No other County has yet followed the example of Green Briar," Jemmy said. "The approaching meeting of the Assembly will probably allay the discontents on one side by measures which will excite them on another."

Franklin chuckled. 'Twas easy to under estimate Jemmy. He was tiny, quiet, inassuming, easy to pass over, yet exceeding formidable in his way. Patrick Henry, Mason, Lighthorse Harry, and other Virginia opponents of a national Government might in concert not overcome the Sprite standing before Franklin. Especially not at a ratification Convention where Chancellor Wythe possess'd the loyalty of the jurists and judges, and General Washington the military officers.

"You intend to New York then?" Franklin said.

"Nay," Jemmy said. "I intend not."

"Intend where then?"

"I may bide in Philadelphiay for some days," Jemmy said. "Put the period to my Notes whilst the proceedings remain affix'd in my mind. Then intend to Montpelier and copy them in Splendour and Comfourt, absent Mobs, crime, poverty, shamblings, disease, putrid malaria that would make a Hog vomit."

Franklin chuckled.

"You sound as Thomas when slandering Cities. And what of the Constitution?"

"When the plan comes before Congress for their sanction," Jemmy said, "a very serious effort may be made to embarrass it."

"Yet you would sequester editing your Notes rather than shepherd the Plan?"

"My presence in the Congress of consequency not," Jemmy said.

"Nay," Franklin said.

"Nay?" Jemmy said.

"Would you say your presence in Convention of consequency not?"

"When I see how little the plan reflects my Principles and Phylosophies, aye."

Franklin pursed his lips and peered at Jemmy stern.

"Act not the Brat nor pout as a Sex," Franklin said, "painting the failure to gratify your every Fancy as the gratification of nothing. I counsel intending to Congress to prevent Mischief on the part of Opponents."

Jemmy sighed long and deep.

"I would rather perfect the Draught of my Notes," he said.

"I preferenced Experiments," Franklin said, "to intending to France as Minister Plenipotentiary."

"I shall consider your counsel," Jemmy said.

"A promise to consider," Franklin said, "is not a promise to intend."

"I proffer no such oath," Jemmy said.

"Virginiay shall also require your Stature," Franklin said, "after the Congress transmits the Constitution to the several States for ratification. Ironical that the state of Washington and Wythe may be the most contested ground of Battle."

Jemmy nodded severe.

"Mister Mason being now under the Necessity of justifying his refusal to sign," Jemmy said, "he will of course muster every possible Objection. His conduct has given great Umbrage to the County of Fairfax, and particularly to the Town of Alexandria."

"And when ratification secured?" Franklin said. "You stand in need of some Profession, if you would take a Wife."

"I fancy Reading my profession."

"I fancy'd it fretting," Franklin said. "And reading 'tis not a Profession."

Jemmy's face stiffened slight.

"A profession would beget an insufficiency of time for Reading," he said.

"Your readings of every Thing certain included the Law. Might you not pass the Bar?"

Jemmy frowned prodigious.

"I had ponder'd the Senate."

"Your tempermeant" Franklin said, "seems ill suited the politician."

Jemmy bristled.

"I have served a Deputy in Virginiay's lower House," he said, "a Burgess in its upper House, a Deputy to Virginiay's Convention of Constitution, as Virginiay's Deputy to the Continental Congress, and now a Deputy in Convention."

"The politics of a Nation more barbary," Franklin said. "Right bloody barbary. Perhaps if you continue to strive to the penman, the committee-man, in the mode of Thomas."

"I am discertain what I suit," Jemmy said. "My tempermeant and constitution ill suited to all but Reading. Tho' as you observe, I stand in need of some profession. Politicks seems the least disagreeable."

Franklin laughed long and so hard he aggravated his Stones.

Jemmy's naïveté knew no bounds!

Silence descended.

"Do speak plain, Good Doctor," Jemmy said. "Your tendency to act the Diplomat is most vexsome for those attempting to solicit a direct opinion."

Franklin chuckled.

"I favour Tact," he said.

"Or perhaps evasion."

Franklin chuckled harder.

"I favour Candour with you, Sir," he said. "Not Diplomacy."

"I stand ready to receive your Candour full bore," Jemmy said. "If you please."

Franklin truncated his chuckle. He resisted the urge to laugh at Jemmy's inapt use of a military metaphor. Jemmy, who looked as if a girl turned of eight might dispatch him.

"You are unseason'd for the Senate, would be eclipsed by the litany of elder statesmen in Virginiay, and would find yourself absent office," Franklin said. "By such a over arching of Ambition you would squander your endowments and deny Americay benefit of them. You are suited to the first House."

Jemmy nodded glum.

"Even could you attain to the Senate," Franklin said, "you can effect greater service to Americay in the first House. The first House shall originate bills adding a Declaration of Rights. Bills incorporating the Government and affixing its character. In the Senate you would be but a whelp, in the first House rather an Eminent, having a hand in Legislating in the first instancy upon tariffs, duties, instituting Departments, the Judiciary, census, naturalization, Patents, crimes, copyrights, Indian intercourse, and cetera."

"I had pondered such," Jemmy said. "Mister Adams has oft marvel'd how few of the human Race have ever had the opportunity of chusing a System of Government for theyselves and they children."

Mr. Adams had to be John Adams. Samuel Adams was incapable of such Perspicacity.

"To legislate a government in its entirety from nought," Jemmy said, "one of the republican form especially, would seem an opportunity sim'lir singular."

"Indeed," Franklin said.

"I can but hope," Jemmy said, "that I wield more influence in Congress than Convention, and can craft a government more consonant with my core Principles."

"So you would subvert the Constitution?"

Jemmy frowned.

"I think you liable to Frustration," Franklin said, "but 'tis no shame to sire a second Bastard."

"Then why did you not?"

"Is that a lampoon?"

Jemmy frowned.

"General Washington," Franklin said, "will need an Ally in the first House he can trust compleat."

"Declaration of Rights?" Jemmy said.

"There will be no ratification without an oath of a Declaration of Rights," Franklin said. "Make no errour on this point. The Violent Men will agitate on such Deficiency. Agitate energetick and ceaseless. They can be neutered expedient by a Promise to proffer amendments constituting a Declaration of Rights in Congress the First."

"If a Declaration of Rights the sole Price of ratification," Jemmy said, "the purchase an Œconomy. Tho' I scruple the Violent Men neuter'd as painless or expediential as you fancy."

"I make no claim to omnisciencey," Franklin said. "And Mister Madison?"

"Aye, Doctor Franklin?"

"Treat your electors to Spirits this time."

Jemmy frowned. In 1777, he had sought seat in the Virginia Assembly, the lower House of Delegates, and was thought nigh certain to attain to Office. Jemmy refused to proffer Spirits to voters, however, while his opponent Charles Porter provided copious Lubrication. Voters cast their lot with the candidate that proffer'd the Quenchers, and Jemmy was defeated.

"I am opposed to personal solicitation and the treatment of voters to food and drink," Jemmy said. "I find it inconsistent with the purity of moral and republican Principles."

"Then you are opposed to holding office."

"Opposed to Bribery and Corruption to attain to office."

After his defeat, Jemmy petitioned the Committee of Privileges and Elections of the Virginia Assembly, arguing that Mr. Porter had made use of Bribery and Corruption during the election, and that it ought be set aside. The Virginia Assembly rejected the Plea, though Jemmy had been elected to the House of Delegates in 1783, without resorting to spiritous Liquors.

It took prodigious effort not to laugh at Jemmy's Naïveté. Franklin knew the Defeat smarted his young friend, so maintain'd his expression indifferent.

"If you would be a politician," Franklin said, "you must be pragmatic. 'Tis a tiny Ill to effect an excessive Good. Even Washington proffered spirits when he stood for Burgess. Think you he dishonest? Stooping to Bribery and Corruption to attain to office?"

"Invoking His Excellency's character doesn't render your Malconformation consonant," Jemmy said. "'Tis the Principle. Small Evils beget mighty great Evils."

"'Tis a long walk or ride to Vote. Proffer a few quenchers."

"A few quenchers?" Jemmy said. "Mister Porter proffered beyond a half gallon of Spirits per man. They were so pissed they might have electored king George without inkling."

"The custom is long entrenched," Franklin said. "Fancy you the one to reform it?"

"You paint me the Fool," Jemmy said, "for belief Revolutions can be effected?"

"Not wherest Spirits concern'd. I learnt this as a Water American."

Sadness crept into Jemmy's eyes.

"I was anxious to promote the moral mode, and reform," he said. "By way of my example."

"You was rendered the example," Franklin said.

Jemmy exhalt deep and nodded.

"I trusted to the new Views of the subject," he said, "which I hoped would prevail with The People. Alas my Abstinence was mis-represented as the effect of pride or parsimony."

Franklin laughed.

"Providence forbid," he said, "that a servant of The People evidence Parsimony."

"I can but hope that my Competition for the fœderal House," Jemmy said, "will not have been tavern keepers as was Mister Porter."

Franklin chuckled.

"Rum luck that," he said. "Mister Porter knew his business, right certain."

"I shall give thought," Jemmy said, "to proffering Spirits. Tho' I remain disinclined to the Corruption, I am proper thankful for your Counsel."

"We help people," Franklin said, "when we can."

"Any final words of Wisdom, Good Doctor?"

"Find thyself a Wife," Franklin said. "Let her lampoon you, and laugh."

"Belles are sparse in the South."

Franklin thought belles sparse wheresoever Jemmy happened to be.

"Visit the North," Franklin said. "Or the City. Tho' even in the city, Wives fall not from bookshelves."

Jemmy laughed.

"If only they did."

"You would have a Harem."

Jemmy laughed harder.

"Had you but consummated Mistress Floyd," Franklin whispered.

Jemmy stiffened and glanced about chambre, nervous that bystanders might have eavesdropp'd.

"No one is present," Franklin whispered, "or I wouldn't dare such utterance. Nor shall I ever ditto such discussion, upon my sacred Honor. But fancy you honest that no one knew of the Dalliance?"

In 1783, whilst serving in the Congress, Jemmy had become smitten by Kitty Floyd, the daughter of Deputy William Floyd, a signer of the Declaration of Independency. Mistress Floyd was with her father at Mary House's, a Philadelphia boarding House, where Jemmy was also resident. Jemmy made love to Mistress Floyd, and they even exchanged miniature portaitures drawn by Peale. She was turned of fifteen, ripe, of marrying and breeding age, vivacious in spirit, and exceeding Handsome. Most men married by their middling twenties at the latest, but Jemmy was so shy that Mistress Floyd was his first Proposal, at age 32. When Mistress Floyd absented Philadelphia to repair to her home in New York, Jemmy rode sixty miles in Coach with her. She rebuffed his letters thereafter, having soon found another

Suitor who she betroth-ed. Jemmy had not seen her since, and was now 36, with nary a Prospect.

"Mistress Floyd," Jemmy said, "was no Dalliance."

"She was no more," Franklin said, "owing your Impotency."

"I made love to Mistress Floyd for months," Jemmy said.

"Therein lay the problem. All verbiage, no Ballocks. Had you evidenced more Confidency, been more decisive, more aggressive, you might be betroth-ed."

The betrothment supposition was probably untrue, but it mattered not. Was Jemmy not more confident and decisive, he would never be betrothed.

"I worry that Confinement at Montpelier disheartens you at times," Franklin said. "Remedy thy Isolation. Hearken to a City."

"A Capital," Jemmy said.

"You are worthy of a fine belle, Mister Madison," Franklin said. "The finest. Do remember that. And remember that with the Sex, fortune favours the Bolde. One cannot make love to the Sex for months when they have other Suitors."

Jemmy nodded with chagrin then shook his head. His expression rendered sundry glum.

"Perhaps another Congress is what you need," Franklin said.

"Perhaps," Jemmy said.

"You must socialize, Mister Madison," Franklin said. "It is exceeding improbable another Belle will manifest at a boarding House."

Jemmy removed his cocked hat momentary, revealing his balding Pate and disattractive Combature. He sighed deep and seemed as if he might sob.

"I do apprehend," Jemmy said, "that I shall always be alone."

Such fear was unfounded not. Jemmy cut not an alluring figure. Short. Balding. Sickly. Nervous. Serious. Shy. He would never make the Sex swoon, to be sure.

Which left but one recourse.

"Look to Widows," Franklin said. "Young Widows, with numerate children, in need of Benefactors."

"Desperate for a husband, you would signify."

"I fear desperate for a husband may be a stark Insufficiency. Destitute for a husband."

Jemmy sighed deep again.

"If Mister Gerry can betrothe one of the handsomest Belles in Americay with his squint and stutter," Franklin said, "you can find one on the whole of the bloody continent who can countenance you."

"With the Sex," Jemmy said, "fortune favors the Fortunate. They wed the Wealth, not the man."

"'Tis no Law of Gravitation."

"'Tis the Law of Attraction. Of animal Magnetism."

Franklin chuckled and quelled a Lampoon on the Law of Repulsion.

Yet he also felt a certain Puzzlement. With Montpelier, Jemmy ought not want for wealth nor income. Did he lavish in Opulence yet a souse in Debt, as so many Planters? Franklin knew not the peculiars of Jemmy's worth. Yet he could not help but envision Jemmy taking a Wife yet forsaking a profession, passing first owing his fraile Constitution and propensity to fret, and widowing his Lady destitute.

"If a Sex enjoy your society and you bring them Laughter," Franklin said, "much else may be overlooked."

Jemmy but frowned at this.

"Mister Gerry is possess'd of a prodigious Fortune," he said. "I am not and never shall be."

"Fortune can favour other Endowments," Franklin said.

Jemmy chuckled. And then smiled. 'Twas an endearing smile oweing its seeming Innocence.

"If you did that more oft," Franklin said.

Jemmy frowned.

"Did what?" he said.

Franklin sighed.

"You may be hopeless, Mister Madison. I pray I foreshadow not in leaving you alone. You was first to arrive at the Convention, its most diligent Deputy, and I shall grant you the Honor of vacating last."

Franklin sensed this was what Jemmy wanted. He rose, fought the Pain, and curtsied to Jemmy as best he could. Jemmy curtsied in return, a full curtsy of greater grace than Franklin expected. Perhaps Jemmy danced tolerable? This, a shaving of the head, and a-fashioned wig, might aid his snaring a Wife. Assuming he could be wrested from his Study, and forced to call on a barber and attend a Ball.

Glancing at Jemmy once last, Franklin wondered if history would remember the Sprite of a scholar, or even recognize him a first time. Like Thomas, Jemmy preferenced labouring behind curtain, exercising influence, but relegating Huzzas for his ceaseless Toil to Jobbers, Officers, and Coxcombs. Curious to think that in a position of pre-eminence in the Congress, Jemmy might wield more Power than even Washington, or other multitudes of statesmen more seasoned and renown'd, yet history might never know it.

As Thomas liked to say, the Earth belonged to the living. Franklin was soon for the Maggots. Washington would pilot the vessel past the Shoals, but the males in his family had been short lived, and he might not endure long past the new Century. The other Patriots of '76 were ageing and passing, and their Spirit with them.

Though 'twas exceeding difficult, Franklin knew he had to manumit and recuse, trust to Posterity, let it pilot the vessel. Trust to Jemmy and Dayton and Pinckney and Governeur, the Little Lion, Mr. Randolph, Thomas, and cetera.

Franklin glanced at Jemmy twice last and wondered if he and Posterity equal the tasking. Jemmy's diligence and Integrity was above question, yet he seemed grievous Naïve, seemed to suffer that affliction of Posterities of being enamoured of energetic government, and insufficient fearfull of the risk of Tyranny that such government presented.

FIVE

Four burly inmates from the Walnut Street Prison entered the East Room with a burlier guard behind them. They approached Franklin's sedan Chair, which resembled a small, roof-ed coach absent wheels. The sedan was parked in the rear of the East Room, in the large gallery behind the Bar, the area intended for spectators. 'Twas in the northern portion of the gallery, what would be leftward for a person entering chambre and peering at the throne, but 'twas right of Franklin.

The inmates inserted long wooden Bars in hook supports on either side of the sedan, providing four carrying points, two front, two rear. The two inmates on the right removed the right Bar and opened the door which was the sedan's entire front.

"I passed the Bar," the front inmate said.

"On ye way to trial," the rear inmate said.

"To conviction," the front inmate said.

The inmates chuckled, then frowned morose.

The guard helped Franklin approach the sedan. He was bald and barrel chested, with oaks for arms and deform'd knucles that chronicled Brawls, and he wore a barkish hued suit in the mode of Messieurs Fry and Weaver, though of a quality appreciable more middling. The guard dropped Franklin after each step rather than pillowing him down gentle as Washington had.

The sedan exterior was mahogany and stained dark, like a fine piece of furniture. Paintings of nude, æthereal figures fill'd the mahogany below and behind the windows. The paintings felt Græcian and reminded Franklin of the Sistine Chapel.

Franklin had not necessarily been endeared of this motif, and would have preferenced artistry tending more to the Austere, or a sedan absent it, but the sedan had been a sale item, an item available for ready sale. Sale sedans was scarce, owing the fact that most who could afford them had them fashioned to their exact Predilictions, so as to be singular and sport the crackest Stile. At the time, in France, Franklin had needed a Sedan immediate owing the investment of the Gout and Stone, and beggars must not be choosers.

The sedan interior was cloathed velvet cochineal with plush cushions. Franklin entered the sedan and collapsed more than sat, and its wood creaked in Protest as he did so. No need to feign Health for felons as with Deputies. Or for Jemmy.

The inmates wore no shackles and were attired diff'rent, in Dress worn when apprehended, as was customary. Three of the four inmates went trousers rather than breeches, a typicality among the poorer labouring Folk who had scant Hope of ever attaining to a horse.

Franklin's body felt pent and constricted from the rigours of not just the day, but the last four Months. He closed his eyes and sighed several times, breathing within and without deep. The beating of his heart slowed, then his mind did, and the Compression abated.

The guard closed the Sedan Chair door. The chairmen—the inmates—began replacing the right Bar. Franklin leaned out the Sedan Chair's left window. The rear inmate was missing the rear portion of one gruesome scarred ear, it having been cropped, which could be discern'd by the disnatural Cleavage chirurgical strait, so strait the cut Line might have been survey'd. Shears most probably, rather than a knife.

Had the chairman been cropped for Larceny? Counterfeiting? Arson? Perjury? Heresy in the Puritanical North?

The front inmate glanced at Franklin's massive Paunch, galled by the weighty Cargo, but cast his glance downward immediate when he saw Franklin gandering.

"Perhaps I'd find Solitude," Franklin said, "if I took up residency at The Nut."

The left-front inmate smirked and seemed to bite his cheeks to keep from chuckling.

"Could you host His Excellency?" he whispered. "Always fancy'd making his Person."

"His Excellency," Franklin said, "is destined for a harsher Gaol."

Franklin pronounced Gaol in the common mode, that the G sounded as J and it rhymed with snail.

"What gaol?" the inmate said.

"The Executive."

"His Excellency a'n't wanting the Executive. Desirous of leisure as a Planter. So they says."

The inmate pronounced says in the vulgar Tongue, that it rhimed with days. He eyed Franklin, seeking confirmation or denial of the Rumour.

Franklin kept his body still and maintained to an indifferent expression.

Fear dilated the inmate's eyes. His expression became incredulous.

"His Excellency wouldn't not condescend?"

Franklin shrugged.

On the inmate's countenance, fear heightened.

"Crinkum crankum!" he said. "His Excellency must condescend! If nay, what the bloody hell would Americay come to?"

"Don't be jabb'ring at the Doctor," the guard said. "You scally Wigsnatcher."

He fixed the inmate with a fearsome Glare.

"His Excellency addressed me," the inmate said.

"I jabbered at him and am without wig," Franklin said to the guard.

"Careful the Cloyer don't snaffle your hair," the guard said.

"Nature long since purloined it from the choicest acreage," Franklin said. "Any Chess players resident The Nut?"

"Thems kencrackers aplenty in The Nut," the inmate said. "They always be proper Tacticians."

Kencrackers crack'd kens. They cracked homes, was Burglars.

"The tacticians I might prefer," Franklin said, "are cunning enough to avoid residency at The Nut."

The inmate chuckled.

"Ye battled The General in chess?" he said.

Franklin nodded.

"Yorktown him?"

Franklin nodded.

"The General," he said, "but a meager tactician."

The inmate chuckled at the Conceit, but only slight, so as not to disrespect, seeming.

"You and The General in residency," the inmate said, "we'd crack The Nut right sure."

Other inmates chuckled.

"Nut cracking," Franklin said, "'tis a peculiar nemesis of The General. Rather like the Executive."

"If His Excellency can fox the British," an inmate said, "cracking The Nut be but a Trifle."

"No more intercourse of cooping the flash Ken," the guard said. "Or I'll mill your cannisters, Doctor or nay."

"You lampoon me," the inmate said. "About His Excellency a'n't condescending the Executive."

Franklin again kept his body still and his expression indifferent. He saw fear in the eyes of all inmates. Their faces also conveyed increasing Perplexion as they grappled with the incomprehensible prospect of Washington abandoning America.

The guard stood before the inmate Franklin had been having intercourse with. A Truncheon matriculated from his sleeve. 'Twas hardwood, heavy and fearsome. A metal Blandish within a hollow'd centre? Regardless, the instrument was worn and had been baptized in Blood. The guard raised the Truncheon, as if to mill the inmate's Cannister. Knife scars on his hand and forearm glistened in the sunlight. The inmate cowered.

"Keep skirting me like a Bitch," the guard said to the inmate, "I'll clout your jolly nob till the Claret runs."

The guard distanced from the inmate and spoke louder, in a tone even more fearsome.

"That does for alls of you Priggers," he said. "You bloody mouths. You here to transmit the Doctor, not intercourse him."

"Mister Pillings," Franklin said to the guard.

Pillings curtsied deep to Franklin. A profuse Scar on the rear of his neck extended below his shirt line.

"Your Excellency," Pillings said. "Your most obedient and humble Servant."

Franklin curtsied with his head, the minimum which etiquette required.

"I would preference you not mill any cannisters," Franklin said. "Not withinst State House especially."

"I know you fancys the good in men," Pillings said. "But in a Hell Town alley, a'n't a one of these priggers a'n't slice your Throat for a Shilling. With nary a shred of guilt. My employ to protect Your Excellency."

"I am grateful you endeavor to protect me," Franklin said, "but would not have you milling the Cannisters of chairmen the day I affix'd my signature to the new Constitution of Government. Or any day, to be frank. I pray you indulge me this Fancy."

Pillings frowned appreciable, but curtsied.

"As you please, Your Excellency."

"You have my gratitude for your Forebearance and Benevolence."

Pillings' frown deepen'd. He curtsied deep again, revealing his neck scar again.

On a different day, Franklin might have tryed to exercise influence with Pillings and effect Reformation. Alas, man was not to be changed. Not its inmates, nor its rulers.

And Pillings was correct, probably.

Had Pillings' grizly neck Scar, and the scars on his fore-arms and hands, been etch'd by priggers? Franklin wondered how he would treat priggers, had they bequeathed him such Adornments?

The older Franklin turned, the more he wanted refuge from man.

"Up with His Excellency," Pillings said. "You scarly Drom-edaries. And you best be erasing them Smirks, less you want them tawed from your Visages."

The inmates flatten'd their faces. The inmate Franklin had been intercoursing moved to his Position at the left-front Sup-port. The inmates vaulted the sedan. Franklin felt himself a rise and his view of East Room heightened.

"Zounds," the right-front inmate whispered. "What the Doc-tor been bloody scurving?"

The necken vein on the front left inmate was taut.

"Anvils?" he whispered

"Cannonball soup," the right-front inmate whispered.

"Crikey he's a Load," the right-rear inmate whispered.

His voice was hoarse with strain.

Franklin laboured mighty not to chuckle.

"Shut your bloody Clackers," Pillings said. "Next prigger that peeps, knock his teeth out his Arse."

Outside the sedan's right window, Pillings clenched his teeth, which glistened white, having been boraxed probably. Pillings seemed to belated realize he had spoke impolitick. He glanced at Franklin, his expression apologetic, and curtsied again.

Franklin glanced out the sedan's left window. The diminutive Jemmy was standing before the Bar. Did Jemmy weigh even a century? Franklin had seen heavyer hounds.

Jemmy glanced at the distraught expression of the inmate Franklin had spoke to about Washington condescending not the Presidency, and then locked eyes with Franklin. Jemmy shook his head. Franklin allowed a smirk. Jemmy rolled his eyes and shook his head more rapid.

The chairmen lumbered past the East Room's two colossal doors, which seemed designed to accommodate Titans of pre-antiquity. The central Hall was 40 feet north to south, as the Assembly and Court Rooms, but only half their width at 20 feet. Franklin faced the West Room and its arcade, a series of three arched entries on pillars.

The central Hall was white plastered and high ceiling'd, an exercise in columns, corbels, and coffers. Entering, Franklin always felt he was in an antient Græcian or Roman temple.

When riding Bayard of ten toes that was. Alas, the Sedan constrain'd Franklin's view, upward especially. Franklin had the dizzying sensation of peering down a hall that was the sedan interior, through the central Hall, and into another hall that was the supreme Court Room to the Bench. Altering his vantage and fixating upon the central Hall, Franklin could not help but contemplate America's resurrection of the antient principles which the architecture symbolized.

The Sedan flexed up and down as the chairmen drove it. This caused Pinches of pain from the Gout and Stone occasional.

Gentlemen in the hall turned heads or swivelt eyes towards the Sedan, which was not a new sight to most, yet nonetheless always right conspicuous.

The Sedan oriented north, towards the main front entrance of the State House and the route Franklin typical took home.

Peering out the front of sedan and without doors, Franklin saw Chestnut Street, which bustled with traffick a foot and hoove. A wagon brimming with cord Wood fill'd Franklin's vantage, moving west to east, pulled a-plodding by a pair of sweaty black draught Horses. One let out a mighty Grunt which caused its lips to flutter and created a reverberatory Snort. Franklin fancied it a grunt of Complaint rather than mere fatigue, and chuckled.

Without doors, Franklin also saw Edmund Randolph striding eastward on one of the walks a side Chestnut Street, the walk on the north side across it. Randolph's rectanglish, figurine Face was right conspicuous even distant. As was the Allegheny nose of John Dayton, who walked behind Randolph a stretch. Seeing two Deputies who rode Bayard coincident was insurprizing, as most lodged within a musket Shot of the State House.

Though similar in Countenance with squarish Faces and domineering whiffers, Messieurs Randolph and Dayton could not have cut more dissimilar figures. Randolph strode with choppy steps that seemed to belie Agitation and Discertainty, while Dayton strolled leisured and seem'd absent all Care.

"Mister Pillings," Franklin said.

Pillings stood without window upon the instant.

"Aye, Your Excellency."

"Promenade the Garden if you please."

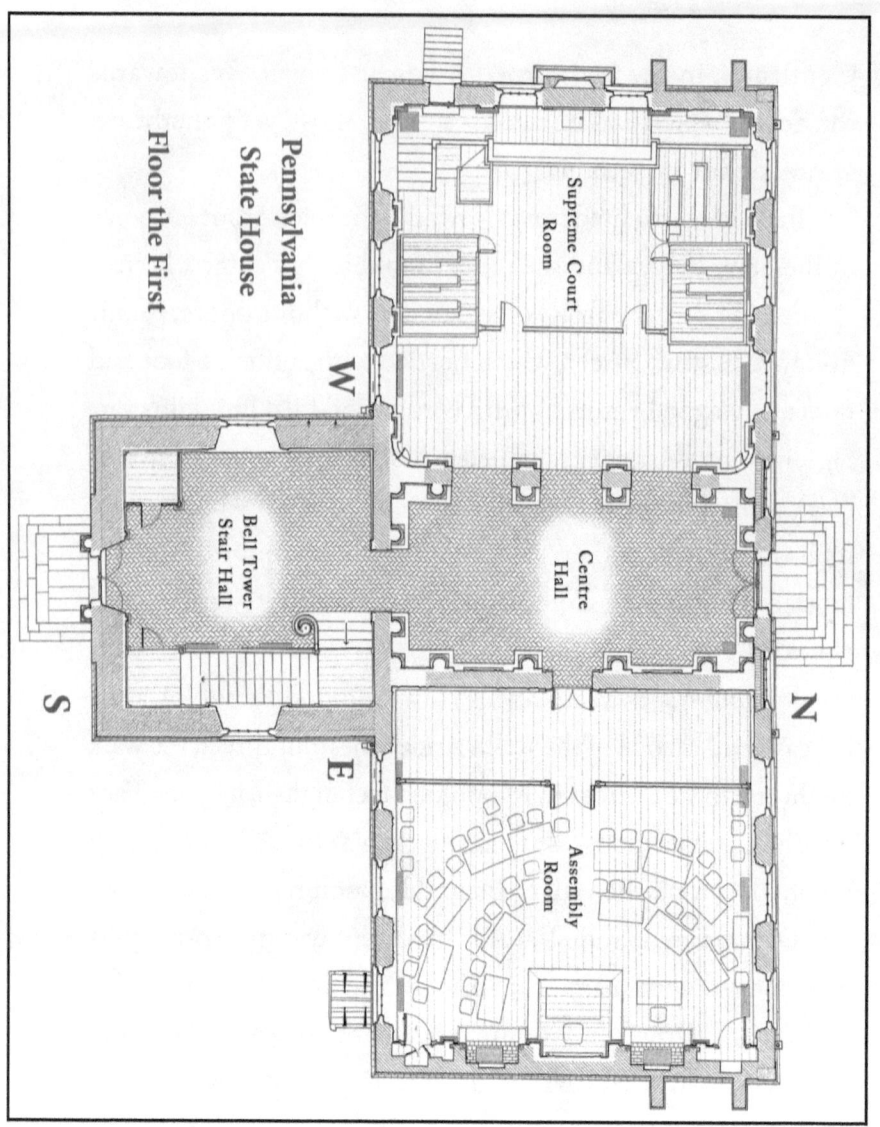

ABOVE: Principal Floor of the Pennsylvania State House.
OPPOSITE PAGE: Close-up of the Centre Hall and the Bell
Tower Stair Hall. This is the vantage of Floor the First. Not
shown: the walkway running above the south entry communicating the two square south landings, the stair way
running upward south to north along the west wall communicating to Floor the Second above stairs.

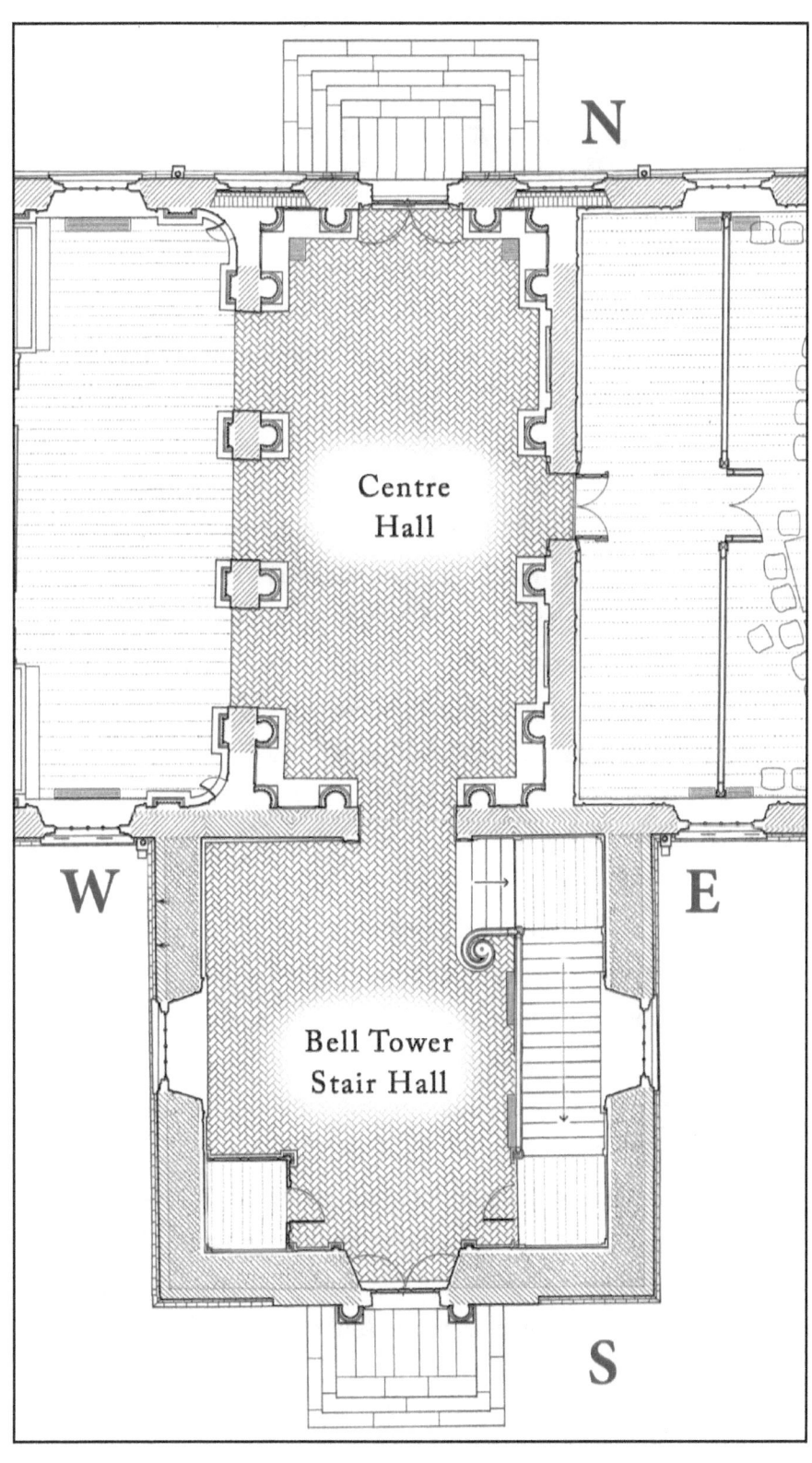

N

Centre
Hall

W

E

Bell Tower
Stair Hall

S

Pillings curtsied while continuing to walk.

"Your most obedient servant," he said.

Franklin needed to Promenade to make his support of the Constitution manifest. Also to gauge publick Sentiment.

"Arse around," Pillings said. "You wretched land Pirates."

Pillings continued to instruct the chairmen with his characteristic Politeness and Compassion, though he seem'd unwilling to oath quite as profligate with a multitude of Gentlemen within earshot. Miniscule consolation, yet consolation nonetheless. Even curses cooled, Pillings' bark remain'd right scalding tho'.

The sedan spun 180 degrees, like the Arm of a clock if time somehow accelerate. The Manœuvre was ambilævous, as the sedan was taller than wide or long, and a trifle tipsy when elevate. Franklin felt the barest beginnings of a nauseate yaw in his stomach, as if a ship lurching on a wave.

The Sedan passed through the south door way, into the Stair Hall of the Bell Tower. An ascending stair way that ran the edges of the walls dominated the room and made it seem cramped. The stair way commenced perpendicular to the entry way. Had Franklin been beating the Hoof, he could have taken a stride or two through the entry way, turned a crisp Left, and been smack a front the first stair

The stair way ascended four steps, levelled into a square Landing in the corner, ascended along the east wall, and levelled into another Landing that ran the entire south wall above the south doorway. At the opposite end of the Landing, the stairway ascended along the west wall, levelled into a square Landing in the corner, and ascended four steps eastward, into a final

Landing and doorway above stairs, direct above the doorway Franklin had just entered.

As above, so below.

Franklin found the sight of his old Nemesis the stair way discomforting. Having seated the Executive Council for three years, and employed in state political affairs for decades, he had ascended the stair way more times than a polymath could cipher.

On Franklin's best days, when the Gout and Stone ceased their investment, he was able to foote the three blocks from his town House to the State House. Franklin relished such days. Yet he still had to ascend this stair way to reach his office, and he suffered a thousand memories of the mortal Coils of the Gout and Stone during ascension and descension. Fortunate for Franklin, the stair way was wide enough to accommodate the Sedan, and he had a shortened poles crafted explicit for the purpose, though even with poles a-shortened, ascending or descending without scraping the walls or tipping required skilled driving by the chairmen.

The Sedan continued driving forward. An alluring Sluice of sunlight swarthed through the south door way. It made Franklin long to be without doors. The south door way was archless, owe-ing the low clearance under the balcony above, and the rectangle doors stretched upward to the underside of the balcony. Though the door Frame was wide, the two doors which each filled half the frame seemed narrow. They would reveal a central seam if closed, yet was opened inward.

The eastward or leftward stair way filched much of the Tower Hall's width, the sedan occupied centre of chambre, and the balcony and ascending westward stair way imposed from above. Franklin felt constricted, cramp'd, hurryed even.

As a few gentlemen dressed in the fine Suits of solicitors entered or exited the south door, they veered westward or east-ward to detour the sedan, most westward into the open Space below the ascending west-wall stair way. Some paused and primped, a-straightening wigs and donning or removing hats, wiping faces with kerchiefs, preening errant specks of wig pow-der, and cetera.

One gentleman in an unornament black suit of the sort Washington might wear was being pursued dogg-ed by a cor-pulent Dandy as he moved along the same tack as the Sedan, from the central Hall towards the south exit. The Dandy wore a suit of the brightest Saffron, was prodigious paunch-ed, and in motion he seemed like an animate Pumpkin. Sunlight reflected off the Watering, the shiney Veneer, of his dry suit fabric.

The Dandy finally caught the solicitor and walked next to him. The Solicitor was gaunt, had severe aristocratic Features, and evidenced œconomy of motion. He glanced at the Dandy with unbridled Disdain and slowed not his step.

"Another fresh suit is it, Mister Winthrope?" the Solicitor said. "Of dyes and ornament grievous luxuriant. As habitual for thou."

The Dandy Winthrope shrugged.

"'Tis but a trifle," he said.

"Saffront dye 'tis never a trifle. The tailors speak of thee as a patron Saint. Those that can render the Miracle of extracting renumeration."

Franklin chuckled. Winthrope glared back with warmth, but turned away rapid when he saw that the sound emanated from the Sedan. All Philadelphians knew Franklin within.

"You must aide me, Sir," Winthrope said.

"Must I?" the Solicitor said. "I recall not thee contracting my Indenture."

"I have called at your Practice repeated."

"And been rebuked of a Purpose. Now thou resort to haranguing me Publick?"

"'Twas not my intent to Affront. Please, Sir. I beseech you t—"

"Is the Sweat that lubrifies thy brow from taking the Exercise?"

Franklin chuckled louder.

"Or is thou sponge-ed?" the Solicitor said.

"The writ has issued," Winthrope said, "but 'tis not yet transmitted to the Bailiffs."

Debtors were incarcerate but temporary at a Sponging House, where they might post Bail or settle arrears to forestall removal to Debtor's Prison. As the name implied, the Sponging House was meant to squeeze renumeration out of Defaulters.

"I'll do bloody any Thing," Winthrope said, "to escape The Prune."

"Any Thing but settle arrears," the Solicitor said. "Had thou Honor, thou would have done so."

"'Tis not a question of honor."

"Cannot be, as thou possess none."

Franklin chuckled a trifle louder. The Solicitor met Franklin's gaze, smirked fractional and curtsied with his head. Franklin smiled and curtsied his head in reply.

"I entreated my creditors," Winthrope said.

"Aye yea," the Solicitor said. "I could help not but hear Tell. All of Philadelphiay recoils at the Infamy. Proffers of reparations at Discounts that make merchants anxious of running thee through. Were we South, thou would have so many creditors demanding Satisfaction as to constitute a Fusillade."

"I made reasoned proffers. Brokered honest."

The Solicitor fixed the Dandy Winthrope with a scathing Glare.

"Labour at The Prune shall be the only honest Endeavor of thy life. How many decades incarcerate does thou reckon to settle thine arrears?"

The thou form was conspicuous to Franklin's ear. Thou forms were reckoned more intimate than common Address, that of you forms, so their use by the solicitor in speaking to Winthrope was curious.

"Thou shall be shrivelt as a Prune," the Solicitor said, "whence paroled at the Last."

Though the matter scarce humourous, Franklin could not help but chuckle at Winthrope's petrified expression. The Fear which the The Prune instilled in delinquents had been rightful earned.

"My west Lands will soon be made productive," Winthrope said. "I oath upon my wife and childs."

"The usual refrain of speculators. One sung far too frequent by thee. Take solace tho'. Enough speculators incarcerate The Prune to quire the hymn with thee."

"Pleaze, Sir. I implore you! If not for my sake, then that of my Family."

The Solicitor sighed deep and darbered Winthrope with a more scathing Glare. He pursed his lips and shook his head rapid.

"I have a pressing docket chock full of Causes I must plead," he said. "And thou is but a Luxuriant with a boundless Appetite of Finery. I have scar—"

The Solicitor and Dandy neared the Sedan.

"Good Doctor," the Solicitor said. "Might I trouble thee for a moment of intercourse?"

"I am yours, Sir," Franklin said.

The Solicitor curtsyed, a discoordinate Bow that was nigh sexish, yet nonetheless low and conveyed deep respect.

"I shall expedite with this scoundrellous scurrillous Defaulter," he said.

The chairmen stopped and placed the Sedan down. The Solicitor stopped walking next to its window.

"I have scarce encountred a dastard so destitute of Œconomy," the Solicitor said to Winthrope. "Thou shall always be in arrears, no matter thine income."

"I learnt my lesson. God and true."

"So the fresh Suit was a celebratory of thy matriculate Œconomy?"

Winthrope frowned.

"Please, Sir. I entreat y—"

"Were it not for the grace of thy Mistress, the promise of thy Son, and the handsomeness and virtue of thy Daughters, I would precipitate thee to the debtor's Dungeon and delight in thy internment. As would a tenth the merchants and artizans of this city. To reckon the matter conservative."

"Thank you, Sir. Thou art a Savior, right and true. Your reputation can a surety mend th—"

"I shan't be party to Artifice," the Solicitor said, "and shall want mine full recompence in advance. Eleven pounds sterling. In hard Currency, not paper Money. And certain not Bills of Credit nor a warrant."

"Eleven pounds sterling is harrowing prodigious."

The Solicitor's eyes dilated with amazement. He laughed sardonick.

"I condescend to render Salvation and thou would complain of mine recompence? 'Tis prodigious. So is thy creditors and arrears. As is the term thou may incarcerate The Prune."

"I meant no di—"

"Call at my Practice the morrow."

The Solicitor eyed Winthrope's watered saffron Suit with contempt.

"Wear a dark Suit unwatered or wave-ed, or other wise Dandy Foppish. Or the closest Approximate in thy wardrobe. If even a shilling of mine recompence be delinquent, the business shan't proceed. In hard Money, not paper Money. And certain not Bills of Credit nor warrants."

"Aye, Sir. Specie it shall be."

"Pawne thy horse if thy must, or huck several of thy suits. One other requisite."

"Aye, Sir. You have but to voice it."

"Make no innecessary Purchases ere the morrow or until tryal. If I hear of even a one, and I trust thee not and shall monitor, I shall retain mine recompence and recuse myself of the Ordeal."

"Aye, Sir. As you'll have it."

"Not even a bloody Shilling on a Frivolity."

"Aye, Sir. So it shall be."

"Enjoy thy fresh Finery, Mister Winthrope, for it shall be thy last."

"Aye, Sir. You have warned a multitude of times on the point, and I am complaisant."

"I must justify mine association with a Disrepute such as thee," the Solicitor said, "to gentlemen and merchants who would disparage and perhaps alienate me other wise. A cessation of thy Profligation answers the question. As does the greater surety of Renumeration to thy Creditors which resultant."

"Aye, Your Excellency. With respect and friendship, I am your most humble and obe—"

The Solicitor held up a halting hand.

"Thou revolt me, Mister Winthrope. Render thyself scarce of mine Sight until the morrow."

Winthrope curtsy'd, and walked off. His eyes shifted leftward as he passed the Sedan, attempting to gander Franklin without making the Act apparent. The Solicitor shook his head in disgust as he observed the departing form of Winthrope and moved close upon the Sedan window.

"Right ironical," the Solicitor said, "to hold such intercourse in presence of thee, an exemplar of Thrift and Œconomy."

"When younger," Franklin said, "as the Way to Wealth. I can scarce lay such Claim now, tho' I am a Debtor not."

"I've faced such a-folly a Thousand times if ten," the Solicitor said, "yet still cannot sound its Fathoms. Winthrope a childe even tho' a man. The ethos to live withinst Purse is compleat absent him."

"Most will live so," Franklin said, "if given Allowance."

"Civilization shall always have need of Debtor's Prisons."

"There is a Way to Wealth," Franklin said. "Yet also a Path to Poverty. All Americans have Liberty to chuse betweenst them. Yet it can be grievous tragick when a man, or nation, won't tack from the one course to the other."

The Solicitor nodded solemn. He carry'd a singular Budget—a satchel—render'd of the thickest leather. 'Twas wrought as if armour and looked not just swordproof, but damn nigh impregnable.

"Another fresh Budget is it?" Franklin said.

The Solicitor chuckled.

"I hath long required a more robust Casing for my Briefs," he said. "Ye olde proved woeful insufficient. When the rain battered, mine briefs oft drenched and the ink run. I also dropped mine Budget recent, had it trampled, and found a horse Shoe watermarked upon nigh every paper within."

"'Tis a fine encasement," Franklin said. "Russiay leather?"

"'Tis. 'Twas the finest available."

"Nigh as luxuriant as saffront dye."

"But paid in Specie," the Solicitor said. "And 'tis Quality procured for Function, not ornament. May it protect mine Briefs as General Washington Americay."

"You expect much of your Budget," Franklin said.

"I think it equal the task. As His Excellency."

Silence.

"Well, Good Doctor?"

"I am indeed," Franklin said. "How does the Practice?"

"Oh come, Doctor. I didn't impose upon thee to intercourse of my practice. How does the Convention?"

"Well, now that adjourned."

"What of the Constitution of Government?"

"What of it?"

Franklin leaned his head out the window and hung one arm out. He preferred intercoursing without the Impediment of view which the Sedan enforced.

"I dislike intercoursing immediate after Sessions," the Solicitor said, "and this inclination oft heightened at the conclude of Trial, one of duration especially. I assume thou is of the same Mind after months in Convention, so would impose for a Brief only."

Franklin nodded perfunctory.

"The Constitution of Government 'tis executed," he said, "and is to be transmitted to the Congress in the morrow for circulation to the several States. They shall put the Question."

"The Charta's character?" the Solicitor said.

"The instrument shall parade the Paper in the morrow."

"And I shall study each word fastidious. But I would know thy Mind."

"I would let the Character of the Instrument represent itself."

"I am disaccustom'd," the Solicitor said, "to Naïveté from one so wise."

Franklin laughed.

The Solicitor waited.

Franklin said nothing.

The Solicitor chuckled.

"Thou conferred the instrument the Sanction of thy Name?"

"Aye, Sir," Franklin said.

"And thou would have this Constitution of Government ratify?"

"Aye, Sir," Franklin said. "Ratification or Death it shall be, for the Confederacy of States."

The Solicitor nodded solemn.

"His Excellency of the same cast?"

Franklin nodded.

"The General conferred the Sanction of his Name," he said, "and would see the Instrument ratify."

"And His Excellency General Washington shall condescend to anchor the new Government?" the Solicitor said. "Render it impregnable as Gibraltar with the weight of his Character?"

Franklin wanted to groan, but mere shrugged.

"What security a Constitution of Government," the Solicitor said, "if His Excellency shan't condescend?"

"Precious little perhaps, at the Onset," Franklin said. "But I am not the Oracle of The General's intentions."

"The Good Doctor and Good General," the Solicitor said, "can be circumspect almost beyond belief. This habitude is right vexing. Thou sure have some inkling of the General's Mind."

Franklin shrugged.

The Solicitor laughed. His smile lines a creased as he did so.

"It is now to The People," Franklin said.

"Who shall be swayed in prodigious Measure," the Solicitor said, "by the pronouncements of thee and His Excellency upon the Question."

"Our weight tho' not a Trifle," Franklin said, "mayn't be the Ballast supposet. At ratifying Conventions, Patriots of the second Pantheon and of a vulgar Cast are requisite."

The Solicitor nodded and peered into Franklin's eyes for a long moment. His gaze was curious yet penetrating.

"What sort of government have ye begot us?" the Solicitor said. "A mixed, a balanced, a divided? Does the new charta not incorporate Montesquieu's triparte system? A Legislative Power, Executive Power, Judiciary Power? Is the Triparte segregate, counter balanced? By what mode? How was the Jealousys of the large States and little States reconciled? Merchant and moneyed Interests counter balanced against the artisan and agrarian?"

The Solicitor spoke rapid yet steady. Franklin could not have interspersed a single syllable, even were he so inclined.

"What security was ceded the South on Slavery to keep them in Convention and cement their Sanction?" the Solicitor said. "What of the Sovereignty of the several States? Shall new States be as Colonies? Where is the tax Power resident, and how energetick? The Power of War? What of the qualifications for Suffrage? Terms of Rotation in office? Jurisdictions of fœderal Courts and state Courts? A fœderal supreme Court? What guarantys in the Declaration of Rights prefixed? What provisions of Amendment? Of what species the Executive and by what mode chosen? Wh—"

"'Tis a monarchy," Franklin said. "Mister Adams of Massachusetts is to be King."

The Solicitor laughed boisterous.

"Samuel?" he said.

Franklin frowned prodigious.

"Bloody hell," he said.

"What is sauce for the goose," the Solicitor said, "'tis sauce for the gander."

They laughed.

"His Excellency John Adams," Franklin said at last. "King of Americay."

"Another Rebellion so soon?" the Solicitor said.

"I shan't lampoon Rebellion," Franklin said. "Let us pray not."

"I seldom do," the Solicitor said.

"One of thy primary Virtues," Franklin said.

The Solicitor chuckled, then his face grew graver right sudden.

"For months I have been consumpted curious of the Nature of the Constitution of Government draughting. Alas mine curiousity isn't to gratify. Might I find thee more receptive whence a few days transpire?"

"Nigh certain."

"I quit thee to promenade then, Good Doctor," the Solicitor said, "and broad-cast thy envaguened support for the Instrument. Why is thy Support so effusive yet evasive, a gentleman wonders? Could it be there is much in the Instrument thou disapprove?"

"I would not chronickle the whole of Convention for every curious Gawker."

"A mere gawker, Sir?"

"I champion the Instrument," Franklin said, "without condescending to agitate upon each minute partickular."

The Solicitor glanced about. No one was within earshot, save the chairmen. He glanced at them wary, leaned in close, and spoke in a lower voice that approach'd the whisper.

"So there is much thou disapprove," he said.

Franklin maintained to an indifferent expression. And silence.

The Solicitor was wise enough, or at minimum considerate enough, not to press further.

"May I call on thee at Salon Mulberry a few days hence?"

"I am yours, Sir," Franklin said. "Tho' if you don't object the counsel of an old man, thous, thees, and thys are becoming archaic."

The Solicitor smiled wry.

"I am all too sensible," he said, "from the keen niggery and naggery of mine mistress. And mine daughters most especially. Alas, I am too bloody olde for Reformation."

"I wish I could pretend such pretext for my Obstinancey."

The Solicitor laughed.

"These thees may please," he said. "Though the thous arouze. Why is thy thee, not thou affection for me?"

"A Bitch of a doggerel Verse," Franklin said. "Neither of us is much the poet."

The Solicitor laughed harder, and then curtsied deep.

"Fate bless thee, Good Doctor. May it abate thy Gout and Stone, at the least for a night."

"Fate bless Americay," Franklin said.

"With thou in service of her," the Solicitor said, "Fate already have."

The Solicitor courtsy'd a final time, then absented the Tower Stair Hall and went without doors.

The chairmen strained audible as they hoisted the Sedan and drove it forward with their musculature. Franklin thought of Winthrope's mistress. She was handsome, but no belle. Jemmy might have a Prospect, if Philadelphia the new fœderal Capital especially. A Widow to The Prune was a Widow none the less.

Having spent years labouring within State House, Franklin knew the exact Count of the main entry steps. Five for the north Front, three for the south Rear.

The sedan angled downward as the inmates descended the south stair exit. Franklin felt as if on a ship, careening downst a wave. The chairmen were skilled and moved slow yet steady. The sedan support beams were pliant and flexed, minimizing the jostling.

As the sedan vacated the State House and moved without doors, sunlight accosted Franklin and his chairmen. They squinted. The sedan leveled out. A wide, southward gravel walk commenced immediate at the end of the downward stairs. 'Twas a pleasing white. The chairmen traversed it. Franklin heard the crunch of the gravel under feet.

The State House was unseen behind Franklin, but he glimpsed the outermost portions of the arcades which extended east and west from it, communicating it to two office House wings.

In the extreme northwest corner of the lot, the new County Court House was demarcate by stakes sunk into the ground and communicated with strings. It was constructing. The basement was digging by labourers whose shovels and picks jutted above ground sporadic, as did jumbles of dirt heaved skyward into carts at basement edge, causing reverberating thumps.

In the extreme northeast corner of the lot were the constructure of the American Philosophical Society and the site of the new City Hall, which was staked and strung though ground not

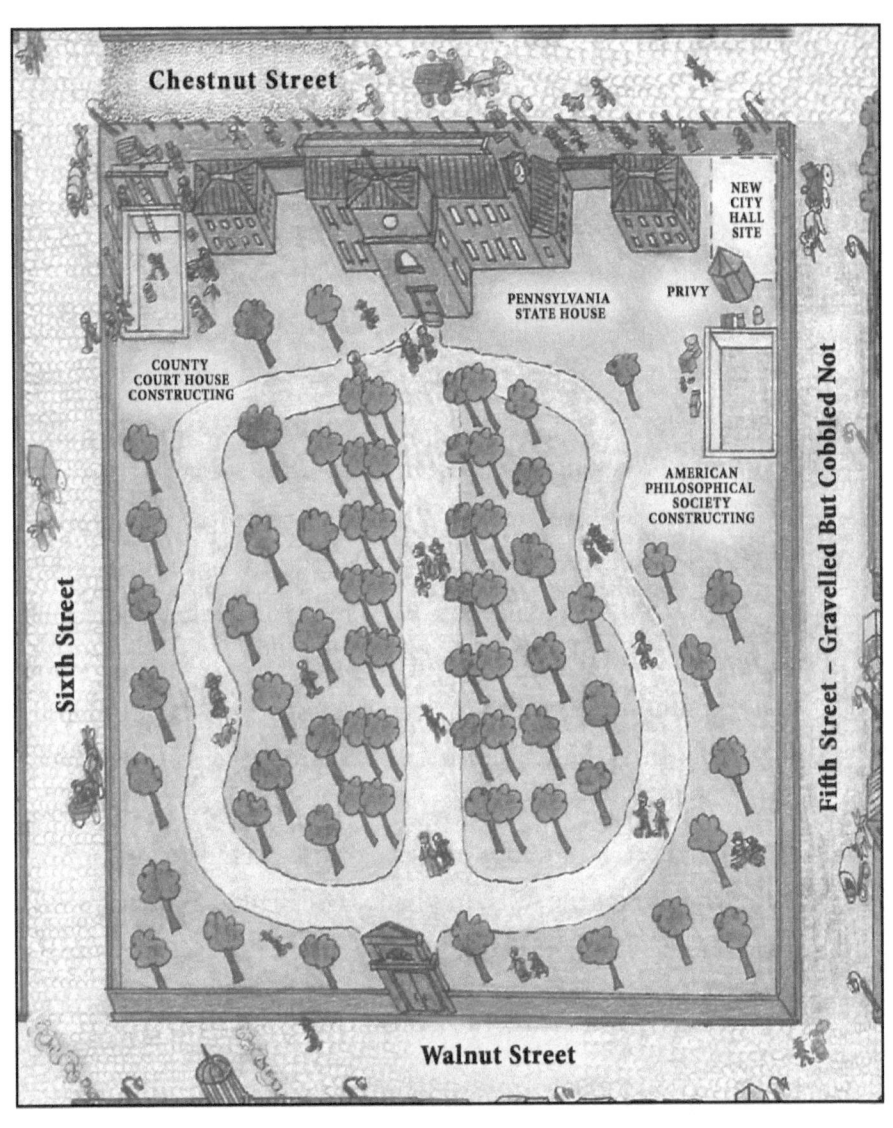

Chestnut Street

NEW CITY HALL SITE

PRIVY

PENNSYLVANIA STATE HOUSE

COUNTY COURT HOUSE CONSTRUCTING

AMERICAN PHILOSOPHICAL SOCIETY CONSTRUCTING

Sixth Street

Fifth Street – Gravelled But Cobbled Not

Walnut Street

ABOVE: The Pennsylvania State House lot, including the Garden, Mall, outer walls, constructures, and south Gate.

yet broke. The Necessary gargantuan and octagonal was nigh impossible to miss and reminded Franklin of a Gazebo. The northeast portion of the Garden was appreciable less herded than others, owing the putrid Odour of the sixteen-holer and the flys it attracted.

In front of Franklin, comprehending south and filling the entirety of the blockwide lot, the State House Garden beckon'd. 'Twas one of the finest publick Parks in America, if not the finest. Seeing it always filled Franklin with Joy and Pride and made him think of his old friend Samuel Vaughan, who had design'd and constructed the Wonder but a few years prior.

The Garden consisted of a beautiful lawn, interspersed with little knobs or tufts of flowering shrubs, and clumps of trees, well disposed. The spacious gravel-walk running through the middle of the Garden was lined with double rows of thriving elms, and communicated with serpentine walks which encompassed the whole area. The Garden was manicured nice, in the english Stile—at least where compleat. The full plenitude of elms was present, but certain knobs or tufts akin to Islands of soil amid the lawn had not the full complement of Plantage. The Garden was nonetheless right pleasing.

Upon a standard day after the noon, at High Mall when the throng of Promenaders at its height, there might be several Hundred, but today's plenytude approached to half a Thousand. Many Promenaders had probably hearken'd to see Deputies adjourn and learn the character of the new Constitution.

The State House lot was 255 feet west to east and 396 feet north to south. The State House itself occupied about 96 feet of the 396 feet of height, including the lawn afront and the rear-protruding bell Tower. This remaindered some 300 feet of north-south acreage for the Garden, which was 255 by 300 feet. Though puny by European reckon, the State House Garden was right splend'rous by American standards.

Yet it felt grievous crowded, to excess. Franklin was disac-customed to his cherished Garden being herded.

Franklin began clicking his tongue against the roof of his mouth instinctual, as if slowing a horse. He truncated his click-ing right sudden, not wanting to denigrate his chairmen. Frank-lin raised his walking Stick and tapped it upon the sill of the window, the usual signal to stop. The chairmen obeyed and broke the sedan.

The gravel walkway was shaped as the letter O, but with the main central southward Walk, or Mall, overlining the middle. It made Franklin envision the capitalized Græcian letter phi, Φ, the Golden Mean. The O walkway was not circular, but rather slithered irregular. Symmetry was requisite in Buildings, but in Gardens 'twas more the crack to simulate the random excen-tricies of the Wilde.

Some five feet south of the door way, and some ten feet east and west of it, were two hexagonal watch Boxes. They were sit-uate upon the outside edge of the O portion of the walk way, wherest it arced outward and southward from the intersection with the central Mall. The watch Boxes were tall and narrow and resembled upright tents, yet were in point of fact made of wood. They were just large enough to shelter a man from the Weather, perhaps two men if cramped. A sentry stood a front of each, facing southward.

The sentries was of a taller cast, handsome, and proper muscled. They wore Pennsylvania Regiment uniforms sim'lar to Army uniforms, bleu coats with carmine cochineal facings, or upturns, at wrist, collar, and lapel, the opposition of the british Colours, of red with bleu facings. Franklin wondered if America would ever chuse new Colours and cease apeing the British. Red, blue, and white were right pleasing though.

Both sentries held their muskets vertical, shoulder Stock on the ground, barrel upward, as if halberds. Muskets being some five feet of length absent bayonet, the barrels were nigh chin high. White straps criss-crossed the sentrys' chests, supporting their cartridge Box, canteen, and powderhorn at the waist. Both was pistol'd, knive-ed, and sworded.

Tho' the sentries possessed Spit and Polish, they nonetheless seem'd more like grizzled frontier Fighters than showpiece Redcoats or French Regulars. This was comforting to Franklin. He wanted Guards capable to the Task if called to action.

The west Sentry approached Franklin. He was middling aged, nigh turned of twenty or nigh past, Franklin would hazard. The sentry was carbuncle Faced, almost as if rouged, and full of Pimples, but his expression was endearing earnest. He curtsied deep to Franklin, with Flourish.

"I beg His Excellency's leave for Imposition," the Sentry said. "Might His Excellency grant Leave for address?"

"Aye," Franklin said. "'Tis no imposition."

"Would His Excellency preference a life Guard?"

"Nay," Franklin said. "I'm but a trifle a cargo."

"His Excellency? A trifle?"

The Sentry's expression became puzzical.

Franklin wanted to sigh. When had the young become so humorless?

"Should marauders or Assassins descend," Franklin said, "I have every confidence my chairmen shall outpace them."

The two front chairmen glanced at each other, expressions partial glum, yet also a portion amused.

"His Excellency might hurl Lightning at them until the Militia can aid," the Sentry said. "In the mode of Zeus."

Franklin wanted to laugh, but feared he would affront the humorless young Sentry. Franklin understood the Hyperbole intrinsic to the comment, but Misconceptions of his prowess with the Lightning also abounded.

"By Providence may it never come to such," Franklin said. "Regardless, I stand not in need of a life Guard."

The Sentry courtsied.

"Does his Excellency require else of the Militia?"

"Nay. The consideration is appreciate tho'."

The Sentry curtsied and began to walk off. He stitched his Step, paused, and turn'd towards Franklin with a trepidant expression.

"Might His Excellency grant leave for another address?"

"Aye," Franklin said.

"Is the rumours true? That the Grand Fœderal Convention have affix'd its signatures to a Charta and adjourned?"

"The rumours stand not in erratum," Franklin said. "For once."

The Sentry's expression became even more trepidant.

"Might His Excellency grant leave for another addre—"

"Aye," Franklin said.

"'Tis true what is spuke? That vulgar men such as I shall Elector?"

"Aye. Representatives to the First House of the Congress shall be Electored by The People."

The Sentry smiled at first, but then his eyes narrowed ever so slight.

"Qualifications for elect'ring to the First House?" he said.

"The first House is stiled The House of Representatives," Franklin said. "Qualification ditto as for electoring to the Assembly in Pennsylvaniay."

"Right and true?" the Sentry said.

"Aye, Sir."

The Sentry's cautious Grin expanded but gradual. His visage became strained, as if given a vexing math Cipher he could comprehend not.

"So I—"

He pressed his forefinger into his chest.

"—will chuse who in Power."

"And who is rotate out of Power," Franklin said. "Should they not heed the Instruction of The People and enforce their Will. Contingent upon you paying Taxes."

The strain in the sentry's Gaze began to abate. He conveyed a Sense of dawning Comprehension. It would be found on many a face in coming days, Franklin suspected.

The Sentry curtsied.

"Your most obedient and humble servant," he said. "If His Esteem'd Excellency requires any Thing of the Militia, it too remains his most obedient and humble Servant."

The Sergeant curtsied once last, repaired to his post, and stood as straight as the Ramrod of his musket.

Franklin focused southward upon the Garden and gander'd the multitudes of Promenaders. They strolled walk ways, sat on benches, stood in small Circles, and a few sat upon the lawn. Hounds and even a Hog frolicked at liberty. A young girl with her mammy walked a leash-ed pet doe.

Many Sexes promenaded, some coupled, paired with their Masters. Scarcer bunches of Sexes intercoursed each other with nary a male. The Garden was one of the few places where it was seemly for unbetroth-ed Sexes, of wealthy families especially, to promenade unaccompany'd without indictment of their Virtue.

An Age of Reason had dawned. It had englighten'd Conceptions, including those of Fashion. One could see the simplicity which was replacing ostentation in the Dress of the Sex, gowns especially.

Most Sexes wore fashionable Undress, not full Dress, which was to say they were clad informal for daily utility, though still a-fashioned. Chemise gowns, the newest Stile, were the most conspicuous, though a far from ubiquitous. Franklin had taught himself Latin, and knew that Chemise was derived from the Latin word for shirt, Camisa. Chemise gowns were cut nigh straight at the Sides and unfitted at the waist or below. They were long, simple, flowing, like the Shift, the undermost garment the Sex wore to bed.

Sashes of varying hue and thickness were tied about the Waist of the chemise Gowns to prevent flutterings and Exposures that might be deem'd lewd and inadvise-ed—by the Sex. The sashes were narrow, not thick Kontush species, but nonetheless made Franklin think of Arabia, of Persia and Turks. The sleeves of the chemise Gowns were plain and ended in Ruffles just past the elbow.

A Herd of the Sex approached. Most went chemise. Several was bushel bubby'd, alas concealed by high Cuts, shifts beneath chemise, and intrusive tuckers, Ruffles stitched about the neckline. Franklin saw Necks creamy and alluring, but scarce more, and could not help but reminisce of Versailles and its low-cut Gowns absent nigh all Concealment. American Sexes ought be more Frenchify'd, though this came at the cost of a certain Sauciness.

Franklin had come to the Garden to parent the new birth-ed Constitution, but also to respite prior to dinner. He was determined to partake said Respite, however brief.

The Herd of Sexes veered eastward onto the lawn and thus approached not the Sedan. A second Herd of the Sex approached in the distance.

Pillings spoke in a low Growl.

"Best be mannersome to thems here upper Sorts," he said. "Or I'll crack your nappers and lace your jackets handsome."

Franklin sighed.

Pillings glanced at Franklin with a repentant expression.

"I wonder," Franklin said, "if you might not pen a pamphlet of poems about trudgeoning inmates."

"I beg forgiveness, Your Excellency."

"Make 'tleast one poem an Ode," Franklin said. "I'd find that pleasing."

The right-front inmate tried his damnedest not to chuckle, to scant avail. As the inmate chuckled, Franklin spied his absent front tooth.

"An Ode to Cracking Nappers?" Franklin said.

"An Idyll," Pillings said. "To Felons Dangling."

Franklin shook his head, but could not help chuckling.

"The habit of speaking such is long ingrain'd, Your Excellency," Pillings said. "I have laboured all the summer to vanquish it and sha'n't cease my Investment. I again beg His Excellency's forgiveness."

Pillings curtsy'd long and deep, and then turned away. Once he did, his repentant expression vanished rapid.

As Herd the second drew opposite the parked Sedan, they eyed the chairmen curious. The chairmen gawked the Sex's duggs and commoditys. Franklin envision'd a lion Herd being shown a massive, glistening Chop. Two of the Ladys seemed discomforted by the carnal glims of the chairmen, but one, the least handsome, in point of fact right homely, smiled sly, pleased by the attention in some measure.

"I pray you mind your distance Ladys," Pillings said. "Get no more close than you would a wilde Beast. Them's Saint Peter's sons, every finger a fish Hook."

The sexes arced wider, increasing their Segregation from the chairmen, passed on, and continued their Promenade.

Fortunate for Franklin, there was no scarcity of Sexes to gander. There were usual more Sexes than gentlemen within Garden, at High Mall after the noon especially, men of business employing at such time. Taking the gaggle of Sexes in a glance, Franklin saw smacklings of the disenfranchized Stiles, most on elder sexes.

A few antient, crotchet hens went Robe à la Polonaise, Robe in Polish. Their overskirts were Polonaised, cutaway, draped, and swagged. Swaths of fabrick were allowed to sag, and pressed upward at fulcrum Points, creating arcing, crescent overtures. The swags atop a theatre curtain might have been transplanted to a gown. Sexes were difficult tempests to gauge, Predilictions of Fashion especially, but ostentation aside, the intent of à la Polonaise seemed to be to imbue the Bum with plumage.

Other crotchet hens promenaded Robe à L'anglaise, Robe in English. This signify'd pleats. Prodigious pleats. Vertical'd usual. Gowns were awash in them. Robe à L'anglaise resemblet the main central curtain of a theatre, if compacted so the Pleats were a scrunch-ed, and a-fastened so as to flow from a sex's hindquarter.

Sexes Robed à L'anglaise and à la Polonaise took dainty Steps about the walkway. Naught a one braved the lawn. They was robed for Stile, not Function. Their Bums wiggled to and fro as they walked, and their Pleats and swags jiggled rhythmic, attracting the glances of many a gentleman. To Franklin, sexes promenading à L'anglaise and à la Polonaise seemed like Ducks with a lumps of coal inlaid up their arses. Some seemed as if trying to evacuate Worms.

Franklin could not help but chuckle.

How vile the vagaries of "Stile."

Many Sexes carry'd parasols, small umbrellas of the East, to shield from Sun, the Face especially. The parasols were scarce shoulder wide and fashioned of luxuriant dyed fabrics.

All Sexes wore hats. To go publick absent hat was lewd for a Sex, without doors especially. Sexes absent umbrellas wore exceeding wide-brimmed shepherdess Hats with low tops, often plumed with whirlwindish Feathers of the autruche, guineafowl, jungle Cock, Amazon parrot, macaw, and cetera.

A third Herd of the Sex approached. Several younger Sexes went à la Polonaise or à L'anglaise rather than Chemise, probably enforced by mothers who strolled with them.

'Twas a pleasing View. On the front, the gowns à la Polonaise and à L'anglaise

hugged the underbodices, the Stays and stomachers, which Sexes wore. Stays and stomachers enforced a rigid upright Carriage in Sexes. They also uplifted and mash'd the exposed duggs so prodigious tight it seemed that the Stitches of the gown would scream or the dairy erupt.

Franklin watched several other Herds of the Sex pass by, and intercoursed some. He soon felt less burdened and happy'r.

"Mister Pillings," he said. "Let us proceed."

"Aye, Your Excellency," Pillings said. "Lap the loop?"

"Alas nay," Franklin said. "The Mall straight away."

Franklin pronounced Mall in the common Stile, that it rhymed with shall or pall.

Pillings curtsied.

The chairmen rose weary, less than enthraled. The language of their bodys suggested a protracted Groan.

"A'n't a request," Pillings said. "You beast-ed Mules. Now up with the Good Do—"

Franklin disattuned the scalding Bark of Pillings as best he could and continued his survey of the Garden. More proper, the Sexes within it.

Now upon The Mall, Franklin could not but help think of The Mall of Britain, in the Park of St. James, which led to Buckingham Palace and was also flanked by pairs of trees upon each Side. Perhaps because Franklin had been resident in France more recent, he also envision'd the Grand Cours, or Grand Promenade, the Avenue des Champs-Élysées. Franklin liked the nomenclature Élysées, the Elysian Fields, the Græcian abode of after life for the Blessed. Far better, nomenclature such as Elysium, than some christian saint. And far better a Mall that led to a Republican State House than a royal palace.

The Mall felt more regimented and artificial than the other portions of the Garden. This was in large measure due its perfect straitness and the a-lined pairs of elm Trees on both edges. At times, Franklin expected pillars rather than elms.

The Mall was the most thronged by Crowds of any portion of the Garden. All eyes seemed to fixate upon the Sedan. Some Promenaders pointed, others waved. Franklin waved back. He was a tourist attractor just as sure as the Repository for Natural Curiosities, Hell Town and the Three Jolly Irishmen, the High Street Market, and cetera, a Spectacle which shopkeepers promoted enthusiastic. Franklin knew his role, and played it.

A brick Wall some eight feet high ran the entirety of west, south, and east Sides of the State House yard, enclosing it compleat. The maroon Brick was contrasted by a white stone ledge atop it.

At the termination of the Mall, exact centre of the south Wall, the largest Gate in Philadelphia, and perhaps in America, loom'd. 'Twas impossible to look south in the Garden, down the Mallway especially, and not observe the Edifice.

The Gate was of brick, merged seamless with the wall, and was pond'rous high, some thirty or forty feet, with two colossal doors fifteen feet High at the least. A faux arch topped the doors, and above arch was a tri angled pediment, as on a house. The Gate was taller than the middling trees, and not prodigious shorter than the larger trees. People entering and exiting was positive dwarfed by the Gate and seem'd nigh Lilliputian.

The Sedan undulated steady upon the graveled walkway. After noon was gradual yielding to evening, one alluring Cool. It had been Spring when the Convention convoked in May yet was now September and Fall hearken'd. Franklin had the fanciful Sense that he had entered the State House yesterday in Spring and was quitting now a day later in Fall. Months of Debate had felt like Epochas while suffering them, yet now that the Convention adjourned there was a mental tendency to compress the Time, to file it in the archive of the past and move forward.

Franklin became cognizant of the Crowds. Hundreds withinst Garden, all looking to Franklin to tell them that the Constitution a Perfection and ought be ratified. Across America, some hundreds of Thousands, perhaps Millions, desirous of the same.

Franklin could not fulfill such Burden alone. Deputies knew it and many promenaded the Garden. Citizens congregated around them, questioning the new Constitution. Tall Boy was the easy'st Deputy to identify. An elm tree without Mallway was larger than others, and he stood under it. With his height and wooden Stump, Tall Boy seemed nigh an extension of the Elm. A small Crowd encircled him, most Sexes, and many laugh'd as he spoke with animation. Franklin spied several betroth-ed Sexes, one batting her eyes at Tall Boy repeated.

Tho' more distant than Tall Boy, the Little Lion was also easy to discern, as he was encircled by a veritable Ballet of parasols, many a-twirling. The Plan to retire to City Tavern with expedition had been abandoned, it seemed, by all save Robert Morris. Sexes tended to have such Effect.

Two young Sexes prodigious handsome stood a distance behind the Little Lion and glimm'd him carnal. One Sex leaned in towards the other, said some Thing, and they both giggled, without diverting their eyes from his Bum. The Little Lion turn'd whilst speaking, and the Sexes repositioned to maintain their vantage of his Pratts.

The Little Lion might have many a criminal Conversation with scant pursuit or effort, Sexes such as these often prostrating theyselves before him. Franklin again felt disease at a man so reckless and ambitious being so enamoured by Washington and empowered thereof.

In the south of the Garden, just without Mallway, The Pinckneys and several south Deputies had also convened Court, with the mammoth CC the most discernable Figure, towering over onlookers with Washingtonian grandeur, and also dominating discussion it seemed. Citizens nodded solemn as he spoke, but laughed occasional.

Other Deputies could be seen in intercourse with Crowds, or beelining the Mallway to the monumental south Gate. They would visit their lodgings in various Quarters, inspect the packet for posted Mail, perhaps sponge their Pits and vitals, change into shirts and drawers not soiled by perspiration, perfume and powder themselves, use the necessary, and respite brief against dinner.

Unsurprizing, Washington was without sight. He was an exceptional fast Walker, and traveler in general, and had nigh certain absented to Robert Morris' home with expedition. As Morris' home was but two Blocks north of the State House, Washington hadn't had far to repair.

Washington's stratagem of a hurried Exit made Franklin envious. Ever shrewd, The General had avoided that investment by the Curious which other Deputies suffered. Like Robert Morris, Washington preferred to leave the intercourse to lesser men.

Elbridge Gerry had liberated himself from the harangues of Mr. Mason and walked so rapid he was nigh a-trotting the central Mallway towards the Garden exit. Few would question Gerry because of his Stutter and Squint. Though gaunt and plump not, Gerry nonetheless seemed like a turkey being chased.

Where was Mr. Mason? In his mind's eye, Franklin saw Mason standing upon the stair way platform astride the south Exit, haranguing the Publick with his Objections to the Constitution, sullying their approbation in the first instancy. Such action would provoke response from Washington, right certain. Mason would wait upon his Repair to the Old Dominion before commencing his investment of the Constitution. All that might be hoped is that Fate might conspire to aid, as it had so oft during the Revolution, and that a coach wheel might crack or horse pull up lame, delaying Mason's intention.

Caledonia James began to walk from a Crowd that had encircled him, but an artful Sex twirling her parasol grabbed his Arm, stood close to him, and smiled whilst leaning her ample bosom forward. Franklin could not help but chuckle. A most unsavoury Tactic. Also a most effecacious one. Caledonia stay'd and suffered more enquiries.

The sedan soon neared the equator of The Mall, its north-south centre. When it did, the State House tower bell began a-ringing, a drawn, methodical series of uniform'd Rings, a second apart, approximate. Had the bellman been watching from above, a waiting the instant Franklin reached this juncture?

The chairman broke and stopped driving the Sedan forward. Pillings barked not at them. Promenaders began to assemble, encircling the Sedan. For months, The People had been assured that when the Convention at last adjourned with finality, sine non die, if successful, the State House bell would be rung thirteen times in succession.

The rings concluded.

There was a pause.

The Rings commenced again, louder this time, another bout of thirteen seeming.

More promenaders congregated about the Sedan.

Franklin had to speak loud to be heard over the bell.

"I fear the bellman a trifle exub'rant," he said.

Promenaders chuckled.

"How many reprizes the Good Doctor instruct the bellman to ring?" someone in the crowd said.

"The Convention gave no such instruction," Franklin said. "But hopeful not thirteen."

Promenaders laughed.

A few rows back in the assembled crowd, Franklin saw a father crack his son a back the head.

"A crown your bloody hat," the Father said.

"We's without doors," the Son said.

"That's Doctor Franklin," the Father said.

He raised his hand to brow another blow.

The Lad's expression became contrite. He donned his cocked hat right rapid.

More promenaders encircled Franklin's Sedan, expressions of benevolent Curiousity upon they faces. They soon number'd a Hundreds and was thick as hasty Pudding.

As Jemmy and Adams had observed rightful and perspicacious, for most all of history, systems of government, even those of a republican Character, had been dictated to The People, not chose purposeful by them. For a People to craft a government of their liking, even indirect by their Representatives, was not just novel, but revolutionary. For The People to feel Liberty enough to stand in question of a new system of government, absent fear, was equal revolutionary. Ever wise, The People seemed to appreciate the moment of what wroughting.

Franklin and other Deputies had been given a sacred Trust and had honoured it. The Temptation of perversive Despotism had been resisted compleat and never serious a-contemplate by any Deputy, save perhaps only the Little Lion. Standing before The People, basking in their Love, Franklin felt greater joy and satisfaction than even that which accrued affixing his signature to the Constitution of Government.

Franklin envisioned a different scenario, of a despotic System of government wrought by Convention, him surrounded by The People inable to tell them the Truth, lest he be dismembered. Had such been the case, Franklin could never have promenaded, or might have done so only with a contingent of life Guard. Despots need necessarily fear The People, but for a true servant of The People, a true Republican, there was no safer Place than nestled in their Bosom, as Franklin was and felt now.

One bracket-faced Lady a front the throng had peacock Plumes fanned upward from her hat, that the num'rous eye-spots appeared as if gazing outward, watching Franklin vigilant. Franklin found this metaphor of a vigilant People, each with numerant eyes of over Sight, pleasing.

The bell compleated its thirteen Tolls.

The crowd a waited expectant for another reprise.

None manifested.

Someone in the crowd shouted.

"Providence bless His Excellency General Washington!"

Another shout rang out.

"May he condescend to head the new Government!"

The crowd roared its approbation furious loud.

Staccato shouts rang out.

"Providence bless His Excellency Doctor Franklin!"

"Providence guard The Doctor and The General!"

"Providence bless the Constitution of Government and Americay!"

Then an even louder shout.

"Three Cheers for Doctor Franklin!"

The bell began ringing again, but the Crowd shouted over it.

"Hip hip Huzza! Hip hip Huzza! Hip hip Huzza!"

Merriment reign'd. Huzzas were general shouted three times only, but they nonetheless continued. Promenaders throughout the Garden joined in, and the Huzzas become nigh deaf'ning. Franklin fancy'd king George hearing them in England and growing warm.

The bell rang numerate times, thirteen presumable, yet still the thund'rous Huzzas continued. Eventual they ended, but Cheers equal thund'rous continued for nigh half a minute. Pistols and even a musket were discharged skyward, producing small explosions of Smoke that lingered above the heads of the crowd for an instant and then dissipated.

Silence descended, save laughter and chuckles.

Then the inevitable Questions flurried.

"Well, Good Doctor," a Male withinst crowd said, "what sort of Government have you begotten us?"

"The People have Power," Franklin said.

"How much Power?" a Sex said.

"How much a Voice?" a Male said.

"More a Voice than ever prior," Franklin said.

"Does your Constitution," a Sex said, "not decree His Excellency General Washington the President of the Executive Council?"

No Constitution of durability could speak to a specific individual, even one as worthy as Washington.

"Does your Constitution," a Male said, "not decree you His Excellency's Second?"

The Vice Drooler.

"Does the Constitution not explode Slavery?" a Sex said.

Such Constitution would never be ratifyed.

"Does the Charta not enforce Paper Money?" a Male said.

"Uniform the currency?" a Male said.

"Pray tell," a Male said, "how does we elector Executive and Judges and Legislators?"

"How large the Legislature?" a Male said.

"What quantum of Taxes need a Gentlemen pay to Elector?" a Male said.

"Shan't the Ladys elector?" a Sex said.

"They better serve-ed," a Male said, "adhering the wifely Arts."

Men chuckled. Sexes' expressions grew warm.

"Did the little state Deputations done rake the large?" a Male said.

"What insurance against Monarchy?" a Male said. "Tyrannick Taxes?"

"And wanton War?"

Franklin let the Crowd continue to dissipate. Dozens more Questions were floated, nigh all egregious in misconception, or so complex as to defy simple answer to a Crowd.

Franklin was determined not to speak until every member of the Crowd had been given Voice. He sat silent until the Deluge of Questions slowed to a trickle.

At last silence.

Franklin let it linger.

Glancing about crowd, Franklin met a Herd of eye Pairs, all fixated anxious upon him. What a curious Power to wield. How fortunate for America that such Power was not wielded by the unworthy or Devilish Evil.

At last Franklin spoke.

"I am disinclined," he said, "to intercourse upon the peculiars of the Constitution with those reading it not. Even worthy Citizens such as ye."

"But you support the Charta?" a Male said.

"Of course he support it," a Male said. "He bloody penned it."

The crowd chuckled.

Franklin was careful not to frown.

"You's enamoured of its provisions?" a Sex said.

"Pleased of the result?" a Male said.

Franklin's desire to frown or sigh increased. Instead, he maintain'd his expression indifferent. To answer indifferent Honest was to do incalculable Harm to the cause of ratification. Franklin had not the luxurie of speaking the Truth, and could not convey even this Truth.

"None will ever mistake this Constitution of Government for a species of perfection," Franklin said. "But there will be this Constitution. Or the Confederacy of States will dissolve in rabid Anarchy."

Franklin was not at all a certain, even now, that he believed this prognostication.

But 'twas incumbent on him to say it.

If he or Washington were seen to waver in Support of the instrument even a Pinch, 'twould never ratify.

"We have done our proper Best these many months in Convention," Franklin said. "Providence as my Witness. No new assemblage hath any Hope of a surer result. Now it must be put to The People. The worth of the Charta is for you to weigh, and render your Verdict, not for I to decree."

"But you drew and support the Constitution?" a Male said.

"Aye, Sir. The instrument hath the sanction of my Name. I would sacrifice my life in Support of the principles it manifests. And in significant Measure have."

"And General Washington?" a Male said.

"The instrument lustres the sanction of his name," Franklin said.

"And His Excellency The General supports the Constitution?"

"I am always grievous reticent to place words within The General's teeth, lest they prove false. But I hazard The General would give the last Drop of his Blood to ensure the instrument receives a fair tryal."

The crowd Huzza'd Washington three times, furious loud.

"So His Excellency The General will condescend the Executive?" a Man said.

"President," Franklin said. "The Executive in the new Constitution of Government shall be stiled President. Should the instrument withstand ratification."

"So His Excellency The General will condescend to President?"

"You'll have to put the question to him," Franklin said.

"When shall I do that?" a Man said. "When I dines The General or brushes by him at Mass?"

"When you sluices your gob with him at the Three Jolly Irishmen," a Man said.

The crowd chuckled. The Three Jolly Irishmen was the most notorious pub in all of Philadelphiay, a den of Thieves and Murderers which no gentleman of quality patronized.

A Male spoke prodigious loud.

"We must campaign His Excellency!" he said, "Ensure he condescends to President!"

Murmurs and ayes was uttered.

"So Your Excellency and The General both support the Constitution?" a Sex said.

"Aye. We pledge our Lives, our Fortunes, and our sacred Honor to ensure the instrument receives a fair tryal."

"If They Excellencys The Doctor and The General champion the Constitution," a Man said, "then so shall I."

"And I," a Male said.

"And I," a Male said.

A cacophony of ayes filled the air. The Crowd might have been Knights of a Round Table, swearing fealty to a king and Quest.

Franklin wondered if the throng would support the Constitution of Government once they had read it.

"May we convey your Posture to others?" a Man said. "And that of The General?"

"You may."

"Providence's blessings," a Sex said, "Your Excellency."

"And to you all," Franklin said.

"All sha' be excellent well," a Male said, "so long as The General stays the Helm."

The need to campaign Washington to condescend the Executive was reprised by the Crowd.

When silence returned, an austere solicitor a front the Crowd stepped forward and curtsied deep.

"Your most obedient and humble servant, Doctor Franklin," he said.

The solicitor stood, glanced at the Crowd behind him, and then curtsied again. The entire Crowd, some two Hundred at the least, curtsied deep in unison.

Franklin's eyes welled with Tears.

By Providence he loved The People!

Franklin curtsied back to The People with his Head, proffered well Wishes, and then tapped the side of the Sedan. The chairmen lift'd it and drove it forward with their musculature.

The Crowd curtsied in unison once last, and spoke in unison as well.

"Your most obedient and humble servant," they said to Franklin.

"As I am Americay's," Franklin whispered. "Until my dying hour 'twould seem."

As the sedan drove on, Franklin basked in the Love of The People, until a breeze blew in from the southwest. It might have been bellow'd out a furnace. Franklin wished he had a lady's Fan to cool himself with.

Or something more ingenious.

Franklin envisioned a miniature mine fan mounted beneath the ceiling of the sedan, penetrating the roof and attached to a rotating array of sails atop it. A wind fan rather than a wind mill, one that would cool rather than grind grain. Franklin drew the invention in his mind, and revised it. A project for the winter perhaps, if Franklin could obtain an instant of free time.

A handsome pair of the sex drew close upon the Left, moving from the lawn to the Mallway. Fixation upon them shut contraptioneering from Franklin's thoughts. One Sex was a tallish, curled blond who wore a lighten'd Indigo chemise, and looked thin and fragile, even her angled face. She made Franklin think of a Færie. Her short companion wore a pinkened rose chemise patterned with flowers. She was more voluptuate, with dimples at the cheeks, a Face that seemed always to laugh, an Arse that might have made an elephant prideful, yet a heaving duggs that made one forgive her Arse.

Both of the Sex waved at Franklin with coquettish grins. Franklin was waving back when a gentleman approach'd the sedan and walked next to it, pacing himself that he remained perpetual a front of Franklin's window, blocking his View of the Sexes. The "gentleman" seemed oblivious to Franklin's irritate expression.

The "gentleman" was starched—stiff and prim—and fashioned in an opulent bright cochineal Suit. The suit had bright gold trim Sewings, and the combination of the cochineal and gold rendered it exceeding conspicuous. A more foppish conflagration of Colour was difficult to conceive.

Flies accosted Franklin for the first time since moving without doors, a disencouraging Omen.

The Maccaroni's gangly legs reminded Franklin of a horse's, especially the knobb-ed knees, and they scarce filled out his silk stock drawers. The Maccaroni's face evidenced the affect haughtiness typical of the english Aristocracy. Yet his expression was annoying earnest, indefatigable earnest, so much so that Franklin suspected he would follow indefinite, sullying the vantage of the Sex indefinite. The Maccaroni courtsied elegant while continuing to walk, no mean feat, and offered an English name Franklin recognized not.

The Maccaroni Club often made Franklin chuckle, but the thought of intercoursing a Maccaroni at this instant was displeasing. The Maccaroni Club was an informal Junto of entitled young British gentlemen who visited Italy on the Grand Tour and repair'd exhibiting pretensions of Fashion, language, and manner that were prodigious exaggerate and oft ridiculed. The Maccaroni Club was stiled such because gentleman on the Grand Tour often developed a taste for maccaroni Paste, a novelty few outside of Italy had savoured, though the delicacy was spreading and becoming quite the Crack wherest adopted.

The singular ornament of the Maccaroni, aside being dressy travelled and a front the Fashions, was the wig. Maccaroni wigs were upon occasion a foot high, exaggerate curled, and the caps atop them were at times removed with the sword, such action being thought clever and stilish by Maccaroni. Franklin had seen Maccaroni wigs so towering it seemed an eagle might be nested atop, with wearers scarce able to enter a coach and forced to crouch through doors.

The Maccaroni haranguing Franklin wore a subdued incarnate of his Order's infamous wig, which still rose vertical above the forehead nigh eight inches, as if forming an embankment or Hedge. The wig contained a central insect-abdomen-shaped bulb of towering hair flanked by two smaller, gradual expanding and ascending cylinders of hair. Though Franklin had seen such "stile" many times, it nonetheless took prodigious effort not to laugh at it.

Franklin tried to peer a left and a right of the Maccaroni, to gander the handsome pair of Sexes, but he could not locate them. Franklin tapped the sill of the Sedan with his walking stick and the chairmen broke. Franklin press'd the Maccaroni gentle out of his vantage using his walking stick.

The Sexes were absent.

Spooked?

Zounds.

Bloody bugger Maccaroni!

The Maccaroni slid back into view.

"Your Excellency," he said. "I beg leave for intrusing. We met in France."

"Doctor Franklin," Franklin said. "Not Excellency."

"Ah, yes. I oft forget. You Americans shun Royalty."

"Shun Tyranny."

"From a Sedan?"

Franklin pursed his lips.

The Maccaroni smiled his hawkish smile.

"Apologies, Doctor Franklin."

"None needed, Your Excellency."

The Maccaroni's face stiffened momentary, but then recovered.

"This would seem to be your Sedan from France," he said. "Though I seem to recollect the poles shorter."

"I resorted to longer poles," Franklin said, "to ease the jostling of the Gout and Stone."

Franklin tapped the window sill of the sedan with his walking Stick. The chairmen drove forward.

The Maccaroni alas paced. He seemed to prance as much as walk. He had unusual tiny feet that many a lady might want on herself. On the Maccaroni, they were unmanly, and heightened the Sense he a pratt Dandy.

"Sedans are curious scarce in Americay," the Maccaroni said. "This the first I saw. Though I expect I may in the South wherest Slaves to porter."

Promenaders stared at the wig of the Maccaroni, some even pointing. He smirk'd with smug satisfaction as they did.

"Forgive the foggyness of an olde man's Recollect," Franklin said. "We acquainted where?"

To be continued …

THE
FOUNDING
FATHERS
RETURN

Part the Third

For information about *The Founding Fathers Return: Part the Third* please visit LawrenceRowe.com.

To receive a notification when *The Founding Fathers Return: Part the Third* is released, sign up for Lawrence's e-mail list at his website.

www.ingramcontent.com/pod-product-compliance
Lightning Source LLC
Chambersburg PA
CBHW020536020726
47494CB00006B/1784